Praise for *All That's True*

"*All That's True* is a genuine Southern-style page-turner. What makes this book shine is the authentic voice of its young narrator, a winning and warmhearted girl on the verge of womanhood learning what it means to be human."
—Joshilyn Jackson, *New York Times* bestselling author of
Backseat Saints

"Miles is a master at creating characters to care about, and *All That's True* is a triumph of the spirit. Rarely do you find an author who writes with as much heart and raw talent as Jackie Lee Miles. Andi St. James is the good, troubled girl in all of us. You'll tear up and cheer for her as she navigates a topsy-turvy world of misbehaving parents, innocent crushes, and honest-to-goodness truths about what it means to be family."
—Nicole Seitz, author of *The Inheritance of Beauty*, *Saving Cicadas*, *A Hundred Years of Happiness*, *Trouble the Water*, and *The Spirit of Sweetgrass*

"*All That's True* is an absolute page-turner that will have you smiling one minute an͏ ͏he next. You'll journey with thirteen-year it like it is when it come͏ loss, and betrayal. And j͏ she discovers all that's tru͏ Beautifully told."
—Julie L. Cannon, author of *Truelove and Homegrown Tomatoes* and *I'll Be Home for Christmas*

"Meg Cabot and Jennifer Weiner, watch out! For the many readers who, like me, love juicy, realistic stories of intelligent young women and their quandaries, Jackie Lee Miles's new novel *All That's True* is a literary feast. Perfect in voice and detail, chock full of girl talk and seat-of-the pants crises, Miles's book is a winner—that rare, truly hard to put down book that even the most sophisticated reader will enjoy."

—Rosemary Daniell, award-winning author of
*Secrets of the Zona Rosa: How Writing (and
Sisterhood) Can Change Women's Lives*

"Through my writing I search for the deepest expressions of feelings in our relationships; after reading this story I realize I am not alone in this pursuit. Ms. Miles is searching for, well, all that is true. Her title stands for something—real relationships deal with the fun, the sorrow, the challenges, the fear, and the hope that define our emotional connections. For those of us looking for relationships that feel authentic, you will find them in this novel!"

—Edward Mooney, Jr., author of *The Pearls of the Stone Man*

"Jackie Lee Miles has honed her talents over the past few years and now has written her best novel yet in *All That's True*. It is created with a writer's eye for the warm, the wild, and the wicked. Miles emerges from these pages as a talented author whose future success is limitless."

—Jackie K. Cooper, author of *The Sunrise Remembers*

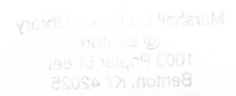

Praise for *Cold Rock River*

"A powerful story of family, love, and loss that will keep you up into the wee hours. Absolutely wonderful! Beautifully told and straight from the heart of an exquisitely talented writer."

—Dorothea Benton Frank, *New York Times* bestselling author

"Jackie Lee Miles brings her rich talent to a higher level. The journey of two young brides…from sensitive adolescence to women of substance…makes for a very fine recipe."

—Earl Hamner, Emmy-winning creator of *The Waltons*, bestselling author, and award-winning screenwriter

"A compelling story you won't want to miss! Well told and deeply true to its time and place."

—Haywood Smith, author of *Queen Bee of Mimosa Branch* and *The Red Hat Club*

"Warm, fresh, funny—the characters leap off the page! Miles is a fascinating new voice in Southern fiction. Readers will rejoice."

—Karin Gillespie, author of *Dollar Daze, Bet Your Bottom Dollar*, and *A Dollar Short*

"*Cold Rock River* is an absolute gem! Filled with humor, sometimes subtle, sometimes out-and-out hysterical."

—Ann Kempner Fisher, editor of *B.O.O.B.S.: A Bunch of Outrageous Breast-Cancer Survivors Share Their Stories of Courage, Hope and Healing*

Praise for *Roseflower Creek*

"Once you start you will not stop until the last gripping page. The lyric prose will thrill you, the story is unforgettable, and the characters will stay with you forever."
—William Diehl, author of *Primal Fear* and *Eureka*

"*Roseflower Creek* is a compelling, fast-paced narrative that captivates from the first page to the last. It is beautifully written and sensitively told. Don't miss it!"
—*New York Times* bestselling author Haywood Smith, author of *The Red Hat Club* and *The Red Hat Club Rides Again*

"Lori Jean will jam her thumbprint into your heart forever!"
—Carmen Agra Deedy, children's book author and commentator on National Public Radio's *All Things Considered*

"I may be through with this book, but [it] will never be through with me."
—Barry Farber, nationally syndicated radio talk-show host

"Jackie Lee Miles writes with rare simplicity and grace, telling Lori Jean's story in a voice as pure as new milk and as genuine as a child's smile. Like Lori Jean, this small, delicate novel has a very large soul."
—R. Robin McDonald, author of *Secrets Never Lie* and *Black Widow*

"A powerful, extraordinary novel. The characters haunt the reader long after the last page is turned."
—Earl Hamner, creator of *The Waltons*

All That's True

JACKIE LEE MILES

sourcebooks
landmark

Published by Sourcebooks Landmark, an imprint of Sourcebooks, Inc.
P.O. Box 4410, Naperville, Illinois 60567-4410
(630) 961-3900
Fax: (630) 961-2168
www.sourcebooks.com

Library of Congress Cataloging-in-Publication Data

Miles, J. L. (Jacquelyn L.)
  All that's true / by Jackie Lee Miles.
    p. cm.
  (pbk. : alk. paper) 1. Teenage girls—Fiction. 2. Brothers—Death—Fiction.
3. Families—Fiction. 4. Bereavement—Psychological aspects—Fiction. 5.
Life change events—Fiction. I. Title.
  PS3613.I53A45 2011
  813'.6--dc22

                              2010014377

        Printed and bound in the United States of America.
          VP 10 9 8 7 6 5 4 3 2 1

For my new granddaughter, Madelyn Grace.
Welcome to the world, baby girl!

Chapter One

My LIFE WAS CLOSE to being perfect until my brother Alex got killed. Then my mother started drinking and my father starting having sex with Donna, my best friend's stepmother. She's not even thirty years old. Me and Bridget—that's my best friend—we saw them through the window of the pool house and nearly stopped breathing. You would not believe the moaning. For a life that was moving along really well, right now everything sucks.

We haven't told anyone, yet. We still can't believe it ourselves. Besides, we're not sure who to tell: her father, or my mother, or maybe a priest. It's complicated. For now, we're just watching them boff each other. It's disgusting, sure, but we can't seem to help ourselves. Now that we know what they're doing, we camp out in the bushes behind the cabana that's behind Bridget's house and just wait for them to show up. Mostly they do the same things to each other, over and over, but we watch like it's the very first time.

Mondays are good. They're always there Mondays. And Wednesdays, they never miss Wednesdays. My mother's at her bridge game and Bridget's father's at church. He's a deacon. And sometimes on Friday nights they're at it, but not tonight; tonight's my mother's fiftieth birthday party and our house is so lit up it looks like it's on fire.

"It's a significant occasion," my father says, sounding and acting perfectly normal—like nothing out of the usual is going on—and he's screwing Donna like he's a sex machine, and he's over fifty, which makes it like a miracle. I didn't know men could even do it that old.

He reminds my sister Beth and me, for the umpteenth time, to make my mother's birthday a joyous occasion, his exact words. So, he still must love her, or he wouldn't care, right?

"Regardless of the circumstances," he says, meaning Alex is dead, but I'm thinking of him and Donna and those circumstances, and grunt, "Humph."

My sister Beth nods politely and assures him we will, then turns and bugs her eyes out at me, which is her way of telling me I should nod, too, right now. I'm sick of her being older and wiser, not to mention bossy. She's getting married this year after she graduates from Vassar and is on the dean's list, so she thinks she's hot stuff. I'm flunking algebra, so I'm on everyone's list, except my mother's. She loves me more than God.

Beth is still eyeballing me. I pretend I'm catatonic. My father stands and waits patiently; he's familiar with and respectful of Beth's signal system. He calls her Elizabeth and says her name like it's a prayer. That makes me want to hate her, but mostly I'm not able; it's in the blood or something not to, but sometimes I think I do anyway, so maybe I have bad blood.

Beth tucks her arms across her chest and glares at me. My father has his hand wrapped around her shoulder. They're staring and waiting. Their expressions are obvious. They think I'm going to ruin the party. I stare back, my face a blank sheet of paper, but really it has invisible ink that says, "What?—Do I look like an idiot?"

The guests are arriving now—two-by-two—and I'm thinking Noah's Ark, and with our luck a flood will follow. Vivian's here. That's my mother's best friend from before I was born.

"And were you a surprise!" she joked, when I stayed with her once, which turns out isn't a joke. I was a big surprise, my mother said.

Vivian always smells like she's just come from the hairdresser.

"I have!" she says, and laughs. "With hair like this, I live there." •

She hugs my shoulder and walks with me snug at her side like we're glued together. "What do you say we crash this party, sweetie? Show these fools how it's done."

Her husband Howard is pouring my mother another glass of wine, and my father smiles like that's fine, but it's really not. Tonight he'll pretend it is, but normally when my mother's on her third glass he shakes his head and makes a face like there's a skunk in the room. And this might be her fourth; I lost count. Now I'm back to paying attention. I get afraid for my mother. She drinks too much and slurs her words, and she hugs people too hard, and my father points it all out the next morning, even if Rosa's there clearing the dishes. I want to tell him, "There are worse things, you know—you don't hug at all. And you're screwing Donna! And you're hardly ever home."

When he is, Desert Storm and my mother's drinking are his favorite topics. He says George-Herbert-Walker-read-my-lips Bush, Sr., needs to get rid of Saddam Hussein now or there'll be all hell to pay later, and then he tells my mother she's disgusting.

"Absolutely disgusting, Margaret," he says, and I want to spill my guts.

My mother sits quietly and nods her head, "I know, I know," all the while my father is berating her. If she only knew what I know… and I almost blurt it out, but it would hurt her so bad, so, of course, I don't. I sit quietly and watch her, like I'm the babysitter. She's still so beautiful to look at. Like Barbie with some gray in her hair, and maybe a few extra pounds, but not many. My mother doesn't eat much, but when she does, it's all the right foods.

For tonight, my parents are all smiles. The kind you paint on. I don't blame them. It's all any of us can muster, seeing as Alex is dead, and it's only been two months, hardly any time at all, and it feels like last night the police knocked on the door to tell us, and no one answered, so they pounded on the door; it was the middle of the night—what did they think? And they had their blue lights flashing in the driveway, scaring half the neighborhood awake. A nightmare, that's what I was thinking, but even then, I could tell it was real. My mother was screaming like a serial killer had hold of her, throwing herself against the marble columns in the front entrance hall. My father grabbed hold of her and held her so tight I thought he'd bruise her worse, but I've never seen him so tender to her in my entire life—and thirteen years, two months, and eight days is a long time, any reasonable person can agree.

Alex was my most favorite person in the entire world, next to my mother, who is next to my best friend Bridget, who's next to no one; she's like my salvation, but that's another story. Alex liked me better than Beth. He told me once he found her shallow. I was nine at the time and hardly knew the meaning of the word, but what did it matter? It sounded perfectly wretched, but more important he insisted I was not, capital, N-O-T—nor ever would be, shallow. It was a sacred moment. I asked him if we could prick our fingers and join our blood. He laughed and said, "It's already joined, you nut," and made like he was tossing me a football.

For tonight, for my mother, I want to look happy—really happy, not fake happy, so she'll think I'm happy, and she won't worry about me and start drinking double—but my face refuses to cooperate with my heart, which right now is heavier than a baby elephant, and just two weeks before Alex got killed it was lighter than air when Dennis Luken kissed me on the mouth, but that's another story, too—and a real tearjerker.

"Andi?" My father taps my shoulder and brings me back to reality just as the doorbells chime. They're very irritating; they sound like they belong in a cathedral, but my father picked them special. Rosa rushes to get the door and welcomes the last of our guests. It's Murray and Loretta Levinson. They have a lot of money, and always manage to be very disgusting about the fact that they do. My father shakes Murray's hand and then kisses Loretta's cheeks, first one and then the other, European-style. Alex taught me that. I try to smile, but it's no use. I nod my head and watch them join the others. Everyone seems to be enjoying themselves, which is probably good, but I'm having a hard time with that. I mean, people you love just up and die, no warning, no good-bye, nothing—poof—they're gone. And then McDonald's opens the next day and sells hamburgers, and Rich's holds their biggest sale ever, and people are rushing to get to work, get to the cleaners, they're booking cruises, signing up for aerobics or doing yoga, taking in a movie; they're going out to dinner—stuffing their faces and talking and laughing—the entire world just continues on as usual, like nothing has happened to yours. I tell my father this in one long sob.

"Life must continue, Andi," he says gently, and pats me like I'm a baby in need of a good burp. He says "must" with great emphasis, like he's trying to convince himself, and I notice his eyes are watery and I've never even seen them moist before, except maybe once, when he accidentally poked himself with his thumb trying to open a cabinet door that was stuck—but not as stuck as he thought—and he yelled, "God damn!" And my mother yelled, "Arthur!" We're Catholic; it's a mortal sin, and then he used Visine in them and they got watery-runny, and it was Friday, so we all went to confession. What a night that was.

I take the handkerchief my father offers. It smells like Herrera for Men, like him, and has his initials on it. My mother buys them special-order from Neiman's—Egyptian cotton; they're soft as butter. I dab at my eyes, glad I'm not wearing mascara tonight—I'm not allowed to until my birthday, but I sneak and put it on at school anyway.

My grandmother, Nana Louise, is here. She's sitting opposite my mother in a matching chaise longue, drinking apple juice from a martini glass with an olive in it. She's eighty-something and lives at Sunny Meadows Nursing Home, only it's not really so sunny and there's no meadow. But there's a very nice sign out front with lights that turn on by themselves at dusk, and the building is painted white with dark green shutters, and the front porch has enough rockers for the entire state of Georgia, and flowers in all the beds, and a reception area that's nicer than my father's, and he's an attorney. When people walk in, they think they're dropping granny or grampy or Aunt Dodie off on heaven's doorstep, so what's the problem? If they visit enough times they'll realize Sunny Meadows is not even close. My father put Nana Louise there an hour after my grandfather died. His brain was like eighty-five going on thirty. The doctors all said he was healthy, too. Shows you how much they know. He took really good care of Nana Louise. She doesn't do well on her own. We take her to dinner on the third Friday of each month; it's like a sacrament. Nana Louise has no idea who we are, but she always smiles and gets in the car when they wheel her out, which I find amazing. When old folks forget people, do they forget not to go with strangers, too?

Tonight she looks scared. Her eyes are searching the room like she's lost something very important—maybe her mind—and maybe it's close by, and maybe if she keeps searching, she'll find it. I go to her side and take her hand, and she lets me. For a split second her eyes grab mine and snap to attention. I think she knows me! The place in my heart that hurts so bad—the part I'm convinced will never feel good again—flutters like a little butterfly. The spark I take as recognition in Nana Louise's eye is gone, but still, it gives me hope. I breathe in deeply and let out a sigh. Maybe my father is right. Maybe life does go on. It just takes a while.

So I start to feel better and then the doorbells chime and Rosa opens the door and you will not believe who's standing there.

Chapter Two

SOMETIMES WHEN ROSA HAS been cleaning for hours, my mother will go around and empty all the wastebaskets. Wherever they are placed—there are many—they match the décor. It's her way of telling Rosa she is doing a really good job, and it's kind of a show of love. But I wonder why she just doesn't give her some extra money and say, "Rosa, I don't know what I'd do without you." Rosa probably thinks my mother thinks she forgot to empty the trash, and she'll go home feeling bad about herself, which makes me feel bad about myself, when my mother should feel bad about herself. What a circus. And then of course, there's the issue of money on its own. People need it. But people who have a lot of it, like my mother, don't realize how bad it is for those that don't have any, and need to count every penny to make sure it will be enough for whatever life hands them that week, like they live on compliments or something. So, my mother should just give Rosa extra money when she sees how hard she's working. I should tell her that, but I don't, so I'm just as guilty. Something about when good women do nothing, nothing is the result. I read that somewhere about men and evil, but it has to include women and regular things, too, right?

For the moment, I'm doing nothing. I need to call Bridget and see if she is, too. My father is out of town on business. I know he's not with Donna—she's home getting the mail; I can see her out my bedroom window. I tell my mother I'm going to Bridget's. She's emptying wastebaskets and smiles as I walk by.

I decide right then and there, if I ever have a maid, I'm giving her a really big raise when I hire her.

Chapter Three

I'M CURLED UP ON Bridget's bed admiring my toenails. They look like Jelly Bellys. It took three tries before I got the right color on the correct nail, so they'd really pop out at you. That's another reason for having a best friend. They don't mind if you change yours after the colors are dry. Bridget just shrugs and picks up the polish remover. I did hers all in one shade, iridescent lime green.

Bridget looks like Winona Ryder, but with braces. Even so, she's totally beautiful. And there's not an ounce of fat on her body.

"Like my mother," she says, then bites her lip. She doesn't mention her mother much. She died when Bridget was eight; some kind of leukemia and it still pains her heart. Her father married Donna, his secretary, last year.

"She had these little cards she carried in her purse in a silver holder," Bridget explains. "'Executive Assistant'."

"That's pretty cool."

"No, it's the same as a secretary," she says, lacing cotton through my toes so the polish won't smudge. "Except they have to pay them more money and they don't make them get coffee."

Bridget's father is a stockbroker. Their house is very fancy, so he must be a good one. Or maybe he had a lot of insurance on Bridget's mother, or both. I don't ask. I just let Bridget talk about her mother whenever she wants and I nod my head to let her know I'm listening really good, but I don't say anything because I can't think of anything to say. I can't imagine not having my mother around, even when she's tipsy, which is a lot now that Alex is gone, except for in the morning. Mornings, she drinks coffee and juice and eats oatmeal, which Rosa brings to her on a tray, which is a big relief. Not Rosa waiting on her, but that she's eating. I read somewhere that alcoholics don't eat, so as long as she eats, maybe she won't be one.

Bridget's the only friend I can talk to about what happened to Alex. Mostly, it's too awful, not just that he died, but the way he did. Bridget listens and then brings extra pillows to plump behind my back.

"Would you like a Coke?" she says. "It's diet." Which is her way of saying she doesn't want my heart hurting as bad as her heart, which makes me love her as a friend forever, and I hope they never move and we never move. And I tell her.

"I know. That's how I feel," she adds, and changes the subject. "Let's go swimming!"

"It's November."

"Yeah, let's get crazy." She opens her top drawer and tosses two swimsuits onto the bed. "Here, pick one."

When you have a friend like Bridget, life can be hard, sure, but then there's all that goodness out there to grab hold of.

"Yeah, let's get crazy!" I say and choose the tank suit, which I'm sure will fit. Bridget picks up the bikini, and we're off.

Now you know why she's my salvation.

Chapter Four

You probably don't want to hear about toenails and nail color. You want to know, like Bridget, what happened the night of my mother's birthday party when the doorbell rang.

"Tell me again!" Bridget says.

We're wrapped up like mummies in oversized bathrobes and huddled in the sauna next to the cabana. It takes a while for the space to heat up and our teeth are rattling like dice.

"Well, she was covered in blood—" I say. Of course, I'm talking about Donna, who showed up that night and nearly caused my father to have a heart attack. It was only her finger that was covered in blood, not her entire body, but it was running down the front of her jogging suit, which was pale peach velvet and matched her lipstick to the letter.

"I was slicing a p—p—pineapple," she wails, preparing dinner for her and Rodger, that's Bridget's father, who isn't home yet, and she can't reach him and she goes on and on between sobs. And can he help her and my father is standing there with his mouth hung open like it's no longer attached.

"Well, of course, of course—" my father says and gently takes hold of her arm and brings her into the foyer, where she drips blood all over the marble floor. Rosa runs up with a clean towel and wraps it around her hand, but it bleeds through quickly and Rosa turns white as Casper and is rattling something in Spanish that sounds like the world is ending, which scares Donna, who seems to agree. She's a mess—and I should be feeling sorry for her, or show some concern at least, but in my brain I'm thinking she probably cut her finger on purpose to get my father's attention. She's stretching her neck around Rosa to get a look at my mother and who's at the party. My mother looks pretty breathtaking in a black velvet dress that shows off her still-blonde hair pulled back in a very stylish chignon, featured in all the latest fashion magazines, and Donna is taking this all in and frowning. Then she leans against my father and cries, "Oh Arthur, Arthur," like they're very close, or something, and of course they are, but my mother doesn't know that and is now standing next to my father and you'd think she'd find the way Donna is clinging to my father and calling out his name in this over-familiar way disturbing, but she simply says to my father that it would be a good idea to take her to the emergency room and would he like her to accompany them? Very strange. Not the words, the fact my mother's not in the least bit suspicious of the way Donna is whimpering to my father. I have this flashback to third grade when I liked this boy Stuart and I wrote him a note and asked if he liked me and he wrote back, yes he did, and I wrote back and asked if he'd like to go together, which meant stand in line to go to lunch together and maybe at the water fountain, and also meet at the front door when school started, which was about the extent of going steady in third grade. And he said yes, and we had an agreement, even though, technically, I was supposed to wait for him to ask me to go with him, but he never asked me one question the entire second grade and I liked him all during that year too, so I figured if I didn't ask, I'd be in sixth grade still waiting and what if I still liked him? So I had no choice but to ask him. Then Darla Myers, this real cute girl who had the prettiest teeth I'd ever seen, comes up one morning when Stuart and I are meeting before the bell rings and she smiles at him—the kind where your eyes smile along with your lips, like they're moving up and down, but they're not, and then she covered her mouth and giggled, and I knew right then and there something was going on. I broke up with Stuart on the spot. Later I found out from Cynthia, this other friend of mine, that I was right all along. Cynthia saw Stuart and Darla in the hallway that leads out the back door where we weren't ever supposed to be and they were showing each other, you know, that kind of showing. The point is, even at eight years old I could tell when something wasn't right. And now Donna is falling all over my father in plain sight and wailing and calling him Arthur, Arthur in a little-girl voice. And my mother is acting like it's nothing.

How much writing on the wall does a woman her age require?

Chapter Five

OKAY, HERE'S WHAT HAPPENED to Alex. Maybe the more I go over the details, the less it will hurt. Alex decided to join this fraternity his sophomore year at Vanderbilt; mostly before then, he wasn't interested, but then he was and he got picked to join Phi Moose or something equally silly-sounding, and part of his initiation had this drinking game where all the plebes—I think that's short for "pledges," because they're not officially in the group until they pass all the tests or something—sit in a circle and drink this concoction like a triple-quadruple kamikaze that has every liquor known to man put in one glass. And they have round after round and the thing is if someone passes out or needs to throw up or can't drink another swallow, they have to follow certain instructions. Like the throwing up part, you have to throw up to your left. And if you can't drink another swallow, then you have to pass your glass to the person on your right. I'm not sure if they have any rules about if you pass out, but I'm pretty sure they don't. If you're passing out it's pretty hard to follow anything but the direction your body heads in.

So, Alex has a guy on his left that passes his glass to him after only two rounds and Alex keeps drinking that guy's drink and his own drink and on and on, and to make it worse the guy on his right is one of those who should pass his glass on to the guy on his right, but keeps drinking it instead, and then promptly throws up each and every round—remember, he has to throw up to his left, which is where Alex is sitting. So Alex is covered in this guy's vomit—I know it's totally gross—and Alex just keeps drinking glass after glass along with this other guy's glasses and before you know it, Alex conks out. He's out cold, really cold. Of course the guys in charge notice, but just drag him out of the circle to sleep it off, but they can't wake him up later when it's all over, so they decide to take him to the hospital, which they do, but they just leave him at the emergency door, ring the buzzer several times and then drive away. Then later, they get to thinking—this all comes out in this preliminary hearing where they're deciding whether or not to have a trial—what if when he wakes up, he tells what was going on and the fraternity gets suspended, so they go back to the hospital and after Alex is settled in his room, they disconnect his IV and sort of kidnap him back. Alex wakes up and says, "Hey, buddy, what's up?" That's what the president of the fraternity says at the hearing. His name is Conrad York III and he has blond hair that's precision cut like a soap-opera star and he is so good-looking you catch your breath. His father is sitting in the first row. He's pretty handsome, too, except now his face is the color of fresh-poured concrete.

So, after they take Alex out of the hospital, Alex passes out again, and they can't wake him up no matter what they do and they try everything: a cold shower, artificial resuscitation, ice packs under his arms, a coffee enema—don't ask—so they take him back to the hospital. These guys are like really retarded. For the second time that night, they leave him at the emergency room door and they ring the buzzer and leave just like before. The emergency technician who found him said, "He was deceased when I got to him, your Honor."

Conrad jumps up and says, "He was alive when we left him. We rang the bell three times. You should have got out there sooner!" And the judge tells him to sit down and be quiet. But he won't; he just keeps yelling at the guy on the witness stand that he killed Alex, he let him die. So they have to remove him from the courtroom—not the witness, Conrad III. His lawyer says he is having some kind of breakdown and requests a continuance so he can have a psychological work-up completed on his client before proceeding.

I'm thinking all of them should fess up like men. But then, I realize they aren't men or even close to it, or they wouldn't have done something so stupid to begin with. I joined Y-Teens one year and we had an initiation too, but all we had to do was squat and quack like ducks all around the square—downtown—during rush hour. It was very humiliating, so why didn't they just do something equally stupid like that, is what I want to ask.

Maybe their attorney is right, it's all a tragic mistake, "Let's not sacrifice their entire lives. There was no intent, Your Honor," he says.

The judge simply calls a recess and orders background investigations on all those involved. Everybody files out of the courtroom. We head to the funeral home and pick out a casket.

Here we are, three months later. The lawyers are still fighting over when to start the trial, or if there should even be one. My father said the charge would be felony hazing. But punishing them won't bring Alex back, so mostly I don't care, but then I remember it might keep others from doing the same, so now I think there should be a trial and some kind of punishment, but what kind? That's the problem, because these are Alex's friends and he'd be the first one to say, "Hey, haven't you ever made a mistake?"

Well, sure—we all have—but this is a pretty big one.

"There's no easy answer," my father says. He hangs his head and turns to go into his study. His eyes are glassy and the edges are beet red. I want to wrap my arms around him really tight. I'm just about to, when he quietly shuts the door.

I check on my mother. She's sprawled on top of her bed with her clothes on. There's an empty bottle of Clos du Bois sitting on the nightstand. She's snoring softly, a nice little feminine snore. Spittle is dribbling down one side of her face. There's no way to tell if she's passed out or just sleeping normal. There's a part of me that wants to think it's just normal sleep, but this other part jumps in and says, yeah, right.

I slip the empty bottle into the wastebasket and tiptoe out of the room.

Chapter Six

My Nana Louise says there is something good in everything. Well, before she lost her memory, that is. But if she could find it, I'm sure she'd insist it's still true. I wonder how that relates to Alex and come up with a brilliant thought: no one will ever throw up on him again.

Now I'm wondering what good will come from Bridget's news, which is totally the last straw. She's going to boarding school and her father says it's not negotiable. Donna needs more time to herself. She's having a hard time adjusting to being a stepparent or something equally full of garbage.

"What are you going to do?" I ask her.

We are sitting on my bedroom floor with our legs crossed trying to do yoga. We haven't been at it long enough to stretch out our limbs and we are all knees jutting into the air like jetties.

She doesn't answer. She rests her arms on her knees and buries her head.

"Maybe I can go, too," I add, knowing it's out of the question. My mother thinks boarding schools make juvenile delinquents out of those that attend them. I'm not sure where she got that idea. Probably from Hollywood; some of those kids are really mixed up and many of them are in boarding schools.

"It has horses," Bridget offers reaching into her backpack.

She hands me a colorful brochure. It's on glossy paper and folds out into four sections.

"Cool."

Westwood Academy is spelled out in large letters. The brochure is impressive. The dorm rooms look like something out of *Southern Living* magazine and the stables show horses with riders in jodhpurs and black velvet hats with chinstraps included.

"But you're scared of horses," I point out.

"Yeah," Bridget says quietly. "My father says that's the idea; to conquer my fears."

"So, you want to go?"

Bridget shakes her head vehemently.

"Well, then don't."

Bridget looks at me like I've lost my mind. Actually, I think I have, or at least what's left of it is growing very twisted.

"It's not that easy," she says.

"Sure it is," I assure her. "Just tell him the real reason Donna wants you out of the way."

Bridget stares at me, her blue eyes big as mixing bowls.

Chapter Seven

MY SISTER AND MY mother are discussing details concerning Beth's wedding. Arguing is more like it, but my mother prefers to use the word discuss.

"It's more civilized," she insists.

Beth is using her outside voice and is about as civil as a war. She is absolutely convinced that ten bridesmaids are not too many. I'm about to leave, it's all so boring. Then I pick up her comment that there will really be only nine bridesmaids; I'm to be a junior bridesmaid. If there is anything worse than being in a wedding you have no desire to be in, it's being dressed up in a kid's version of the real thing and listed in the program as a junior something-or-other. I have a meltdown.

"Oh, look! Your dress is gorgeous," my mother croons and holds out a sketch of a pink chiffon concoction with more layers than the wedding cake. It looks like a ballet tutu; not the cake, the dress; well, okay—to be honest—the cake too. The dress will make me look like an overweight baby elephant—it would make an anorexic look like one—it has about three hundred yards of fabric too much.

"I'm not wearing that," I say. "I'd rather be eaten by pigmies."

"Listen, you little brat—" Beth starts in.

"I'll speak with her," my mother assures her, waving one hand and taking a long sip of wine with the other.

Beth glares at me and leaves the room.

"Now, Andréa, darling," my mother addresses me with her *aren't we being a bit unreasonable?* tone.

She's going to guilt-trip me into cooperating and I'll end up letting her. There's no way out of this. Beth is marrying Parker Barrett—who I admit is a pretty neat guy, as older guys go—and is determined to make it the fanciest, most talked-about wedding of the season. Don't ask me why she is marrying him or even getting married at all. She is never happy to see him. All she does is criticize him no matter what he does.

For the moment, my not wanting to wear the dress she has picked out for me is not going to work. None of my objections are going to hold up. If I don't fold now, my father will eventually be called in. He will make me see things in a new light, which is that I'll have no allowance until I graduate from college and the keys to my car, which I will never get, will vanish as well.

Why bother to fight it? Sometimes it's just better to cooperate and be done with it, and pretend everything is just fine, when really your world as you see it is ending. Life has never been fair around here, but then it's that way for a lot of people. I read in the paper that a woman's health insurance lapsed when her payment was lost in the mail and she moved and never got the notices that it had lapsed and then her little boy got sick with leukemia and now the insurance won't pay, so that's really unfair. It puts wearing a pink elephant tutu in total perspective. It's rather small in comparison. I tell myself I will think of that at the wedding—the entire day—that poor little boy with the leukemia and no insurance, and I'll feel better.

Chapter Eight

My life is falling apart. Ever since I agreed to cooperate for the wedding you would think some things would go right for me—but oh, no—Fate just steps in and says, *Think you are going to be rewarded for being a good daughter and a good sister? Well, think again, you moron, because I am going to totally mess up your life*—and she does.

First off, Bridget called and she is definitely going to boarding school without so much as one simple "I am not!" Her father is going to be working in England on some European investments for his company and he has decided that, for at least one semester, Bridget is to try Westwood Academy and then they'll talk.

"It's reasonable," she says, sounding like my mother. What happened to her being a kid, and unreasonable like the rest of us?

Secondly, Amy is coming over and Jeffrey, Alex's best friend when he was alive to have a best friend, is coming with her. Amy is about my most favorite person in the world, after Bridget, who used to be after Alex.

Alex met Amy when he first started college and was planning on pinning her as soon as he qualified to have a pin to pin her with, and then he was going to be engaged to her, and then get married, which would make her my sister-in-law, and someday they would make me an aunt. Alex didn't say all that; he only said the part about pinning—I thought up all the rest on my own, but they are reasonable assumptions.

Amy calls right after dinner and speaks with my father.

"Amy's coming over with Jeffrey," he explains to my mother. "Something about they need to speak with us—"

"Is it about Alex's trial?" I jump in.

"I guess we'll find out," my father says and picks up the newspaper. "They'll be here within the hour."

I don't know why the hair on my neck stands up, but if it were *The Twilight Zone*, that weird music would be playing.

Then, I remember something that happened after the funeral and it all starts coming together. Rosa fixed this enormous buffet and all the neighbors sent over dishes so—picture this—the entire dining room table is loaded with the most delicious food you can imagine and people start lining up in droves to make their selections. Others are mingling and whispering how sad it is about Alex, and a few are sharing happy memories of being with him. My parents are in the front hall greeting the new arrivals. I'm sitting in a chair nearest the dining room, next to one of the large columns that divides the sitting room from the dining room, but I have a good view of the food. I'm thinking about fixing myself a plate—there is a large platter of macaroni and cheese that looks particularly appetizing. That's when I see something out of the corner of my eye that catches me off guard: Amy is standing in line next to Jeffrey—who is not only Alex's best friend, but has been since forever—and of course goes to Vanderbilt, as does Amy, who followed Alex there.

Amy has on black pumps and a short black dress with three-quarter sleeves and a Peter Pan collar, demure and appropriate. I mean she's sort of like Alex's widow and I'm admiring how beautiful she is, which she is—she looks like Jennifer Aniston—and the next thing I know, she is slipping her left hand quietly into Jeffrey's right hand and then just keeps it there.

Doesn't that grab you as being very strange? That's my reaction, but then I tell myself they are probably hanging on to each other to grieve, and let it go.

And now they want to meet with my parents. They have something to discuss. It's probably about the grieving process, or maybe Alex's trial.

Sure—and the Pope is really a Methodist.

Chapter Nine

I'M UPSTAIRS ON MY bed, face down, waiting for Jeffrey and Amy to get here. I'm thinking about when I was five. The unthinkable happened. My mother lost me. She'd taken me to Lenox Mall and while she was preoccupied with a fitting, I wandered off. The story is she went completely hysterical when she realized the dress she'd chosen for an important fundraiser was divine, but in the interim, her daughter had vanished. They had the entire store personnel scouring the mall. Of course, I'd been taught never to talk to strangers, so instead of picking out someone—like a lady with small children or an elderly man with a seeing-eye dog—and asking for help, I went into the first bathroom I could find that had the lady figure on it and hid in the very last stall. I'm not sure how long I was there. I remember chanting the alphabet song sixteen million times. The reason I chose the last stall in the bathroom was simple. Whenever we were shopping, eventually my mother would say we needed to find a restroom and do so quickly. Something about her kidneys not being what they used to be; they were about to explode, which made me wonder what they used to be like and would they please not explode, at least not while I was there to see it.

Mother always used the last stall.

"Less people use this one, Andréa. Always use the last stall."

I went there knowing eventually she and her kidneys would find me.

Not so. It was a policeman who did. I was curled up in the corner beneath the toilet and this head popped under the stall.

"There you are," he said, a wide grin on his face. He had large even teeth and generous cheeks with a dimple parked in each one.

"We've been looking all over for you," he exclaimed.

"Where's my mother?" I whimpered.

"Well, she's—she's—" He opened the stall door and reached in to get me.

"I need to wait here for her," I insisted, and burrowed deeper into the corner. "Her kidneys will be exploding any minute now."

The officer let out a howl, then reached in and gently pulled me towards him. Once I was free from the stall, he lifted me into his arms.

"Come on, little lady," he said. "Let's go find your mama."

It turned out I was missing all of three hours, which to me was at least three days. The worst part was at the very end, before the nice officer found me. I had this strange agitation going through my heart, like it was going to beat itself out of my chest, but mostly I had this newfound awareness, that life was no longer the safe haven it had been just hours before. Bad things could happen. I realize now I was experiencing a serious case of anxiety. All these years later, it feels just as deadly.

I'm watching the clock, waiting for Amy and Jeffrey to show up at our door. Whatever it is they have to say, I'm pretty sure I won't want to hear it. My stomach thinks it's a washing machine. It's spinning and twisting what's left of my dinner—meatloaf, mashed potatoes, fried okra and cornbread—into one big soggy heap. Then anxiety walks in and takes over like it owns the place. My heart is beating too fast. I can feel it pulsing even in my ears. I go downstairs and curl up on the sofa in my usual spot, hugging my favorite throw pillow, the burgundy velvet tapestry. I close my eyes. It feels like I'm huddled in that bathroom stall, waiting for my mother to appear and make everything right again. Only this time, she won't be able to. No one will.

Chapter Ten

I'M RIGHT. *ALWAYS TRUST your instincts,* Ann Landers says. And she's right, too. Amy and Jeff are a couple. It all happened rather quickly they say. They want us to be the first to know. She's having a baby. They want to do the right thing—the old-fashioned way—a modest ceremony, no fanfare, only their parents there and perhaps a few friends. Would we like to come? "You see…" she continues, but my ears have lost their ability to hear.

I jump up from the sofa and toss the pillow onto the carpet as hard as I can. I want it to hit the floor like a brick and smash into thousands of pieces, but it's a pillow, so it just drops where I toss it and plays dead. I run up the front staircase. It twists and turns in spirals and is longer than I ever remember it being. Finally I reach my room. I slam the door and fall onto my bed, face first.

"Oh, Alex," I'm sobbing. "She's a little slut—a slut—a slut! Didn't you know?"

There's a tap on my door. I answer with dead silence. The door opens. It's Amy.

"Can I come in?" she whispers.

I sit up and stare at her. She's gained a bit of weight, not enough that I would have suspected she'd gotten herself knocked up, just enough to take away some of the sharp angles of her face. And her cheeks have a tad more color in them. She has always been beautiful. Now I see what the magazines have been saying all along is true. Pregnant women glow. At least Amy does. That's it. That's the last straw. Alex is dead, Alex has been betrayed, my life sucks—and she's glowing. Life isn't just unfair. It's full of crap, too.

Amy walks over to the bed. She sits on the edge and takes my hand. "Andi—"

She says my name like my father says Beth's—like it's a treasure that's just been discovered. My heart leaps! Why? Why? Why?—I've loved you just like a sister, it wants to say. Instead, it breaks in two.

"You cheated on Alex. You said the baby's due in May, which means you were cheating on Alex in September, it means that while he was alive and loving you—" I'm counting on my fingers one more time to make sure. Yup!

Amy wraps one arm around my shoulder and pulls me close to her.

"Andi, Andi," she croons like I'm a baby. "You're wrong, sweet girl. You don't understand." She brushes at a loose strand of my hair, soggy with my tears, and tucks it behind one ear. She's still the same attentive Amy. She smells the same, too—Estée Lauder's Beautiful. It was Alex's favorite. Everything about her was Alex's favorite. How can I hate her? She's as special as ever, so there's no way around it. I have to find a way to forgive her. I have to. No matter what she's done, she's still part of Alex. It's so confusing—

"So wrong, sweet girl," Amy repeats. She takes hold of my shoulders and leans back and stares at me straight on. "Don't you know what this means?" she asks.

I nod my head that I certainly do!

"It means—the baby is Alex's, you silly goose. That's what we came to tell you," she says, and beams like she's part of the sun.

"And Jeff is going to stand by me. And we're always going to have a part of Alex with us."

If my face were in a cartoon, my eyes would be triple their normal size. *Jeff is going to stand by me.* Sort of like what brothers were told to do in the Bible. I've died. I've died and gone to heaven. I sit on my bed like I've been hit with a stun gun. I can hardly believe it. Just when I think I have everything figured out, and when I've had about all that I can take, life pulls a fast one on me. Just up and throws me another curve. Stands right up in my face and says, *So, Andi, how about this?* And I brace myself for another bad hit—and what do you know?—it hands me a rainbow.

Chapter Eleven

MY MOTHER ANNOUNCES AT breakfast that she has exciting news for me. Whenever my mother has made similar announcements in the past it has been something totally gross, like the time she enrolled me in a foreign language class that had me conjugating verbs every Saturday morning at 8 a.m. I got out of that by convincing her I'd hang myself.

I'm sure she has something equally disturbing to share with me now, but have no idea of the extent she will go to make my life miserable, regardless of her intentions to the contrary.

"You have been selected to be an altar server!" she exclaims, like I've just been named America's Junior Miss. She stops stirring her coffee and waits for my reaction. The look on her face tells me she expects me to dance around the room while hugging myself.

"Isn't it wonderful?" she says.

About as wonderful as having a terminal case of acne, I want to tell her. My father clears his throat and nods at me, a clear signal I'm to show my gratitude; I'm to thank my mother profusely, like a good daughter.

"You start your training on Saturday," my mother continues, her cheeks glowing. "Over one hundred candidates were considered and only six were chosen, Andi. Isn't it exciting?"

Absolutely—all my life I've wanted to dress up like a Cossack and be an altar boy. When Gloria Steinem burned her bra, did she give any thought to the Catholic Church, and what it might lead to? Obviously not—but then, I think I read somewhere that she was Jewish, so what did it matter to her that altar boys would eventually no longer be boys, but girls, as well.

"Just think," my mother is babbling. "You will be carrying the cross during the processional and ringing the bells during the Eucharist Prayer. Can you imagine?"

I can imagine, I assure her. I can see it all so vividly that I have to get up and leave the table.

"Where are you going, Andi?" my mother calls after me.

"I'm going to throw up!"

"Oh, dear," she says. "I had no idea you'd be this excited." She tucks her napkin neatly at the side of her plate and quickly follows me.

Chapter Twelve

WE ARE DOING OKAY with the holidays. It's our first without Alex, but it's not nearly as depressing as I thought it would be, which I should find disturbing, but really, I'm happy for the grieving to be less intense and so relieved to find that it is, and say Hail Marys and Our Fathers all day in gratitude, hoping it will stay that way.

My father has the entire house decorated inside and out by At Your Service, just like always. They bring and store all the items and obviously take very good care of everything. The lighting is as beautiful and shiny and opulent as ever. Our home looks like a hotel. Even the iron gates leading up to our front door are covered with piles of greenery. The smell of fresh pines is everywhere. I breathe in deeply. It sticks in my nose for hours.

Rosa is singing and baking. She's like Mary Poppins, bouncing around the kitchen. She is extra happy this time of year. Her family is coming to visit from Mexico and will stay through the holidays. My mother insists that she take home some of everything that she makes.

"So make plenty," she says, opening up another bottle of wine.

Rosa barely rests, working from morning through dinner. Heavenly smells spread like fire to every corner of the house, filling the rooms with cinnamon and nutmeg and yeast bread and cookie dough. My mother is busy shopping and wrapping gifts in shiny foil paper with elaborate bows. They're for the less fortunate, so that's good. No one in this house needs another thing for at least twenty years. My mother's a bit tipsy all day long, so Mr. Porter, the gardener, drives her when she goes shopping. She gives him a large tip for doing so.

"Mum's the word," she says, placing one finger over her lips, like no one will ever know she's half-smashed if he doesn't mention it.

My father is gone long hours as usual, but passes out hundred-dollar bills to Beth and me like there's no end to them.

"There isn't, silly," Beth says. She's home from Vassar and driving everyone nuts with her wedding plans. She has six months left so I don't understand the problem, but she's frantic every other hour, checking things off her list and rechecking with my mother to make sure the right cake was ordered; she changed her mind again, remember? She hasn't once made plans to see Parker. This is the guy she's marrying. You'd think she'd be crazy to call him. Oh no, she's worried about the gifts for the bridesmaids—have they arrived? And if they have, where in the world are they? On and on she goes, so I leave the house and go see Bridget, who is busy packing for school. She leaves right after New Year's, so for once I don't want it to show up. It hurts to see that she is excited. Of course, I don't really want her to be miserable—she's my best friend in the whole world. Still, it would feel really good to walk in her room and find her lying on her bed sobbing—at least for, say, a half-hour.

The door to her bedroom is open, so I walk in.

"Hi," I say, trying to sound cheerful.

"What do you think?" she says, holding up Westwood Academy's uniform.

It's a navy blue jumper with short pleats at the bottom of the hem, and has a fancy gold crest on the right breast pocket. Bridget is beaming.

I suck in my breath, let out a deep sigh, and offer a weak smile. Finally, the sobbing starts, but I'm the one doing it.

Chapter Thirteen

ALL THOSE HAIL MARYS and Our Fathers have paid off big time! The most amazing thing has happened and I have my mother to thank for it. I will never second-guess her decisions again, ever. This is in stone.

I am now an altar girl, thanks to my mother adding my name to the list of those to be considered. I started the classes at St. Lucy's, and just as I figured they are a zero. Then the first Saturday after New Year's, Father O'Malley says we have one more addition to the class, Anthony Morelli. His family has just joined our parish, having transferred from Our Lady of St. Catherine's.

"Anthony has been an altar boy there for over three years," Father O'Malley explains proudly, as if he had something to do with it, which is okay by me if he did, because who do you think walks in the door? My future husband is all! And he is the most gorgeous creature God has ever created. He has black hair and black-brown eyes the size of quarters and olive skin. Obviously he is true Italian, and a magazine article in *Cosmopolitan* said Italians make the best lovers, which doesn't concern me yet, except to say that I do get a warm feeling down there a little bit, when I think about it, but that is for much later—I don't want to be a slut, so I remind myself to keep my thoughts pure. Basically, I can hardly breathe when I think of Anthony, and when he accidentally brushes up next to me, like when we are passing the cruets of wine and water for Father to put in the chalice, I can hardly remain standing. Somehow the floor is no longer under my feet. If that isn't proof that Anthony and I are meant to be man and wife, what is? All this is unfolding directly under the crucifix. It's a totally holy and incredibly sacred moment. All because I am an altar girl. And to think I was mad at Gloria Steinem.

My mother is right: It's best not to draw conclusions and much better to reserve judgment. You just never know who you will be grateful to.

Chapter Fourteen

It's eight o'clock. I'm doing homework when the phone rings. I'm convinced it's Anthony and my heart flips right out the window.

"Hello?" I say as whispery as I can.

"Andi? Is that you?"

It's Bridget, who I am very happy to hear from, yes, but I was prepared to hear Anthony, so it takes me a moment to get my real voice back.

"Ah, yeah, it's me—"

"You sound funny,"

"Oh, I was, just, just deep in—into my homework, is all," I lie.

"Well, you will never guess. Listen to this," she says.

She's all excited about school, having joined the Equestrian Guard and is now after only three weeks jumping hurdles. I am thoroughly convinced she will break her neck and end up a mega-quadriplegic and tell her she must reconsider this dangerous sport immediately.

"You will not have any fun in a wheelchair," I say.

"Don't be silly. We have experts teaching us."

I want to tell her I am getting married probably sooner than I ever imagined and would very much like her to remain in one piece for the wedding as she will be my maid of honor. I don't get a word in. But it's okay. I haven't heard Bridget this happy in a very long time. And who's to say. Maybe she was born to jump horses over perfectly manicured hedges. I decide to say extra Hail Marys in her honor in case that is not the case and let it go.

"I'm bringing a new friend home for the weekend," she adds.

"But I thought you and I were going to the mall."

"We can still do that," she says. "She'll come too. You'll like her. Her name is Madeline. She's from Savannah."

"Great," I say, thoroughly convinced I'll hate her.

"Well, we'll see you this weekend," Bridget chirps.

"Right," I answer and hang up the phone.

Madeline—she sounds like a spoiled rich girl. Then I realize, she'll probably think the same thing of me. This is all Donna's fault. If she wasn't screwing my father, Bridget would never have been sent to this school and no one named Madeline would be moving in on a perfectly wonderful friendship. I have to get Donna and my father to stop seeing each other. Not just for me—for everyone, my mother, Bridget's father, not to mention Donna and my father's eternal souls. It's a matter of life and purgatory, plain and simple. What won't be is finding a way to do it.

Chapter Fifteen

THERE'S A SMALL PROBLEM concerning Anthony Morelli. It seems the fact that we are meant to be man and wife—by divine order I might add—has not occurred to him. He is playing up to Rachel Martin. It's almost like a mortal sin, going against holy orders. Normally, I would turn to Bridget and talk things over before determining what I am to do about all of this, but Bridget is totally preoccupied with her new school, horses—who would have thought it, she used to get hives just watching them on TV—and Madeline, who she says is just so cool. And granted, that's not an exaggeration. I was prepared to totally hate her, but she is a very interesting person to be around. She knows everything about makeup and skin care and she can look in your closet for about three minutes and put together an awesome outfit right under your nose from what was already in there to begin with and you never even noticed before. It's like magic.

So now, I have four perfect Madeline-inspired ensembles to tantalize Anthony with, but do you think he notices that I have just the right fashionable clothes thrown on in just the right order? Oh no, his eyes are glued to Rachel Martin. They have sparks flying back and forth between them and all I can wonder is how did this happen? I was standing at the altar doing perfect altar girl duties, experiencing a complete hallowed moment regarding Anthony. How could he not have felt it, too?

I decide to talk it over with Bridget and Madeline next weekend. They have been alternating weekends at each other's houses, which thoroughly annoys me, yes, but now I have more important matters to concern myself with—like a future husband who is already cheating on me.

Chapter Sixteen

MY MOTHER IS REALLY losing it. Now she has decided that I am to be an Angel. Not the heavenly kind, mind you. An Angel is a teenager who volunteers their time at Sunny Meadows Nursing home—the very one my grandmother Nana Louise resides at, which is how my mother found out about it. Mostly, the Angels go to the rooms they are assigned to and read stories to whoever they find there, which is sometimes not the person who belongs there. These elderly people, even those in wheelchairs, wander all over the place. Which makes me wonder immediately: is anyone watching them?

This Angel business started when a local girl volunteered to read to a person at Sunny Meadows that she was no relationship to, and she just happened by chance—at least that's what she told the newspaper reporter who wrote the article for the local paper—to select a room that had a resident that was a former school teacher and loved books, but her eyesight was failing her, and when the girl was reading to her she said, "Oh, you are an angel," and it just so happened that a nursing assistant overheard this and mentioned to another visitor that wouldn't it be wonderful if there were more "angels" around here, and wouldn't you know, that particular person that this nursing assistant mentioned it to was none other than the Woman Volunteer of the Year and so, of course, she organized a squad of volunteer "angels," and now my mother has volunteered me to be one.

Do I object? Before I answer that, let me explain that my mother always announces what she has in mind for me in the presence of my father. This time, it was not at breakfast, like when she gave me the news that I was to be an altar server. This time it was at dinner, which is even worse. When my father manages to be home for dinner he is so wrung out he could wipe the table down. So, no, I do not object. It would be pointless. My father would simply lose it, and my mother would ask Rosa to open another bottle of Chardonnay.

"Andi," my mother says, naturally over a glass of wine, "I forgot to mention; you are now officially an Angel at Sunny Meadows."

How does one forget to mention she is ruining her child's life?

The details of my assignment are not complicated. I am to show up each day for an hour after school and read. One hour. How can I possibly get out of this? Let me tell you: I can't.

I am here now for my first day. Reading to Nana Louise is not a problem. I was doing that already, just not on a regular basis. Being an official Angel—I have a little gold badge with those letters spelled out that I must wear while I'm here—I have been assigned to an additional room that I go to after I finish with Nana Louise. They've given me Room 225 which is home to a married couple, Howard and Mavis Sterling.

The Sterlings are close to ninety; they have to be. They have so many lines on their faces they could both be road maps. I'm not trying to be unkind here, just honest.

This is how my first day with them goes:

"Hi! I'm Andi and I'm—ah—an Angel," I say, feeling very stupid. I point to my badge. "And I'm going to read to you for a while. How will that be?"

"Say what?" Mr. Sterling shouts.

"She's going to read to us," Mrs. Sterling shouts back.

"Well, tell her to speak up. I can't hear her."

I'll have laryngitis after two days, guaranteed.

Now I know I stated that I would never question my mother's

judgment again—after meeting Anthony—but I am thoroughly convinced that I lied.

Chapter Seventeen

MADELINE AND BRIDGET ARE spending the night. We are camped out on my bedroom floor and I'm the entertainment. I'm doing my best imitation of Mr. Sterling and they are laughing so hard one of them may wet her pants.

"What'd you say, girlie?" I shriek and cup my ear like Mr. Sterling does. "I said the man was never seen again!" I'm telling about the time I read him and Mavis a mystery story.

"Well, check with Gabby," Mr. Sterling says. He's referring to Mrs. Sharp, the nurse in charge who never shuts up. "She knows where everybody is." I wag my finger in the air high over my head, like Mr. Sterling.

I shouldn't be making fun of that poor old man. He can't help it that he can no longer hear, even with both hearing aids in place and at high volume. When I remember this fiasco will get me ten Hail Marys, I change the subject.

"Let's make some popcorn," I say.

"Let's sneak out of the house instead," Madeline suggests. "Don't you have a hang-out where there are lots of boys?"

Bridget shrugs her shoulders. I give Madeline a blank stare. Bridget and I are not much into sneaking out, unless it's to watch my father and Donna in the pool house. But it's Saturday night. They won't be there. Besides Bridget and I haven't shared this secret with anyone, so even if they were, we probably wouldn't invite Madeline to join us.

"Come on. It'll be fun," Madeline says and starts to put her shoes on.

"We have some guard dogs in our neighborhood," I point out. "They're bound to give us away." Part of this is true. There are some dogs, but I have no idea whether they'd make a fuss.

Madeline tosses her shoes aside and opens her overnight bag. She dumps the contents on the floor.

"Check it out," she says, the suggested foray into the night forgotten.

"Where did all this stuff come from?" Bridget asks, sifting through an assortment of enamel bracelets. She pops one on her arm, then wraps a silk scarf around her neck. There's stretchy tops loaded with rhinestones, some leather belts, a red leather Coach wallet, scads of makeup, and a dozen bottles of perfume. I pick up a bottle of Arpège, my mother's favorite. Sample is stamped on the bottle.

"I can get as much of this stuff as I want," Madeline explains. "It's fun!"

There are bottles of Dior Eau Noire, Narciso Rodriquez, Tabu, Obsession, Poison, Chloé and Oscar de la Renta. I'm not sure where this is going, but I have a pretty good idea. The Coach wallet alone costs at least a hundred dollars. I realize Madeline's parents are wealthy, but still, there are limits to a parent's generosity.

"These are just samples, but they smell the same," Madeline explains. "But I can get you the real thing if you want."

My eyes are bulging out of my head.

"Trust me," she adds, "It's no big thing. I'm very good at it."

Madeline turns to Bridget who is eyeballing the loot.

"Cool, huh?" Madeline says, perfectly convinced.

Stealing is definitely not cool. Suddenly I am fearful for Bridget, who has grown very close to Madeline. She idolizes her. Bridget could get into a lot of trouble. I don't know what to say or what to do. I do know I would like all this stuff to disappear. What if the cops have some type of sting operation going on and we are surrounded? It's giving me the creeps. I peek out my bedroom window. No one is out there that I can see. Even so, I have a feeling in my chest like something very heavy is resting on it. I take a deep breath.

"What's wrong?" Madeline says.

I don't answer. Bridget picks up a bottle of Chanel No. 5 and dabs her wrist. "Is it me?" she says, and holds out her arm. "What do you think?"

I think I'm going to be sick. And I think it was a big mistake for Bridget to end up at Westwood Academy. And for sure I think it was a major mistake the day she met Madeline.

Chapter Eighteen

IT'S SEVEN O'CLOCK ON Sunday night and I have a book report to turn in tomorrow. Once again I've waited 'til time is no longer on my side. We are to pose questions regarding the purpose of the narrative and then give answers. I've chosen *The Great Gatsby*. It was on the list and I liked the character Daisy, even though I don't think we're supposed to. So far my list of questions includes:

1. Why did Jay Gatsby have this obsession with Daisy to begin with?

2. Why didn't Daisy love him back?

3. Why did Nick just watch and never do anything?

My answers are a blank sheet of paper. Consider question number one. Why do any of us feel attracted to someone? It's very complicated to explain. If we could figure that out then when we find we really like some jerk, we could stop liking him, and that's not how it works. And as for Daisy not loving Jay Gatsby in return, that sort of follows question number one. And Nick was the narrator, so maybe his sole purpose in the book was just to relay the facts, but if that's the case, why didn't F. Scott Fitzgerald remain the narrator himself like many other books that have been written? So there has to be some reason Nick was there observing and not really doing anything. Maybe my questions are not very good ones. I'm thinking of starting over when Beth taps on the door and comes into my room. I never can figure why people knock if they are going to just barge in without waiting for a reply. Beth is home from school and she couldn't have chosen a worse weekend to do so.

"Andi, what is this doing here?"

She has an Arpège perfume bottle in her hand. I have a feeling it's the one stamped sample and I can't understand what she's doing with it. Madeline shoved all that stuff back in her bag before she left. I watched. She said, "It's no big deal, Andi. They have insurance for stuff like this when it's lost."

Lost was not exactly the word I had in mind and it is a big deal. To begin with somehow she left one behind and now I'm the one having to explain it. If I tell the truth, I'll be grounded. If I lie, I'll feel bad about myself. This is not a win-win situation. All because of Madeline's thievery—and we're not even talking the big picture here, yet. Bridget. She'll be next.

"Andi? I'm talking to you," Beth says. Her lips are twisted to the side like she is really enjoying this. Like she knows her question is rhetorical—another word Alex taught me—and her face has the answer. I stole it. That's what it's saying and saying it with pleasure.

"Ah," I say. "I—I—"

"Thought so," she says and leaves as quickly as she entered, the bottle still firmly clutched in her hand.

It is hard for me to understand why a flesh-and-blood relation can take so much pleasure in another's discomfort. It makes me think we're not related. That there's something my mother's not telling me and I was really fathered by someone else, say a long-lost love that came back into her life for one brief night. I know that's far-fetched, but still at times like this I can't help but think it. Right now I don't need to be thinking on it. I need to get to my mother before Beth does. She'll have her convinced I should be in reform school. And she'll enjoy convincing her.

There's another reason why parents should never have a drinking problem while their children are growing up. Say you want to talk to them about something very important, something that is near eating your insides up, and they are just lying on their bed at seven o'clock on a Sunday night and they look like they're sleeping, but they're not. They're so far under the influence they don't answer no matter how many times you call their name or shake their shoulder.

Chapter Nineteen

JUST WHEN YOU THINK you have all your priorities straight and know what's important—and what's not—life steps in and says: Nothing doing. You are way off-track, buster. Take this morning for example. Beth has left to go back to school and the day is nearly perfect. I'm trying to find a way to approach my mother about Madeline, and the perfume bottle, and the entire mess I'm sitting in, through no fault of my own, and the phone rings and everything is turned upside down.

"Oh, good Lord!" my mother says. "When?" A slight pause follows. "How bad?" My mother's face is the color of cement. "Uh-huh, uh-huh, oh no!" On and on she goes, shaking her head side to side as if to deny whatever it is she's hearing. I hate it when people on the phone don't repeat what's transpiring on the other end of the line and you're left picturing the worst. My mother lays the phone down and yells for Rosa.

"What? What?" I chase after my mother who is still trying to find Rosa. Finally, my mother stops and explains. We have to go to the hospital immediately. Amy has gone into labor. It's way too soon. My mother's hands are shaking so hard she can barely hang on to the car keys. Rosa runs to get Mr. Porter. He's poking around in the garden as usual, but gets behind the wheel and pulls the car around while we wait at the front door.

"Andi, you best go to school," my mother says. "There's nothing you can do—"

"No!" I say.

This baby is all we have left of Alex. How am I supposed to go to school like it's an ordinary Monday? Sometimes my mother doesn't think clearly.

"Well, alright then," she says. "Get in." She turns to Mr. Porter and says, "Mercy Hospital. And hurry!"—like he's a taxi driver.

Mr. Porter nods his head. He's a small man who might have had a nice physique had he been born a woman. His shoulders are narrow and pointed and his hands are almost delicate. His fingers remind me of tulips, but I'm not sure why. Maybe because he spends so much time in the garden and everything grows green and lush within days after his hands sift about in the soil. He caresses the folds around the plants, like the small piles of dirt gathered in his hands are little blankets and he's tucking in his babies.

"I can't understand this. I just can't understand this," my mother murmurs and squeezes my hand. I feel very important when she does this, like we are in on this together and of course we are, but still, it's nice that she is letting me get close to her anguish. I really do love my mother even when she oftentimes isn't there for me. She's here right now and she's very distressed and she's sober. If this was going to happen, at least it happened in the morning before her oatmeal. She never drinks before her oatmeal.

Mr. Porter drops us at the emergency room door and leaves to park the car. He'll be in the coffee shop, he says. In case we need him. My mother rushes to the nurses' station where we find that Amy has been admitted and taken to a private room on the third floor.

"I forgot to call your father!" My mother rests her hand on my arm. "Stay here," she says and turns and rushes back to the nurses' station. I watch as her heels click on the poured-concrete floor. She's like a thoroughbred. She glides easily across the surface.

I enter Amy's room, careful not to make a sound. A nurse is by her side. Amy's resting comfortably, she says, but someone needs to tell Amy that. Her eyes look like an animal's that have made contact with the headlights of a car. She's on the phone with her mother who lives in New York. She's divorced from Amy's father who is some sort of diplomat. He is currently out of the country.

"I don't know, Mother," Amy laments. "They haven't told me anything. They're trying to stop the labor, is all I know. And I'm not calling Jeffrey until I know something."

Jeffrey's at Vanderbilt and Amy's living in an apartment by herself off North Druid Hills Road, not too far from us.

My mother makes her way into the room. Her face is no longer soft and serene. Her brow is creased and her lips are pinched. She's worried. The last time we were at this hospital it was so my father could identify Alex. My mother insisted I wasn't to go with them, but I cried 'til hiccups wracked my body and my father convinced my mother it was best to stay together. That night is still fresh in my heart. It sits there like an open wound, ready to fester with the slightest encouragement.

The doctor strides into the room and picks up the clipboard at the end of Amy's bed. He is young and stout, with greasy hair parted on one side. He's wearing large, black-rimmed glasses and I want to laugh out loud. He looks like a doctor ready for a sketch on *Saturday Night Live.* But this is not a laughing matter. The doctor explains to Amy and my mother about the medication in the IV and what they hope to accomplish by administering it, which I find rather strange. Not the IV, but the fact he's giving us all this information. He doesn't even know who we are. He hasn't even introduced himself. I guess this doctor is too busy to bother with formalities and assumes since we are in the room, we are family and takes it from there.

"The medication is not without side effects," he cautions. He explains that Amy is being given a steroid drug called a corticosteroid, which will help the baby's lungs mature, along with antibiotics, to help prevent infection since the baby's immune system is immature.

"We're also using ritodrine," the doctor explains. "Dr. Charles" is stenciled on the pocket of his white coat in red letters. "As I said, there's a possibility of side effects, naturally."

I'm reading the inscription on the IV bag and there certainly are! It says possible side effects for the mother include rapid heartbeat, fluid in the lungs, poor blood flow, low blood pressure, fast heartbeat, high levels of sugar in the blood, high levels of insulin in the blood, low amounts of potassium in the blood, reduced amounts of urine, changes in function of the thyroid gland, shaking, nervousness, nausea or vomiting, fever and hallucinations. All this from a drug Dr. Charles insists is the proven drug of choice to stop premature labor.

Possible side effects for the baby are equally disturbing: fast heartbeat, high levels of insulin in the blood, low or high levels of sugar in the blood, enlarged heart, poor blood flow, low levels of calcium in the blood, jaundice, low blood pressure, and bleeding within the brain or heart.

This poor little baby. We found out last week it's a boy. They did the sonogram and the doctor said, "No mistake here. It's a boy!"

❖❖❖

When my father arrives, I know that I'll feel better. It is a big disappointment to discover that I don't. He is very somber after speaking with the doctor, who explains that so far the treatment is not working.

"It doesn't look good," my father says when the doctor leaves. My mother has her arms wrapped around her waist. Her head is moving side to side in slow motion, like she has seen the outcome and no longer believes in possibilities. My father puts his arm around my shoulder and I bury my head in his sleeve, squeezing my eyes shut to hold back the tears. I don't want Amy to see. I don't want her to know that our side of the family has given up hope.

Chapter Twenty

THERE'S NO GETTING AROUND it. Beth is beautiful—absolutely, positively beautiful. And I'm not. I'm staring in the bathroom mirror, trying to figure out what makes my face different than hers when it's so much like hers to begin with. Yet, mine's not even close to beautiful. We both have long blond hair. We have the same eyes, brown and very round. I decide mine are maybe spaced too close together, but I can't be sure. I'm feeling extra miserable as it is totally out of my control. Like Amy. We left the hospital after several hours with no change. Amy was still having contractions. But my mother decided I needed to get some dinner and get to bed early so I would for certain make school in the morning. As if I can concentrate on school.

I call Bridget at Westwood Academy, but she is not in her room. Probably she's at the library. She's doing a report on Stalin for her history class. Bridget is getting all As and her father is totally convinced Westwood Academy is the best school in the world for Bridget. Now she'll never get to come back to Parker Junior High. Why couldn't she get Cs or maybe even C–s? But no, she gets As. And she's never gotten As before, which is a real mystery to me. So I'm triple miserable. There's Amy, and my face in the mirror, and Bridget, and of course, my father is still sleeping with Donna. I mean there's nothing to indicate he's not. He still sneaks over to the pool house every Monday and Wednesday and sometimes Friday. Bridget's no longer with me to witness, so I no longer watch, but

I see him walking through the thick hedges making his way to the pool house and sometimes if I'm still awake when he returns, I hear the front door open and his footsteps as he climbs the long winding staircase back to my mother. I picture her waking, still tipsy from her wine.

"Long day, darling?" she says.

"Very," my father replies.

I close my eyes tight at the thought, willing the image to leave me. My life is mostly a disaster. Especially considering what just transpired with Anthony Morelli. It's hard to believe it actually happened. I went to altar class on Saturday and found out Rachel Martin has moved. She's the one Anthony was all ga-ga over. Her father took a job in Dallas, which is really good news. Dallas is fairly far away, so I don't think she's going to be a problem anymore.

After class—Easter's on its way and we were going over what each of us is to do when it's our turn to assist the Mass—Anthony said he wanted to talk to me and motioned for me to go up to the balcony. I waited until everyone left and Father Murphy was busy putting everything we were practicing with back in its little cubby-hole, the chalice and the crosses and the cruets. Once Father left I followed Anthony up to the balcony and my heart was pounding and I was thinking he's probably going to ask me to go with him, so I'm in heaven. When we get up there, he turns around and puts his hands on my chest! There's really not much there, so I'm wondering why he's so interested, but I'm going to marry him so I figure it's probably all right in the long run. And then he starts kissing me and other than when Dennis Luken kissed me right before Alex died I've really never kissed a boy before, so I'm not very good at it. Then Anthony sticks his tongue in my mouth and I'm really grossing out, but I want him to like me so I kind of mush my tongue back at him, trying not to gag. Then he starts putting his hands on my chest again and if that's not bad enough, he reaches down with his other hand and puts it up my skirt. I'm going shopping at the mall this afternoon with Bridget and Madeline so we decided to wear skirts and try to look sophisticated. Even though I'm determined to marry Anthony and am probably destined to, his hand up my skirt is not a good thing and I'm about to push it away, when he pulls me closer and puts his hand right down my pants and that is the last straw, marriage or not! We're not even engaged yet, so all that stuff has to come later. I'm about to shove him away and in walks Madeline.

"Gaaaawd, Andi," she says.

And I'm like to die. When Anthony kissed me, I forgot all about Donna picking me up to take Bridget and me and Madeline over to the mall. It's like my brain and my feet and my stomach no longer resided in the same body. Nothing else mattered, so naturally I forgot all about the time.

I yank my skirt back down and run after Madeline.

"Wait up," I yell. "Let me explain!"

Madeline turns around and smirks.

"You better be careful," she says. "I've got something on you now." And she laughs, but it doesn't sound like a normal laugh. It sounds like a cackle.

Chapter Twenty-one

SOMETIMES I SWEAR THERE are two people living inside of me, an angel and a beast. I can have such nice thoughts about people and then they do something and I want to kill them. Or I picture them getting hit by a bicycle and breaking an ankle. What is that? Good and evil married to each other right inside me. Beth has decided to let me choose the dress I will wear at her wedding—so long as it's pink—and I want to hug every inch of her neck. Then she says I'm to wear flats, not even short pumps but flats. End of story.

"Why?"

Because I'm the junior bridesmaid, that's why, she says, and reminds me I'm already taller than Joanne, one of her regular bridesmaids. A pigmy is taller than Joanne. I hope Beth gets hit by a motorcycle and breaks both ankles and has to hobble down the aisle in walking casts. I do, I swear.

At least I found a dress I really like. It's light pink and has a satin top that makes me look like I have real breasts instead of bumps. There are pleats on the bodice and it has an Empire waist and the rest of the dress is a sheath made from chiffon. It's very sophisticated, but of course I don't say that, because I'm still supposed to be a junior bridesmaid and I'm hoping Beth doesn't notice. She's busy with the cake and flowers and a gazillion other things, so maybe she won't, but even if she does, the dress is already paid for—it cost four hundred dollars—so my mother would probably be on my side.

However, something more important is going on right now,

something very strange. It has my full attention. My mother has invited Rodger and Donna to dinner. She is going over the menu with Rosa.

They will have Caesar salad, followed by beef Wellington and twice-whipped potatoes and creamed corn, and cognac and an assortment of cheeses and fruit for dessert. Don't ask me how Rosa knows how to prepare all these things, but she does. It's like she went to culinary school, but I know for a fact that she didn't.

"She's a natural," my father says.

"Gifted," my mother adds.

The fact that my father finds nothing unusual in my mother's invitation is perplexing, considering the fact that he spends more time screwing Donna than he does playing golf.

The dinner party is all set for tomorrow night, Friday, which means my father and Donna will have to give up their rendezvous in the pool house. They can hardly excuse themselves between the main course and dessert and go at it.

My mother insists that I will attend. Beth doesn't have to. She's back at Vassar. I wish Bridget were home from school. Then she'd have to be at the dinner, too.

"You'll have a lovely time," my mother says.

Well, of course, I'm thinking. What could be lovelier than having dinner with a woman who is trying to steal my father from my mother right under her very nose?

Donna needs to receive an academy award for her performance tonight. If I didn't know what she was up to with my father I'd never suspect what she was up to with my father. So I can hardly blame my mother anymore for not knowing. I'm thinking of writing an anonymous letter to my mother to tip her off. Something simple like: *I am screwing your husband. From your neighbor.* She'd have to know which neighbor. The only other women on our street are Mrs. Reed, who's about eighty, Mrs. Anderson, who weighs at least three hundred pounds and Mrs. Decker who has a face that is the spitting image of her Doberman. But if I do write a letter, it's bound to break my mother's heart. And what with Amy still in the hospital and the wedding coming up, it would be wrong for me to destroy my mother's world, so writing the letter right now is pretty much out of the question. I pray during Mass that my mother doesn't find out about what's going on all on her own, at least until after things calm down. I light a candle. I light two more. I pay money. It better work. I spent the last five dollars from my allowance.

Chapter Twenty-two

Today is a special day at Sunny Meadows Nursing Home. It's Mr. and Mrs. Sterling's sixty-fifth wedding anniversary. I'm getting attached to them so I'm actually glad to be here. We Angels decorated the activity room with crepe-paper wedding bells and streamers and the kitchen staff made a cake. It's supposed to be a wedding cake, but it's a long sheet cake, so it hardly resembles one. It has pink and blue bells and the number sixty-five in the center with pink icing. A minister from the chapel is coming to have them renew their wedding vows. I can just picture that. Mr. Sterling will be saying, "WHAT'D YOU SAY? SPEAK UP!" And Mrs. Sterling will say, "HE SAYS, 'DO YOU WANT TO MARRY ME AGAIN?'" Which is exactly what happens except no one counted on Mr. Sterling saying, "WHY WOULD I DO THAT?" And everyone starts chuckling, pretending he's joking, and Mavis, that's Mrs. Sterling, pats his back and smiles at everyone.

The minister skips over the "I do" part and says, "Bless this couple in their rededication one to the other," and Mr. and Mrs. Sterling shuffle over to the cake. All the residents are having a nice time. Andy Williams's love songs are playing on an old record player one of the nurses brought in. Nana Louise is sitting next to another elderly woman, Ms. Moorefield, who's actually the oldest person living here. She's ninety-eight. Neither one of them knows what's going on, but they eat the cake and look up at the ones dancing now and then and smile. The dancing is not real dancing; it's more like feet stumbling here and there, but still, it's nice to see them trying. Nurse Sharp—ole Gabby herself—is twirling Mr. Bailey around and around in his wheel chair. "Are we having fun? Huh? Huh?" she asks and he just sits there looking like he'd like to stand up and belt her one if he could find a way to stand up without falling over.

One of the other Angels, Allison Whitley, has invited me to come over to her house. She lives on a regular street and her mother drives a regular car, a Chevy, and Allison is like a regular person, but very interesting to be around. She says some unusual things.

"My Dad was changing the oil on my mother's car last night and he kicked the oil pan over and you should have seen the mess! He was hysterical trying to clean up the garage floor so my mother wouldn't have a fit." And last week she said, "We're getting a new color TV this weekend." And the way she said it, you could tell that it was a very big deal. So most of what she says is really entertaining, plus she's just a very nice person, so I'll probably go over to her house when she asks me again.

Right now I'm just hanging out with Bridget and Madeline. They're still alternating going to each other's houses on weekends. Trying to stay friends with Madeline is nearly impossible. We went to the mall again last weekend and were just hanging out and looking at this and that and I was watching Madeline to make sure she wasn't snatching any more perfume bottles, and then out of the blue she says, "Look, there's Baskin-Robbins. Let's get ice cream," and sure enough they've added a Baskin-Robbins store. So we go there and as I'm taking out my wallet to pay for my cone, what is sitting in the bottom of my purse but a gold chain! It still has the price tag on it. It's not pure gold, but it's a Monet, the kind guaranteed not to tarnish for life. I turn to look at Madeline and she is grinning like a Cheshire cat and I start shaking.

"What did you do?" I said.

"I saw you admiring it," Madeline says, "so I got it for you."

"You stole it!"

"Sssssshhhh," Bridget says and takes my arm.

I hand the clerk two dollars for my ice cream and don't bother to wait for change. I walk off with Bridget, shaking my head. I can hardly believe this.

"I need to take this back," I say.

"You can't," Bridget points out. "You'll get arrested."

"Maybe I could just slip it onto the counter real casual-like," I tell her and bite my lower lip.

"Someone could see you," Bridget says, "and you'd still get arrested!"

Of course, she's right and then I realize I could have been caught with it in my purse. What if another shopper had seen Madeline place it in my purse and thought I was in on it all along. I start shaking again.

"Don't ever do that again, Madeline!"

"Lighten up, Andi," she says. "It's just some crappy old chain."

She's licking her cone, running her tongue around the edges in a circle and I want to just push the whole thing right into her face.

"It's stealing! And don't ever do it again!" I say, "or I'll—I'll—"

"What? Tell my parents and then I can tell yours?"

Madeline finishes her cone and stops to toss her napkin in the trash can next to the escalator.

"Oh, don't tell her parents she had anything to do with it," Bridget says, and stops in her tracks. "If they thought she was shop-lifting, they'd ground her for life."

But it's not shoplifting that's on my mind at the moment, it's Anthony Morelli and what Madeline saw or what she thinks she saw that has me worried. Being grounded for life is one thing and being sent to a convent is another thing entirely.

Chapter Twenty-three

AMY IS BEING RELEASED from the hospital! The doctors stopped her labor and they think she may be fine if she can stay off her feet until she's further along.

"Every week counts," they say.

My father is convinced that the stress of her and Jeffrey living apart and her being alone in an apartment is too much for Amy. He's buying them a house, which Jeffrey outright refused, so my father said, okay he'd buy it but they'd pay him rent, but he'd write a contract that they're actually buying it from him. It's called a lease-purchase agreement. Jeffrey agreed, and the deal is he will come back to Atlanta from Vanderbilt and transfer his credits to Emory University. It's very expensive, but my father says not any more expensive than Vanderbilt, which Jeffrey's parents have been paying for part of and the rest is from a scholarship. My father explains Emory has scholarships available, too, and with Jeffrey's grades it won't be a problem. My father seems to know everything.

Right now, I'm helping them move in and Amy is resting on the sofa. They don't have a lot of furniture yet, but Jeffrey says they'll worry about that later. The important thing is to get Amy settled and resting properly.

I'm putting their dishes away. They do have a nice set of dishes—stoneware, with yellow and brown flowers in the center. They were a wedding present from my parents. They got married at the court-house by a justice of the peace. Amy's mother cried the whole time, which really irritated my father. I mean it's bad enough Alex is dead and Amy's having his baby, without her mother boo-hooing because there's no big church wedding. Well, that's what my father said, and I have to agree.

"Thank God they're getting married and the poor child is getting a proper name," my mother says.

Appearances are everything to my mother. That and the right street address. She's not overly wild for North Druid Hills Road where their new home is located, but it's respectable enough and in a section of Decatur where the land grows more valuable each year.

"A good investment," my father points out. "And affordable for them," he adds. "I rather like the fact Jeffrey insists on making his own way. He's got character."

He says it like it's a reflection on Alex. And maybe it is; he *was* Alex's best friend.

"Can I get you anything else?" I ask Amy and hand her an iced tea and some magazines I found lying in a box full of books. *Cosmopolitan*, an old issue of *Reader's Digest* and *People* magazine. She picks up the *Reader's Digest* and I notice it has an article on the front entitled "The Truth About Miscarriage." God! I reach to take it back, but she's already turning pages. She stops at the joke page, but then continues on.

"Maybe we could watch TV," I chirp gaily.

"Cable's not connected," Jeffrey points out.

I'm hoping she's not going to have a meltdown and then my parents and Jeffrey find out I gave her those magazines. Jeffrey says, "Keep her company, Andi. We'll unpack."

Oh, I'm good company, alright. I sit down next to Amy, keeping an eye on what page she's up to. She stops on page 167. It's where the article on miscarriage starts.

Oh brother. This world and I are not getting along.

❖❖❖

I'm home lying on my bed waiting for dinner and thanking God that Amy read the article and then just put the magazine down and picked up the *People* and never said a word, when the phone rings and it's Bridget. She's all excited because Madeline won class president. Like I could care. It's a big deal, Bridget insists. It means Madeline is the most popular girl at their school.

"And she's like my best friend," Bridget says.

"Thanks a lot."

"Well, next to you, Andi, you know what I mean—here at Westwood, she's my best friend." She's a bad influence is what she is.

There's a tap on my door. It's my mother. She asks if she can come in and waits for me to answer. My mother always gets it right.

"Sure," I call out.

"Honey, there's something I've been wanting to talk to you about," she says. "Is this a good time?"

There's never going to be a good time. My blood pressure is higher than the ceiling.

"Sure," I lie, and tell Bridget good-bye.

My heart starts to pound. What is it my mother wants to talk to me about? I'm thinking Madeline called. No, Donna called. No, my father's told her—

My mother wobbles over to my bed and sits down next to me. I can smell the wine on her breath. She sighs deeply, like what she is about to say is more difficult to discuss than when she brought in the book on sex.

I sigh deeply, too, but try and force a small smile onto my face. It feels like it's stuck on with scotch tape.

"Andi, sweetheart, I'm going away for a little while," my mother says.

I knew it. My father told her. He just up and told her and tore our entire world apart and here we're having a wedding in a few months. That's just like him.

I hate him. I do.

I put my arms around my mother and hug her tight.

"I'm sooooo sorry, Mommy," I say. That's what I used to call her when I was little and right now I feel smaller than I've ever been.

Chapter Twenty-four

My mother is going to Peachford. She'll be gone for thirty days. Peachford is for those addicted to drugs or alcohol. This means my mother is an alcoholic, which I find hard to believe. I mean, she doesn't even drink before breakfast. How can she be an alcoholic? She has a home and nice clothes, and friends, and still helps Rosa around the house. Alcoholics lie down in the street or stumble home and pass out in the doorway, don't they?

She's leaving in the morning and I've decided to bury myself in my school work. Maybe I can become an absolute scholar and surprise my mother when she returns. She'll be so happy with my progress she won't ever drink again. The only problem with this plan is my teachers. There is not one of them I like. Well, maybe Mr. Majors, the choir teacher. He's alright, but he has some strange habits, like he clears his throat constantly as if something lives in the back of it and he prefers that it didn't. But the rest are crazy. So burying myself in my studies and becoming a scholar to grab my mother's attention is not going to be easy.

Peachford is different than I pictured and so are the people stuck here. They have a nice lounge area where family and friends can come and visit and there are lots of plants and large windows—which have mesh inside the layers of glass; I guess so nobody can break out—to look out onto the grounds which are well-kept and full of flower beds. My mother has made friends with another woman with a drinking problem, Dixie. It's hard to imagine my mother making friends with a woman with a nickname that sounds like she lives in a trailer. I find out that she does.

"Come over some time," she says to my mother. "I got a cool double-wide."

My mother says, "Double-wide what?"

Dixie grabs her sides and laughs so hard she starts coughing. Dixie is thin and nervous and chain-smokes Lucky Strikes. It's hard for me to picture my mother and her being friends. I think about my mother's soft voice greeting her in the morning, "Lovely day, isn't it, Dixie?" and Dixie's frog voice calling back, "I ain't noticed. Hand me one a' them coffee cups." It's too much for my brain to handle on short notice. I smile and put my hand out to shake hers when my mother introduces us, like I've been taught to. Dixie gives mine one good awkward shake and then lets go real quick.

"Nice kid," she says and lights up another Lucky Strike.

Vivian's here, you know, my mother's best friend who's married to Howard.

"Andi, sweet girl," she says. "Come right over here and give me a big hug. You're as tall as me."

It's true. Now I am. But then she's only like five-foot-three, so that's not saying much. I give her a hug and then turn to my mother to give her one.

"How are you?" I ask, not sure what else to say. "Is it okay?"

"It's fine, honey. I'm right where I'm supposed to be."

Great! Right where she's supposed to be—smack in the middle of the nut ward with all the other nuts.

"Okay?" she says.

I stare at her. Oh just peachy.

Chapter Twenty-five

I DON'T THINK BETH said anything to my mother about that perfume bottle. If she did, my mother is keeping it to herself—at least for the time being. I feel like I'm getting off scot-free, which means I really can't count on it for sure. It all goes back to Dred Scott, the slave that never got free.

I buried the necklace out in the backyard in a part of the garden Mr. Porter mostly leaves to nature and I buried what Anthony did to me as deep inside of me as possible. I saw him for the first time since the incident this past Saturday and told myself that I should stop liking him, pronto. But telling myself to and actually stopping is not the same thing. When I look at him my heart still does this little dance like it knows how to polka. Maybe I'll just keep liking him but never go to the balcony with him again. That should be okay. I'm still trying to figure out what got into him. Maybe he feels we are destined to be married someday, too, and just got impatient. Either that or he's a sex fiend and I don't like to think of him being one of those types, seeing as I can't help myself that I still like him. So like I said, I'm off scot-free.

Alex's fraternity brothers are for the most part, too. There's not going to be a trial. The guys involved pleaded guilty to the lesser charge of aggravated hazing, which my father explained is a fourth-degree offense, whatever that means. And all they got was probation and a million hours of community service. It didn't upset my father.

"It's not going to bring back Alex," he said.

"Well, maybe it would make other people think before doing something stupid like that," I told him and he just nodded and then changed the subject.

"Would you like me to take you to visit with your mother?"

Not really. "Sure," I say.

She's on her twenty-fourth day and goes to these AA meetings every day faithfully. They have to while they're residents at Peachford or they lose their privileges. I'm not sure which ones they're referring to, maybe they don't get dinner and they have really good food there. I got to join her for lunch on Sunday and it's cafeteria style, but real fancy with a chef and all sorts of meat to choose from, roast beef slices and ham, all sorts of fresh vegetables and a salad bar better than many restaurants, and desserts to die for. Maybe that's why this place is so expensive, the food is heaven.

"Can we go for lunch?" I ask.

"Not this week," my father says. "I've got a deposition to work on, but I'll take you this afternoon."

Afternoons aren't as fun. Everyone just sits around and drinks coffee or soda. And there's candy and crackers in a vending machine, which is better than nothing at all, but not by much.

I nod my head and go off to read for a while. Sundays are very boring days. After mass there's never really anything to do, unless Bridget is home for the weekend and this is her week to go to Madeline's. Madeline used to invite me sometimes but not since I told her not to steal for me anymore. I paid the price.

Instead of reading I decide to write a letter to Donna, not to mail to her, but just to get it on paper. Maybe I'll feel better. My dad is seeing her almost every day now that my mother is out of the house. Rodger, Bridget's father, is still in Europe but he's coming home next weekend and he's taking Bridget and Madeline and me to the mall and then to dinner and a movie. It's all planned. He and Donna are going to shop by themselves and then we'll meet up with them at Longhorn's Steak House. I've already decided what to wear. One of the outfits Madeline put together for me. No sense in going back to dressing like a dunce just because I'm mad at her. I went to confession and told Father Murphy that I have hate in my heart for a friend and he said if I can't forgive to ask God to do it for me, and gave me ten Hail Marys and two Our Fathers, and then absolution. I did ask God to forgive Madeline for me, but if he did it hasn't done any good. Maybe it takes a while 'til I feel that I'm not mad at her anymore. So far I still am. Maybe God's not listening to me, which is probably the case, because I did not confess what Anthony Morelli did up in the balcony. Father Murphy knows my voice so I couldn't. I wanted to go to confession at another church so I could confess it to a strange priest that's never heard me before but I couldn't figure a way to ask my father without him suspecting I'd committed a mortal sin and get very nosey and start asking questions. So I just decided to leave it out of my confession entirely. Besides, I really didn't do anything wrong. Plus I didn't even like it, except for the first part of the kiss before Anthony pushed his tongue into mine. The first part was very nice. My stomach dropped a mile. And then out of the blue it took off like a roller coaster.

Chapter Twenty-six

MY MOTHER IS COMING home next weekend and my father has planned a big surprise. We are all going on a cruise to the western Caribbean. We're not leaving next weekend, of course. We leave the week after school's out and I get to take Bridget! This will be my first cruise and Beth says she will help me shop for just the right clothes to wear. She has very good taste in clothes. She's like Madeline that way. My father said Beth could come, too, but the wedding is two weeks before we leave so she'll still be on her honeymoon.

I don't want her to go anyway. She'd just be trying to play tour director every day and Bridget and I just want to roam around the ship by ourselves. My father has sworn me to secrecy. I'm not to say a word 'til my mother is home and he presents her with the news. Howard and Vivian are coming, too. I can't wait. It's just so exciting—first the baby's due and I'll be an aunt, then the wedding, and then the Bahamas, the Cayman Islands, Costa Maya, Cozumel. My life couldn't be better and to think I thought it was going all wrong. And I'm hoping that my father will fall madly in love with my mother again and when we get home he will have forgotten all about Donna. Stranger things have happened. So it could happen.

Bridget says, "Don't count on it." But I am counting on it. One should always be hopeful. It fills the air with positive ions, or something like that, positive energy fields. Ms. Schaeffer, my science teacher, insists it's true.

Madeline and Bridget and I are getting ready to leave for the mall. This is the weekend her father takes us and then we all meet up for dinner at the steak place. This is going to be an outstanding, memorable day. You know how you can just feel it almost to your bones? That's what I'm feeling—all tingly inside. Plus my hair turned out. It's long and blonde and the edges are cut just right, kind of like a gypsy shag. Beth took me. She's turning into a real person. She wants me to look good for the wedding, so she had them experiment with me with putting it in an up-do before we left. But now I've combed it out and it looks great. I'm wearing my favorite jeans and a white shirt and a tapestry vest and these western-style boots I've had since Christmas. Madeline said, "Too cool," when she saw them. I'm not sure why her opinion still counts, but it does.

I can't remember who it was that said never count on anything being what you think it will be, or you'll be disappointed. Maybe Nana Louise when she was still in her right mind. But whoever said it was right on target. Today did not turn out anything like I counted on. If I had counted on it being my worst nightmare then I would have counted on it correctly.

Chapter Twenty-seven

ONE DAY IN MATH class, a girl—Virginia Stuart—started her period right out of the blue. Virginia was wearing pink, pale pink, a skirt and a matching sweater and I swear her face just turned green and she raised her hand and said in the softest voice I've ever heard, "Ms. Hadley." And Ms. Hadley must have had some experience with girls wearing light pink and speaking in a soft voice with a look on their face that they'd rather be in China, because she walked right over to her and took off her sweater—I might have forgotten to mention those sweaters she wears around her shoulder. They almost reach down to the floor. So, Ms. Hadley walks over to Virginia, wraps the sweater around Virginia's shoulders while she escorts her to the door and whispers something in her ear, and Virginia leaves, and Ms. Hadley goes on with the lesson and asks Billie Martin if he knows how to solve the latest algebra problem, which I've forgotten even what it is.

The point is Ms. Hadley is now my favorite teacher. I mean if I'd started my period at school, which I didn't—I started last summer when I was twelve—I would want it to be in her class.

I'm not sure why I thought of Ms. Hadley just then, when what I want to do is think through what happened at the mall to see if it could have turned out any differently. Maybe if I'd been more alert. I don't know. Everything is just a mess and to add to it I have failed to be the type of person I have always counted on being. To start with, I hate Madeline. She is the entire reason there is a mess in the first place. I go over and over what happened in my mind: We are shopping at Saks Fifth Avenue, which is Madeline's favorite store—naturally—but about the only thing I can buy is maybe a handkerchief; my father gave me fifty dollars and everything in here starts at a hundred. So we are just walking along and this security guard comes up to Bridget and says, "Come with me, miss." And he takes her by the arm and Madeline just stands there looking all innocent with a look on her face like, "What? What?" And I have daggers in my eyes aimed right at her.

I run after Bridget and another security guard says, "You two girls follow me." And my heart is pounding like it's leaving my chest. And I'm thinking what if Madeline put something in my purse! I should have been watching her like a mother watches an infant learning to walk.

I just know I'm going to be sick. There is a bad taste marching up my throat. I swallow hard to force whatever it is back down. My knees are limp as a dishrag, my head is swollen up three sizes too big for my body and my ears are ringing out of my head—which is thinking, you could go to reform school. This is Saks! This is the part in the movies where the music gets very deep and loud. Only it's not make believe, it's real life and I am being led away by store security personnel who have already taken Bridget away, probably to beat it out of her that she's a thief, which isn't true. It's Madeline who's the thief and she's looking like she can't possibly understand what all the excitement is about. In fact, the look on her face is one of boredom. I think this explains a lot about her. Not even a security guard dressed up like a regular cop with an official looking badge and a gun gets her excited. She has major problems.

Chapter Twenty-eight

I'M SITTING IN FRONT of the security guard trying to picture the look on my face, whether it says I look totally innocent or maybe I have one of those faces that always looks completely guilty, like the ones on the mug shots in the post office. Then I stop worrying about this because they are taking Bridget out of the room in handcuffs. Handcuffs, like she's a criminal. The main security guard, who acts like he is the boss over the others, says Madeline and I can go. Go where? Go about our life like nothing has happened? They didn't find anything in either one of our purses, but they discovered Bridget had half the junior department in hers.

"You better not tell," Madeline whispers. "Or else."

I don't need to say or else what? Or else she'll tell my parents I'm a slut. This is not good timing. My mother's coming home, and we're having a baby, and we have a wedding, and we're going on a cruise. And now I wonder if Bridget will even get to come? Will she be on probation and not able to leave the country? I could just kill Madeline. But then I'd have to join Bridget in the slammer, if that's where they have her. The guards show me and Madeline to the door. We walk over to Longhorn's Steak House which is across the street from the mall. This is supposed to be where we order Shirley Temples and an appetizer and wait for the best steak you can sink your teeth into. Instead, here we are, having to tell Bridget's father that she's been arrested.

"You do it," I tell Madeline and just make my eyes as thin and mean as a Siamese cat with an attitude.

Bridget's father and Donna are waiting in front of the restaurant. Donna smiles brightly but right away Mr. Harman's eyebrows arch upwards, like, *what gives? Where's Bridget?* And the part of my stomach that is convinced it lives somewhere else marches up my throat again.

"Mr. Harman," Madeline says. Her voice is all syrupy-sweet. "Something terrible has happened. Bridget's been caught shoplifting."

Mr. Harman takes hold of one of her arms. "What did you say?" he says, and leans in a little closer, like maybe he hasn't heard her correctly. He has his head cocked to the side and one ear turned toward Madeline.

"I just don't know what got into her," Madeline says. She opens her eyes wide and shakes her head from side to side.

She's a total liar, but she doesn't look like one. She's very convincing. If I didn't know better, I'd think she was being sincere, too. What I need to do is explain exactly what I know happened, but do I do that? Oh no, I just stand there with tears running down my face and my shoulders heaving like a five-year-old.

Donna walks over to me and puts her arm around me. "Don't worry, Andi," she says, "It's going to be okay. These things happen."

She pulls me tightly against her and pats my back and I'm thinking I could just love this woman. Go figure. She's like my enemy. Now how can I send her the letter I've been working on? This is all getting very complicated.

Rodger Harman doesn't look like he thinks these things happen. He looks like he's ready to start a war.

"Let's go," he says and nods his head toward the car.

"Are you okay, Andi?" Donna says. "Do you want me to call your father?"

So that's it. She wants me to call my father. She wants to see my dad. And here I thought she was starting to be someone I could like.

❖❖❖

Bridget has been released into her father's custody and we are sitting with my father in our library. At times like this it's very inconvenient having an alcoholic mother. I would really like her to be here. She would be sitting next to me with her arm around my shoulder. I just know it. My father is sitting across from me and watching my every move. Madeline has been taken back to Westwood Academy. She boards in, which means she lives there except for when she spends the weekend at Bridget's or goes home to Savannah, which I wish she would and then just stay there. Bridget has been crying and her eyes are very pink around the edges and her face is blotchy.

"Why would you do this?" her father asks her. "What got into you?"

Bridget doesn't answer. She just shakes her head and swallows hard like there's a rock caught in her throat. There's a major one in stuck in mine. Mr. Harman turns to me. "Did you know this was going on?" His jaw is set in a firm position, and he lowers his head and gives me a harsh look. It is a look that says, *Don't lie to me.*

"No," I say weakly.

Which is the truth—I did not know it was going on this time; and I only knew about the other times after the fact, so I'm being completely honest here. But I know I should tell them the truth and not worry about my parents finding out about the necklace buried in the backyard and all about my incident with Anthony. I'll live in a convent until I'm of age, but it's better than Bridget living in a juvenile center.

But I'm a coward so I sit there and watch Bridget, who is keeping the secret, too. Why would she do that? Why would she take the blame when it all belongs to Madeline? Is it all just to be popular? To be part of the in-crowd and if she tells Madeline will let everyone know Bridget is a snitch, which I guess is worse than being a thief. I picture Bridget walking down the corridors at Westwood Academy and everyone clearing a path to get out of her way. A tear is floating down her cheek. The whispers on both sides of her easily reach her ears: tattletale, stoolie, ratfink, stool pigeon, SNITCH.

"It was Madeline!" I say. "She's been stealing for ages. She put that stuff in Bridget's purse. She did it once to me, too. And she brought a bunch of stuff over here one night and showed us, and we never said anything and we should have!" The words fall out of my mouth one after the other like a waterfall. "She put a necklace in my purse! It's buried in the garden." I turn to my father. *I'm sorry* is plastered on my face. Bridget is looking at me, pleading with me to be quiet. There's desperation in her eyes. I stare back. I feel my eyebrows scrunch together like they have a mind of their own. They try to convince her we are doing the right thing. Lies heaped upon lies have gotten us into this mess. All that's true is sitting on the table like a delicious piece of pie, piping hot from the oven, warm and all inviting, waiting for someone to take that first bite and say, yes, this is good, this is what dessert is all about. All that's true—it's something to savor.

Chapter Twenty-nine

I'M SITTING WITH MR. and Mrs. Sterling, reading them *The Great Gatsby*. Mavis says, "Why doesn't he kiss her?" She says it almost every other paragraph and I'm thinking maybe I'll read into the story that Gatsby does kiss Daisy and shut her up, but then I decide that changing the story may be worse than plagiarism, and I've been in enough trouble lately, thank you. Howard—that's Mr. Sterling—says, "What'd ya say?" and Mavis shouts back her answer. "He didn't kiss her!"

"Who cares?" Howard says and slaps the air. "Got any Mickey Spillane?"

He likes murder stories. I tell him I'll check the library for next time. I've already read him two, but it is very hard to shout out the details of a crime. Actually it's hard to shout out any book. I'm thinking of checking at the desk and explaining that Mr. Sterling's hearing, I mean lack of hearing, is making it impossible to read. I'm probably getting cancer of my vocal chords from all the irritation. Maybe some arts and crafts would be better, anything that doesn't involve hearing.

Guess what? Remember when my grandmother said there is good in everything? Well, she is making a believer out of me. Bridget is no longer attending Westwood Academy! She's back at Parker Junior High. No charges were brought against Madeline and the ones against Bridget were reduced to a misdemeanor and she has to make restitution and she got forty hours of community service, too. It didn't matter when we told them Madeline actually did it. Since no one can bear witness that they saw her put the items into Bridget's bag, Madeline's off the hook. For Bridget's community service, they've assigned her to Table Grace Kitchen where people bring in food products that aren't perishable and then they are distributed to families in need. Bridget gets to sort through all of the canned goods and put them into different piles to be passed out, so everyone doesn't get ten cans of green beans and nothing else. They take volunteers too—not just who Juvenile Court sends them—so I volunteered and you would not believe how many hungry people there are around here. We are always low on food. They don't take any perishables except bread. And they really like getting Pampers and other baby needs, and also grooming aids. I'm sorting through deodorant and toothpaste and shampoo to make up different packages to be included with the food boxes. One woman brought in L'Oreal shampoo and a matching bottle of conditioner and I kept them together in the package and imagined the lady that gets it thinking, wow, God really likes me. I picture her face lit up like a Christmas tree, and then I get kind of sad thinking what a silly thing to get excited about, if that's all that poor lady has to get excited about and I put in a bottle of hand lotion that looks like it came from a gift shop. Really make her day. When you do something like work at a share kitchen you just know it's an important thing. Your heart steps back and takes a good look at itself and says, ah, this feels really good. That's what mine's doing now.

Something sad happened on our street. Mrs. Reed died. She's the lady who's eighty something and lives next to Mrs. Anderson, the fat lady. What's really spooky is Mrs. Reed wasn't even sick that we know of. She gets up one morning, pats her cat on the head, has her tea and toast and *boom*, she's on the floor dead. We're gathered at her house now. My mother's here. She's home from Peachford and looking really good. Her skin is prettier than ever and there's a glow on her cheeks that's bound to get my father's attention. She goes to an AA meeting every evening at six o'clock and then we have dinner when she gets back, so Rosa stays late. Mrs. Reed's grandson is here. He's been serving in Iraq in the Gulf War and happened to be back on leave when she died, so that was nice. He is so good-looking I almost grab my chest just looking at him. His name is Rodney Hall. His mother is Mrs. Reed's youngest daughter, Pamela. Mrs. Reed has two other daughters, but they haven't arrived yet. I think Rodney's twenty years old, but I can't be sure. He fought in the burning fields of Kuwait City when the Iraqi soldiers set the oil wells on fire, so he's probably a hero and has saved many lives. I'm about swooning and Anthony Morelli can just forget it. Now I understand why divorce is so prevalent. Had I been able to actually marry Anthony I would have made a big—big—mistake. Now I'm in love for real. Anthony was the puppy kind, but it was hard to know until the real kind showed up right out of the blue. And all because Mrs. Reed keeled over. That part's really sad, but true love will have its way, no getting around that.

Chapter Thirty

EASTER DINNER. WE ARE having ham and scalloped potatoes and creamed corn and fried okra and cornbread and rolls and iced tea and every kind of pie there is. Beth is here and Amy and Jeffrey and Howard and Vivian. There is laughter in the house again and everyone is smiling and eating and seeming to have a perfectly good time, except for me. I am hopelessly in love and feeling miserable, like I can't get enough air into my lungs.

"What is it, Andi?" my mother says, and puts her hand to my forehead. "Do you have a fever?"

Yes, I have a major fever of the worst sort.

"No, I'm just not hungry," I say. It's true. I'm not. If there is one thing love is good for I have noticed is that it is a miracle diet. I have lost three pounds. It seems I've lost it from the head down. I finally have cheek bones.

"Oh look," Beth says. "Andi's losing her baby fat." She holds my chin in her hand and turns my face from side to side. I hate her. She already pointed that out two years ago.

"Why Andi, you're turning into an absolute beauty."

I love her. She might be the sister I've been hoping for. Then I realize how strange she is. She didn't even invite Parker to join us for dinner. So, why is she even getting married if she's going to ignore him?

I don't dwell on Beth. I think of Rodney which makes me sad. There's something I've learned about the other kind of love—the romantic kind. Sad just rolls over you every minute you are not in the same room with the one you love, which is every waking hour I exist. I haven't seen Rodney since the funeral which was eight days ago. But I will see him today. My mother has invited him and his mother to come for dessert. They are having their Easter dinner at some restaurant, I can't remember which one, and will join us later. I should be very excited, but my stomach is too nervous and I am rehearsing what it is I want to say to him. It's very important I choose just the right words, as he is leaving to go back to Iraq and who knows when I will see him again.

"I love you. I positively love you," seems too much too soon. I'm thinking of maybe, "Can I ask you a question?" And he'll say of course and I'll say, "Do you believe in love at first sight?"

But that sounds like it's a script for a movie. So dorky. When he gets here I manage to say, "Hi!" but then everyone is standing around in a circle so what else can I say? But later when I get a chance to talk with him alone, I say, "So, how's the war going?" and he nearly chokes on his iced tea, and I want to kick myself. It's a very serious thing, this war, and it comes out of my mouth like I'm inquiring about the weather.

"It's not a good situation, Andi," he says, "but I think we're making progress."

He's so mature; I could just die on the spot acting so stupid. And then what is wrong with me? Out of the blue, I blurt out, "Do you believe in love at first sight?"

He doesn't blink. "I'm not sure I do, Andi," he says, "but I'm not convinced I don't." And he winks. I am the color of what's left of the ham sitting on the dining room table.

"Would you like to see some photos of Kuwait?" he says, and reaches into the breast pocket of his uniform.

He wants to share his world with me—a world of war and death and suffering and oil field fires. He wants me to see what is going on in his life; to be prepared. My heart starts beating so fast I get the hiccups.

This is absolutely the best Easter of my entire life, bar none. Except for the hiccups.

Being in love for real is like watching the sun set and seeing every color that God ever created sit in the sky all at once. I play music on my stereo and dance around the room. I have my arms held out in a circle with each hand wrapped around one wrist like Rodney is in my arms and I'm in his. Really there's only empty space, but someday there won't be and that makes my heart just stand up.

We'll have such an incredible life together. And three children— a boy and a girl and then a surprise baby; whatever it is we will love it. I am so far in the clouds I don't even mind school anymore. In algebra if Ms. Hadley calls on me and says simplify the expression and writes on the board $2(a - 3) + 4b - 2(a - b - 3)$, I tell her I don't know, like always, but I'm not the least bit embarrassed. Why be embarrassed? I plan to marry Rodney when I'm old enough and raise our children. Why would I need to know how to simplify a mathematical expression? Exactly. And when Mr. Finch in English asks me to define two independent clauses, I say it's two sentences that can stand alone and take my seat (I mentioned I was going to work harder in English), but I don't really care at all that I know the answer. My mind is seven thousand one hundred and ten miles away—the exact distance between Kuwait and Atlanta.

Chapter Thirty-one

AMY AND I ARE folding all of the baby things she got at her shower last night. Two of her friends, Trish and Marsha, held it here so she could just stay on the sofa and rest herself. Amy is eight months pregnant now. It's so nice having baby showers when you know what kind of baby you're having. There are blue rompers, and blue blankets and cute little boy-baby hats and shoes. I wonder during all those years when there was no way to know what kind of baby they were having how many women lined up to return things or just dressed their baby in whatever color was available, say a pink stretchy on a little baby boy and all day long people were saying, "Oh, isn't she cute?"

Lately, being around Amy, I'm amazed at all the things pregnant woman cannot do anymore. It's a wonder the rest of us are alive. The women were talking about it at the shower—how mothers who smoked and drank and took aspirin and ate blue cheese dressing and tuna from a can and never got tested for diabetes. And then after babies were born they were put to sleep on our tummies in a baby crib covered with bright colored lead-based paint. There were no childproof lids on medicine bottles, no latches on doors or cabinets, and kids rode bikes with no helmets. They rode in cars with no car seats or booster seats or air bags. They drank water from the garden hose and not from a bottle. They ate cupcakes and white bread and real butter and drank Kool-Aid made with sugar, but they weren't overweight because they were always outside playing. My mom said they would leave home in the morning and play all day, so long as they were back by supper and then they'd go out again and stay outside until the streetlights came on. No one was able to reach them all day and it was okay. There were no PlayStations, Nintendos, or Xboxes. No video games or movies, and no cable TV, no three hundred channels and no surround-sound. Mostly they were pretty safe. They had lots of friends and went outside and found them. They fell out of trees, or slipped on the sidewalk, broke bones, and teeth and there weren't any lawsuits. It was all part of growing up. They ate mud cookies and worms did not end up living in them. And if they got in trouble at school, they got in double trouble at home and their parents always sided with the principal.

I think of Amy's baby and all the changes in the world since my mom was little and even since I was little and figure maybe it's not so great and then I get scared for him.

I am looking at Anthony Morelli and thinking what did I ever see in this guy? And I am wondering do grown-ups ever step back and think the same thing? God help them. They are more likely to act on their impulses, whereas teenagers have restraint, because of our lack of freedom. It's called "parents." We are limited in our responses to our choices, but what about grown-ups? What do they have? That is a very good question. A big fat nothing and that's why they end up in trouble. Take my father. He is still all over Donna without any consideration as to what this could do to his marriage, our family, life for all of us in general. He's just full steam ahead.

I keep watching Anthony, carrying the cross up to the altar. It's our last rehearsal this week before the first Mass after Easter, known as Prudence, when Jesus showed his wounds to the world. At least I think it is. Half the time I don't listen while I'm here. If someone asked me if I find all of this boring—right now while I'm standing in front of the altar—I'd have to say a big fat YES.

Anthony is doing a good job. "Very nice," Father Murphy says.

Anthony's holding the cross up above his shoulders but just at the right angle so it looks very majestic without being showy. He's a good cross-bearer. I will give him that. But do you think he even cares that I am no longer looking at him with great longing? Not one bit. He is all over Melanie Morrison, who I should really have a talk with. At least I should warn her about the balcony.

Chapter Thirty-two

ROSA'S IN THE KITCHEN preparing dinner. It's very interesting to watch her. She can have four things going on at once on the stove and in the oven and it always comes out perfect. Her face is dotted with perspiration and her cheeks are flushed, like always, but she is smiling and singing along with the radio, also like always. It is possible that she is the sunniest person I know. She has on the Spanish channel. I love Spanish music. It always sounds like they're having a party, no matter the song. Maybe that is why Rosa's so happy. You can't listen to that type of music all day and stay sad.

The kitchen is filled with savory spices. I take a deep breath. Garlic, cumin, cinnamon, saffron and paprika are holding hands and floating in the air. It's like walking into a fine Mexican restaurant. Rosa waddles back and forth between the pantry and the cooktop.

"Oh, Miss Andi," she says when she sees me. "You give me a fright, no?"

"Sorry," I say, then explain to her that it is major important that I learn to cook, immediately.

"I might be getting married much sooner than I planned," I say.

"Married? Too young be married," she says, and pats my arm. "But learn to cook is good. I teach you make enchiladas."

She points to a pile of fresh ground beef sitting on the counter. It's a brilliant red color and still oozing blood.

"I want to learn to cook," I say eagerly, though I'm not quite sure my stomach does. I'm used to seeing food when it's time to eat it.

"First we make beef recipe," Rosa says, picking up a large frying pan.

She heats three tablespoons of vegetable oil over medium heat, then adds a whole yellow onion. It's already finely chopped.

"Now cook three, maybe four minute, yes?" she says and hands me the spatula. This is easy. I'll be an expert in no time. Rosa adds the ground beef along with a teaspoon and a half of salt. When the beef is almost done she adds four cloves of minced garlic.

"Now cook three more minute," Rosa explains. "Is good."

Once I do as she says, she pours in one cup of tomato sauce and two-and-a-quarter teaspoons of ground cumin. I haven't written any of this down and now I realize it's a bit more complicated than I anticipated. I'm not sure I remember the order we've added the different ingredients and wonder if it will be okay if I just add them all at once and cook it an extra minute or two when I make this recipe on my own. Surely, it will taste the same; it will be the same ingredients. Rosa puts three-quarters of a cup of water and one-quarter of a cup of oregano leaves into the blender. After it's blended she motions that I should pour this onto the meat mixture.

"Now cook ten minute, yes?" Rosa nods her head.

I continue to follow her instructions.

"Turn down fire and cook ten more minute." I do precisely what she says.

"Is good," Rosa says smiling. "Is ready."

She sets the dish aside. "Now we make enchilada and Spanish rice and refried beans, *sí?*"

I thought we just made the enchilada. Rosa explains that we've only made the first step. There are three steps before we even get to the Spanish rice or refried beans. First we make the ground beef mixture, which we have just done, next we are to make the enchilada sauce, and then we will make the actual enchiladas. Only then are we able to move onto the Spanish rice and refried beans. In a Mexican restaurant you make your selection and before you even finish munching on the chips and salsa, presto!—a large platter is before you with refried beans, Spanish rice, and your choice of entrée. I had no idea they went to so much trouble to place it there. I will never again take Mexican food for granted.

Rosa assembles the ingredients for the sauce which consists of two cups of chicken broth, four tablespoons of chili powder, one teaspoon of ground cumin, two heaping teaspoons of garlic powder, three-quarters of a teaspoon of salt, one pinch of ground cinnamon, one-third of a teaspoon sugar, five tablespoons of cold water, and five tablespoons of white flour. And that's just the ingredients, not the steps that go along with actually making the sauce.

"We start sauce, yes?" Rosa says.

I don't think so. "Not today," I say, no longer interested in learning to cook. It's far more work than I imagined. Maybe Rodney and I can eat our dinners out and I'll fix breakfast. Breakfast is so much easier—eggs and bacon. Anyone can do that. You just crack an egg and fry it. And bacon—anyone can make that. Put it on paper towels in the microwave and *voilá*: bacon!

Chapter Thirty-three

I KNOW NOW WHY Bridget was getting all As. She was copying Madeline's work. Now that she is back at Parker Junior High, she's in real trouble academically. Her father has hired a tutor. Every day after school this college student Ben Riley—from Georgia State—comes by and spends two hours with her. He is all business, this young man, and looks like Bill Gates, only younger.

"I'm so far behind," Bridget laments. "I'll never catch up."

"Sure you will," I say, hoping I'm right. I can't imagine starting high school next year without her. What if they hold her back? It's too depressing to even think about.

"How about I quiz you with what Ben went over yesterday? How about that?" I smile brightly, hoping she'll see all is not lost. Bridget has always been there for me, except for the months she got sidetracked with Madeline. But that's all behind us now. And something good came of it, like Bridget and I both helping out at Table Grace Kitchen. It's very rewarding. Even Beth congratulated me and said all good women must be stewards to others. That line was really a shocker. Where did that come from?

Donna taps on Bridget's door. "Ben's here," she says.

"We'll go over everything later," I say, picking up my books. Bridget nods her head and purses her lips together. She's not really into her sessions with Ben and who can blame her? We've been in school all day. What a bummer to add two more hours on to that every day. It's enough to make a body want to jump out the window. I realize Bridget's bedroom is two stories up.

"You're not going to jump out the window, are you?" I ask.

"'Course not," she says. "We've got the dance next weekend. I'm not about to miss that."

I almost forgot. It's the annual Sadie Hawkins dance. I haven't invited anybody yet. Neither has Bridget. We'll probably end up going alone, which is like announcing: *Hey, look at us. We're losers.*

"Maybe we could ask the Hanson twins," I say. "They're not so bad."

The Hanson boys don't look like twins. They're fraternal and Joey is much cuter than David. Bridget will pick him, and I'll let her. It's bad enough she has to do school double-time. The least I can do is let her have the better looking guy for the dance.

"I'll take Joey," Bridget says brightly. "Is that alright?"

Do I know Bridget or do I know Bridget?

"Sure," I say.

It won't be so bad. David is kind of interesting. He follows true crime stories and always has some interesting things to share, like the ways people kill each other and how they almost get away with it.

Chapter Thirty-four

WHEN I GET HOME my mother is sitting in the living room and who do you think is there with her? Rodney Hall! I almost keel over.

"Andréa," my mother says. She only calls me Andréa when something important is going on. I feel a tingle climb up my spine. He's asking for my hand in marriage, but why my mother? Isn't he supposed to speak with my father?

"Rodney needs your help," my mother explains and folds her hands neatly in her lap. The phone rings and my mother goes to answer it. Rosa is at the grocery store.

"I'll just leave Rodney to explain," she says.

The phone is ringing again. It sounds more urgent. Phones do that when you don't answer. They just get louder with every ring. But phones don't matter to me right now. I won't talk even if it's for me. It is. "I'll just call them later," I say to my mother all casual-like, but really my heart is bouncing in my chest like it's on a trampoline.

"You need my help?" I turn to Rodney trying to act perfectly normal, but my voice is at least an octave higher than normal. God! I hate myself when that happens. It did that the first time I talked to Anthony, too. Maybe I have a defect and my larynx is connected to my heart.

"Are you alright?" Rodney asks.

I shake my head, and clear my throat.

"Frog," I explain, then, "What do you need my help with?" Talk of marriage will have to wait.

"With my grandmother's things. My mother can't stand the thought of going through them and my aunts have left it up to her." Rodney stands up and rubs his chin.

"Think you could help me out?"

Could I?

"It won't take long," he says.

It can take forever, gladly! I see myself sorting through Mrs. Reed's things for the rest of my life: Rodney is beside me, there's streaks of gray in my hair, thick-soled shoes on my feet, an apron around my waist.

"No problem," I say, pretending I'm my same old self and really my insides are jumping in circles.

My mother walks back into the room.

"So, do you mind helping Rodney?" she asks.

"Not at all."

"I can go with you, if you like."

"Oh no," I say. "I'm—I'm fine. Really." If she goes along it will ruin everything.

I'm not exactly sure what we'll be doing while we sort through her things, but I don't care, I'll act like I'm well versed in it.

"Well then," my mother says. "We'll see you two later. I've invited Rodney to dinner."

She's invited Rodney to dinner! My mother's invited Rodney to dinner! My mother has absolutely, positively invited Rodney to dinner. My brain is stuck in one gear.

"You ready?" Rodney says and motions with one hand toward the door. I follow him across the street to his grandmother's house. There's a large moving van parked in the driveway.

"We're just going to sort through her clothes. They'll get the rest," he says.

I nod my head.

"You can show me what you think my mother might like to keep, for later, when she's feeling better."

"Okay," I say, not sure if I'll know what that might be.

"Handkerchiefs," I say.

"Beg your pardon?"

"Your mother, she might like to keep these," I say and point to the small stacks of hankies resting in neat little rows in Mrs. Reed's top dresser drawer.

"Think so?" Rodney says, and I nod.

"And this," I say, gently folding a lemon yellow shawl. "Whenever I saw your grandmother she usually had this on," I explain. "I'm sure you're mother will appreciate having it."

Rodney smiles. "Then she shall have it." He takes the shawl and places it in the small box on the bed. The handkerchiefs go in next. I don't want this to end.

"I think the jewelry case is something your mother will want to go through on her own." I hand him the case which is encrusted with little pearls and shells in all different sizes.

"Alright," Rodney says. "I think that about does it."

It's taken hours but we've managed to sort through all of her clothing. Rodney decides Mrs. Reed's church can distribute them as they see fit. We grouped them by seasons, the heavier ones on the bed, the lighter items draped on the chair with the matching ottoman. Sweaters are on the dresser. Blouses are neatly folded and sitting right next to them.

"She had a lot of pretty things," I say.

Rodney nods his head. "She was a fine old woman. I'll miss her." He closes the closet door and turns to me.

"And you're a fine young woman, Andi, and I'll miss you, too."

The word woman grabs my heart and says, Here! Have a little more happiness! He called me a woman. For sure he is falling under my spell. And he will miss me. When will this missing part start?

When does he have to return to Iraq? I hate that war worse than before, but I only say, "You will?"

Rodney nods his head and smiles and reaches over and ruffles the top of my hair. And my head starts shouting, this is great! And my future is screaming, Andi, you are right! And my lungs forget they're supposed to breathe. And my heart beats faster than it's meant to. And my feet are no longer on the ground—they're doing a little two-step. And entire world is spinning around me. And there it is again, that feeling that I don't want this to end. I want to grab time and hold it tight and make it stop.

Chapter Thirty-five

I KNOW I HAVE to carry on with my life while Rodney's gone. It's the only way, so I resign myself to everyday things. Here's how it goes with Joey and David. I decide to call David and ask him to go with me to the dance, and then ask him to ask Joey if he would like to go with Bridget. Calling them on the phone means I won't be as embarrassed if he says no, or if they both say no. At least they won't see that I'm embarrassed. If my face turns red they'll never know.

I make the call, but it's Joey that answers the phone when I call. That's where the trouble begins. Why can't this be easy? It's a stupid dance, not a marriage proposal. I'm already covered in that regard.

"What do you want David for?" Joey says.

"Ah, well," I say. Already I'm bungling this phone call. "It's kind of personal," I say.

"You're gonna ask him to the dance, aren't you?" Joey says.

"No, that's not it," I say, hitting the side of my head with the palm of my hand.

"Why'd you call then?" he says.

Silence. During a phone call, silence is even louder than it normally sounds.

"I'm calling to ask David if he wants to go to the dance with Bridget. She's got laryngitis."

One lie after another jumps out of my mouth. Just like that. I could win the shot put of lying in the Olympics. The problem with this lie is now Bridget will be stuck with David, if Joey agrees to ask David and David tells Joey to say yes for him, and it's Joey that Bridget wanted me to ask in the first place.

"I don't know," Joey says. "Hey, David. Andi St. James wants to know if you want to go to the dance with Bridget Harman! Can you hear me?" His voice is a loudspeaker. Everyone on the block can hear him.

Joey comes back on the line.

"Tell her yes," he says.

"Yes?" I repeat.

"Yeah, David will go."

Here we go, just like I figured.

"Actually, Joey," I say. "Bridget wanted me to ask you to go and I was supposed to ask David. I got it all mixed up."

"Oh," Joey says.

"So, you want to?"

"Go with Bridget?"

"Yes," I say

"Sure. It doesn't matter to me."

Great, Bridget and I are interchangeable, like Tupperware lids.

"And David? He'll go with me?"

I hear a muffling over the mouthpiece on Joey's end. The phone piece is being dragged over some type of hard surface. He's back on the line three minutes later. I timed it.

"Yeah," Joey says.

"David will go?"

"Uh-huh."

I won't tell Bridget it took so long for David to decide on me. It's bad enough Joey didn't care who went with who. The important thing is they said yes. But I'm glad I'm marrying an older man. They make more sense.

Chapter Thirty-six

BRIDGET AND I ARE at her house, doing nothing really when we get this great idea. When we were at Table Grace Kitchen this morning this girl came in with her mother and she was just waiting around for her mother to fill out her form to get her groceries and this girl says to Bridget that she really likes her top and where did she get it and Bridget pops off, "Neiman Marcus," without thinking, like this girl could march right over there and get herself one. And then the girl just nods her head soft-like, but you could see she was disappointed like maybe Bridget was going to say Kmart and she'd just march over there and beg her mother to buy one for her. She was wearing blue jeans, but not any kind you can be proud of, no name or anything, and a T-shirt with butterflies on the front; not exactly a fashion statement. So Bridget and I were talking about how lucky we are not to have to shop at Kmart and not really have to worry about where we shop at all and Bridget says, "I wish I would've had another top with me. For truth I would have given her this shirt," she says yanking a piece of it away from her body. "I've worn it like a dozen times already."

And then this idea just came to me; just knocked me right in my head plain as pie. And I say, "Why don't we make it so these girls can have clothes like ours?" I tell her I'm thinking we could start a clothes-share just like the food-share. And Bridget goes, "Yeah! We can get everyone to donate really good clothes that they're tired of, right?"

We're going to call it Sweet 'n' Sassy Fashionique. We like the sound of it. My mother said the best way to get it off the ground is to get the daughters of all the Junior League women to help out. Plus those kids all have the best clothes and believe me they get tired of them really fast, so their hand-me-downs are first rate.

Monday after school we're meeting with Mrs. Blakely who heads up Table Grace Kitchen to tell her about our idea and then my mother is contacting the Junior League woman and Bridget and I are going to make a list of all their daughters that want to help out and we're going to set up a boutique, hopefully in the room in back of the food room, that's supposed to be full of food; it's an overflow area, except we never have enough food to fill up the first room. No matter how many donations we get, the food just marches right out the door like it has feet.

So now I'm feeling very happy with myself. There's a warm spot in my heart that just gets warmer thinking about girls like the one that came to the food kitchen and seeing their eyes all shiny and bright as they pick out a complete outfit. That's the idea, they get to come and for an hour shop the boutique and come away with maybe two complete outfits, belts and necklaces and everything. So we're collecting those, too.

Bridget is lying on her bed on her stomach making notes of all of the things we have to do to get it started. The sun is shining through her window and catches some strands of her hair and it looks sort of like a halo. I'm so excited my hands are shaking and my head is filled with twenty happy thoughts at once. When two friends get together, it's amazing what can happen. You just never know.

I'm telling my father all about the boutique. I've already told my mother, but the excitement is still bubbling inside me so I start telling my father as soon as he gets home. He's walking forward and I'm walking backwards in front of him.

"Guess what?" I say, but don't wait for him to answer. I

immediately explain what Bridget and I are doing and plop down on the sofa. He actually sits down next to me and listens and then pats my shoulder and says, "That's a very good idea, Andi. I'm proud of you." My father hardly takes time to talk to me at all and now he's listening to me and talking back. Ever since I met Rodney my life has been filled with miracles. Everything just glows.

Chapter Thirty-seven

WE GOT THE NEWS this morning. Amy had the baby! The doctor was right. It's a boy. He's premature so he sort of looks like a little bird, but a really cute one. He'll have to stay at the hospital until he weighs at least five pounds. Currently, he's only four pounds and some ounces and he doesn't have any hair. Jeffrey and Amy have decided to name him Joshua Alexander. But they're not going to call him Alex for short, which is good. It would hurt too much to hear that name all the time. They'll just call him Joshua, which I really like. Joshua Alexander Beauchamp. Sounds really nice. Maybe not the Beauchamp part, but the parents don't get to choose their last name, so he's stuck with it.

We're at the hospital now. Amy is sitting up in bed with the covers tucked around her waist. She still has on a hospital gown. Jeffrey is handing out blue bubble-gum cigars that say, *It's a boy!* He unwraps one and sticks it in his mouth and does a Groucho Marx routine. He's feeling really good, no doubt about that. But it is a big relief. When Amy started having the baby again, it was still a month too soon, and that's never good. You don't know what will happen. Then again, even when babies are born on time, sometimes things go wrong, so it's just a big relief all around that he's finally here and he's fine. The hospital staff has Joshua in an incubator. He has these little plastic breathing tubes in his nose. Mrs. Beauchamp, Jeffrey's mother insists he looks just like Jeffrey when he was born, which is a rather stupid thing to say. Jeffrey's not really the father. Alex is. But

Mrs. Beauchamp also says Jeffrey was premature, too. That part's a relief. Not that they're related by blood or anything, but Jeffrey is at least six feet tall. Being premature doesn't seem to have hurt him. So, maybe Joshua will grow up big and strong and being premature and getting off to a rough start won't matter. When I think about stuff like that it makes me want to see into the future, but mostly I never want to. It's too scary. It's bad enough when stuff hits you in the face. It's better not to see it coming.

Right now I just want to sit on the ceiling and take a picture of everyone laughing and being so happy. It's like all the families gathered around—Amy's mother is here, too—are related now, some more than others. I think about Joshua having our blood in his veins and it's pretty thrilling. A part of Alex really is still with us.

Amy's mother says we should all be going and let Amy get some rest. "It's been a long morning," she says, and tucks some of Amy's hair behind one ear. Amy doesn't look tired at all. She's positively beaming. But she had a caesarean which I understand is a major operation. It was necessary because when she went into labor the monitor said the baby's heart was beating too fast. Probably from the drugs they put in her veins when she first went into labor. You never know when they're using these powerful drugs what harm they can do in the future.

I go back to the nursery one more time to see how Joshua is doing. They have him in a special nursery where the premature babies are kept. I can see him clearly through his little plastic bed. He's moving his feet and his arms around like a regular baby. The nurse moves his bed over to the window so I can get a better look. It's a very nice thing to do. I smile and wave at her. She probably thinks I'm the big sister and here I'm an aunt. When she turns the plastic bed around so I can see him better, Joshua opens his eyes. His little head turns toward me like he knows I'm there! He blinks twice. He looks so cute with the little tubes in his nose, but I hope they don't hurt him. He's so sweet. His eyes are staring right at me. It's like he already knows I'm family. I lean closer to the window and he just stares away at me. This little guy is really smart. It's like he's thinking, *I know you! You're my Aunt Andi!* It makes me want to pick him up and take him home, pronto.

As soon as we get home I call Bridget. "You weren't at school today," she says. "Are you sick?"

I plop down on my bed and wrap the phone cord around my arm and tell her all about the baby. "He's so tiny, but all his parts work," I assure her. I ask if she'd like to come up and see him. "We're going back tonight."

"I have to finish my homework first," she says. "What time are you leaving?"

I tell her I'll find out and call her back. My mother's not in her bedroom, so I go downstairs. She's in the Florida room arranging flowers in an oversized vase. She has a cup of tea on the table next to the vase. Now that she's not drinking, she does regular things like arranging flowers and having tea. I'm still not used to it, so it's always a surprise. I ask her about what time we'll go back to the hospital.

"As soon as I get back from my meeting," she says. She wraps her hands gently around the bouquet she's arranged and leans over and sniffs.

"You know what I'm thinking, Andi?" she says.

I don't say anything. I just stand there because I'm afraid of what she could be thinking.

"I'm thinking that I like life so much better now that I'm sober."

It's the first time she's used that word, at least while I'm around. I don't know how to put into words what I'm feeling when she says it. It's like someone just blew my heart up like a balloon and they blew in too much air and it's about to burst. I wrap my arm around her waist and rest my head on her arm. I want to say something amazing and meaningful, but I know if I try to talk I'll start crying. I never counted on things turning out this way. I thought life would continue to suck—for the most part—on a regular basis. I still have my arm around my mother and she wraps one of hers around me. She kisses the top of my head softly.

"Oh Andi," she says. "I had no idea it was so bad for you, honey. And I'm so sorry." She pats my back.

That does it. I start blubbering. My father's home, for once—he's reading the paper in the next room. He hears me crying and gets up to joins us.

"What's up?" he says. "Andi?"

My mother pulls a Kleenex out of her pocket and hands it too me.

"It's nothing," my mother explains. "Too much excitement for one day is all." And I'm thinking like too much excitement for one lifetime. First my brother dies, then my mother starts drinking, then my father starts up with Donna, then my mother stops drinking, and I meet Rodney and we have a new baby and Beth is getting married and we're going on a cruise. It's a lot of things filling me up—my cup is running over. I sniff loudly. My mother takes her hand and smoothes the hair on the back of my head and my father takes my chin and tips it gently toward him. And he just stands there holding it and looking into my eyes. I realize it isn't earth-shattering for a father to take hold of one's chin, but under the circumstances at our house, it is a lot. I start blubbering all over again.

Chapter Thirty-eight

TONIGHT IS THE NIGHT of the Sadie Hawkins dance. Mr. Finch, my English teacher is explaining to our class how this tradition got started. To begin with the event is supposed to be held in November, but our school principal says with our homecoming dance being in the fall that it would be better to hold this one in the spring. So much for tradition. Still, the story behind the dance is very interesting and for once Mr. Finch has my full attention.

"It all began with *Li'l Abner*, Al Capp's classic hillbilly comic strip," he says and holds up a yellowed newspaper. "It was popular from 1934 to 1977."

Suddenly, this is starting to sound like a history lesson. Several of the students are shifting in their seats and the guy across from me, Warren Pritchard, is doodling in his English notebook. Mr. Finch drones on.

"Sadie Hawkins was the daughter of one of Dogpatch's earliest settlers. She was known as the 'homeliest gal in all them thar hills'." Mr. Finch is really getting into the story. He thinks his imitation of the cartoon is so funny he stops and snorts. He takes a deep breath before continuing with his monologue. "According to the legend, Sadie grew frantic waiting for suitors to come a-courtin'," Mr. Finch says. Laugh, laugh. He's getting a major kick out of telling this fable and goes on to explain that Sadie's father was even more frantic than she was. In desperation he called together all the unmarried men of Dogpatch and had it declared "Sadie Hawkins

Day." A footrace was set up, with Sadie in pursuit of the town's eligible bachelors.

"Matrimony was the consequence," Mr. Finch explains. He picks up the newspaper strip he has brought as a prop and starts to read from it.

"'When ah fires my gun, all o' you kin start a-runnin'. When ah fires agin, Sadie starts a-runnin'. Th'one she ketches'll be her husbin'.'"

Mr. Finch has done such a good job of reading, the class starts to clap and hoot and holler. Mr. Finch grins like he's receiving an academy award. He lays the newspaper on his desk and leans over and takes a bow. There's too much talking going on in the class for him to continue. He holds up his hands and calls for order.

"There's more," he says. "Settle down." He clears his throat. "Now the town spinsters decided that this was such a good idea, they made Sadie Hawkins Day a mandatory yearly event, much to the dismay of the Dogpatch bachelors. Many sequences of the comic strip centered around the dreaded Sadie Hawkins Day race. If a woman caught a bachelor and dragged him across the finish line before sundown, he had to marry her. It proved to be a cultural phenomenon and schools across the country started holding Sadie Hawkins Day dances. So there you have it, the history of this dance."

Warren Pritchard leans across the aisle and taps me on the shoulder. "So, you gonna ask me to the dance?" He snorts like Mr. Finch. Warren is fairly nice looking but he has more pimples on his face than a polka dot dress has spots. I ignore him and thankfully, the bell rings.

"I'll be waiting for you to call," Warren says and files out the door with the rest of us. Even if I were going to ask him, which I'm not about to, how does he figure I'd ask him on the day of the dance? That's another reason why I'm fortunate to be in love with an older man. Rodney would never ask such a stupid question at such an inappropriate time. Boys are so immature. The only reason I am even going to this dance is because Bridget wants to. Also, I'm thinking it may be important for a school memory when I'm fully grown. So I don't feel like I missed out on things.

The actual dance turns out alright until the last half-hour. I'm wearing this petticoat dress. They are all the latest rage, sort of soft and floaty. Somehow, the back of mine gets caught in my pantyhose, so I end up showing my butt to the entire school. Joey and David laugh all the way home. I know if this had happened with Rodney, he would be comforting me, not laughing at me.

"It's not even funny anymore, you guys," Bridget says and crosses her arms firmly.

She is sitting in the front seat with Joey and David's father, Mr. Hanson, who is driving us home.

"What's not funny?" he says.

"Andi mooned the school," Joey says.

"Yah, her dress got caught in her pants. What a show," David adds and bursts out laughing again.

Their father looks at me in the rear-view mirror. He can easily see that I am humiliated.

"A joke isn't funny if it's at someone else's expense," he says and turns his head toward David and Joey who are sitting next to me. He gives them a stern look, then, quickly looks back at the road in front of us.

We ride home in silence the rest of the way. All the while I want to reach out and hug Mr. Hanson. There is one thing I have learned tonight about humiliation. It keeps a person very humble. I think of all of the times my father berated my mother over her behavior. And she sat there, humiliation resting on her cheeks like face powder. And I realize whether people are laughing or scoffing, the results can be the same. And to think I never said a word to my father. I didn't stand up for my mother. Now I'm so ashamed. I should have come to her rescue. Showed her how much I care. My mother has been very alone with her grief. No wonder it's so hard for her to stay on her program. There's been no helping hand in our household to hang on to. At least Joey and David's dad did something. He was trying to hand me back my dignity and I am grateful to him. But it's possible that I will never speak to David or Joey again.

School's out. I won't have to face the kids at school anymore over the dance fiasco. Maybe by next year they'll have forgotten all about it. I push it out of my mind and remind myself there will be no more homework or classes that I positively hate. Next year, however, I will have to get serious about studying. I'll be in high school. It's the beginning of when you're supposed to figure out what you want to do with your life. For now all I want to do is sleep late.

We have this tradition at Parker Junior High. On the last day of school they hand out your report card in homeroom. You then take it around to all of your classes that day and the teachers get to make comments in the space next to the grade you got in their class. It's embarrassing. How is it any of their business what you got in your other classes? Thankfully, I got some nice comments. Ms. Schaeffer, my science teacher who's always saying, "Listen up," or "Make no mistake," wrote, "Make no mistake, you're a joy to have in class." You tell me where that came from. I hardly spoke all year. Mr. Finch, my English teacher said, "You have great potential. Keep up the good writing." That's probably because I got an A on one of my short stories, but all the others were just Cs, so I don't understand his comment at all. Still, it was nice of him.

All of the other comments on my report card were just ordinary comments, like "Best of luck to you" or "Enjoy your summer." Except for my choir director who wrote, "You should see about voice lessons." He must be totally deaf or have me confused with another student. The last time I checked I couldn't even carry a tune—which makes me laugh as I realize that's what he may have meant. I can't carry a tune, I should get voice lessons.

You may recall I told you about Allison Whitley, one of the Angels at Sunny Meadows? She's the one that lives a totally ordinary life and seems very happy with it. On the last day of school she invites me to come over to her house again. This time I say, "Sure!" So that's where I'm headed now. I'm trying to pick out something to wear that looks average and ordinary. Allison doesn't have very pretty clothes. And that's when I get the idea that she should come down to our boutique and pick out some outfits! I'm surprised it's taken me this long to think of it.

I toss on a pair of cut-off jeans and a white T-shirt. They're pretty ordinary, except the T-shirt has Ralph Lauren splashed across the front. Maybe she won't notice or even know who he is.

Allison lives in a house that has three bedrooms, a living room, a kitchen and a one-car attached garage. If you take the garage off, their house would fit into our family room. Regardless, this is a very happy family. When I get there her mother is shaping hamburger meat into patties and she's humming. I'm pretty sure my mother has never touched raw meat before. If she had to shape hamburgers she'd probably be hysterical.

"Hi, Mom!" Allison says. "This is Andi."

Mrs. Whitley puts down the meat and wipes her hands on her apron. It's the type that loops around your neck and has peaches and pears peppered across the front.

"Well, hello, Andi," she says and holds out her hand. I'm not sure if I should shake it. My mother always insists one is to thoroughly wash ones hands after handling raw meat. However, I don't know how to not shake her hand without making her feel bad. I decide to risk it. It must be alright. I don't get dizzy or sick or anything, even after an hour. Maybe my mother is wrong. Or maybe she means a certain type of meat. I think she mentioned chicken once. Yes, it was chicken. Now I remember. You are never to touch anything or anyone once you touch raw chicken.

"Would you like to stay for dinner, Andi?" Mrs. Whitley says. She smiles and nods her head. "We're having burgers on the grill and homemade fries." She says fries like it's a real treat. And it probably is. I didn't know you could make them at home.

"I'll have to call my mother," I say. "But I'd like to," I add brightly. This will be fun—a regular family just sitting around having dinner, probably on the picnic table. I can see it right outside the sliding glass door. And the patio is made out of plain cement. I've never seen one like this up close. All the patios in our neighborhood have brick or fancy stone work. I feel like I'm in another world completely, but I like it. Nobody puts on any airs.

My mother says I can stay if I like. She'll have Henry pick me up at eight.

"Can't you come?" I ask. I don't want Henry picking me up. He always opens the back door like he's a chauffeur or something, and he sort of is, when he's not gardening, but still. It's embarrassing.

"Well, I'll be at my meeting until seven," she says. "And then a group of us are going out to dine."

"Oh," I say sadly. I'll bet Mrs. Whitley would never say going out to dine. She'd say they were going to grab a bite. I look around the kitchen. It's painted a bright yellow and has white fluffy curtains over the kitchen sink and coffee cups hanging on a wooden spindle. It's a happy kitchen. I can tell. You get a warm, cozy feeling just standing in it. There's a small needlepoint picture over a key rack. It says "Home is where you are loved." Suddenly, I wish I was Allison with just a plain old regular life. My mother would pick me up after being at a friend's house and she'd be driving a Chevy or a Ford or something—anything but a Mercedes. I hang up the phone. It's hooked to the kitchen wall.

I tell Mrs. Whitley I can stay.

"Wonderful," she says and asks Allison to tell her dad the burgers are ready to go on the grill.

Allison slides the patio door open and dashes outside. "Come on," she says. "You'll like my dad. He does impersonations. Tell him who you want to hear. He can do anyone."

I try to think of someone I would like to hear, but my mind is a big blank. Allison's father is tall and very thin. He wears wire-rimmed glasses and is okay looking, except for his nose. It's too big for his face. It's hard to explain, but it ruins the rest of it. Allison introduces me and he says, "Howdy, partner," and nods his head. And I swear it's John Wayne! No kidding. Mrs. Whitley brings out the burgers on a big platter. They're thick and red and juicy. My stomach starts to growl and my mouth starts to water. They look that good and they're still just sitting there raw as ever. The charcoal is ready and I can smell it. Charcoal just smells good when it's been burning a while 'til the briquettes turn white—like the food is already cooking when it hasn't even been laid on the grill.

Mr. Whitley asks me how I'd like my burger. I tell him pink in the center. And he says, "You got it kiddo," and now he's Steve Martin. Allison and I are laughing and having the best time. I'm so glad I came. Allison has two little brothers, Zachary and Addison. "It means son of Adam," Allison says. Zachary is the oldest. He's eight. He's got Addison's head in the crook of his arm and is pretending to make a fist-ball against his head.

"Knucklebone," he says, whatever that means. Boys can act pretty stupid at times. Addison is really cute. His front teeth are missing. He slips out of Zachary's grasp and runs the other direction.

"You boys go in and wash up," Mrs. Whitley says. They ignore her. Mr. Whitley says, "Boys, you heard your mother." Immediately they march right into the house. I'm impressed, but hope he doesn't have a dark side to him and beats them and they're afraid of him, so they do everything he says the moment he says it. I realize my imagination is probably getting the best of me. Mr. Whitley seems very nice. Maybe he just uses a lot of time-outs if they don't mind and they're tired of time-outs.

Mrs. Whitley brings out a big platter of French fries. They're the longest French fries that I've ever seen. Then I remember they're homemade and can hardly wait to try them. My mouth is positively dripping. We each pick up a paper plate. Mrs. Whitley puts an open bun in the center of each one and Mr. Whitley slides a burger onto it. Ketchup and mustard and mayonnaise are already on the table in little plastic Tupperware bowls. I get mine all set the way I like it and am ready to take a big bite when I notice that everyone has their hands folded, except for me, of course. I'm holding my burger. I'm sure my face is redder than the hamburger meat was before it was cooked. I put the burger down and fold my hands. We don't say grace before meals and now it shows. We do go to Mass every Sunday. But there's no way for them to know that, unless I tell them, and it would be stupid to just blurt it out. I lower my head and close my eyes.

"Bless this food, dear Lord and the hands that prepared it. Bless our family and bless our guest, Andi. May we be worthy of all your gifts. Amen."

When our cookout is over Mrs. Whitley says Allison is excused. "Spend time with Andi before she has to leave," she says, clearing the table. She hands Zachary the bottle of ketchup and gives the empty basket of French fries to Addison. Zachary is moaning. "Why doesn't Allison have to help?"

"Hush," Mrs. Whitley says, "you don't help when you have friends over, either."

Allison and I go to her room which is at the end of the hall. It's small but nice. The walls are painted a soft rose color and there's a pink and white striped comforter on her bed and a matching pillow tossed on a rocking chair. I sit in the rocker and hug the pillow. Allison sits down on the bed. Her closet door is open and I can see her clothes lined up—what there is of them. I remember the boutique and my idea to have her come down. I tell her all about me and Bridget's volunteer work and how we got the idea of the boutique and how well it's going and how girls that don't have really cool clothes get to come and pick out two outfits, complete with belts and everything.

"It's called Sweet 'n' Sassy Fashionique," I say proudly. "Would you like to come down and pick out some outfits?" I hold my breath waiting for her eyes to fill with tears and gratitude. But I have it all wrong. Allison looks at me. Her face is a complete puzzle.

"Why would I need to do that?" she says, and holds her hand out toward her closet.

Can you beat that? She's perfectly happy with her wardrobe, with her life, with everything. It's pretty amazing. I sit there feeling very stupid and wonder what it would be like to be perfectly content no matter what life handed you. I'm really embarrassed for making the suggestion and wonder what to say to explain myself.

"Oh, just for some variety," I say. "I get so tired of my clothes. You know how it is."

Allison doesn't say a word. She picks up her scrapbook instead. "Look," she says. "These are the pictures when I went to the YMCA camp last summer. I got to stay an entire week! And I might get to go again, if my father gets his raise."

It's a perfect example of being happy with whatever life hands you. I'd give anything to feel that way. I have so much, but right now, sitting here with Allison, I feel like I don't really have much at all.

Chapter Thirty-nine

I DISCOVERED THIS RADIO station, WYOU. They play all the hits from the 1960s, which you'd think I'd hate, but I don't. I'm not sure why I like this music. Maybe because lots of them are filled with the problems of love and I'm having plenty of those with Rodney. To begin with, I've only received one letter from him and I've sent him five. But I read in the paper that twelve countries have sent naval forces to Iraq. And six aircraft-carrier battle groups have arrived as well, which means a lot of new soldiers. Rodney is probably busy getting acquainted. He's very friendly. I'm convinced he's doing his best to make them feel at home. Therefore, one letter is understandable under the circumstances. I'll write him another one tonight and tell him it's okay to just send a short one back.

WYOU is playing "I Love How You Love Me," by the Paris Sisters. It's so whispery, it gives me the shivers. And of course it makes me drool for Rodney. Next comes "Will You Still Love Me Tomorrow?" by the Shirelles. It has the best beat. I'm making a list of all of them to see if I can find some copies of them or maybe I can order them off one of those TV advertisements, where you join and they send you one every month, whether you want it or not, but then you can send it back if you don't, so it's still a pretty good deal.

Beth is home for the weekend from Vassar and Parker Barrett is here. That's the guy she's marrying. They're going over the guest list. They're having the reception at the Piedmont Driving Club which my mother considers the only place to have a reception. They have to keep the guest list to five hundred people. Two hundred and fifty people each. I didn't know my parents had that many friends. When Rodney and I get married I think we'll just elope and ask my parents to give us the money I'll be saving them. Watching all that Beth and my mother have been going through over this wedding makes me crazy.

Parker is a pretty cool guy, though. He looks a lot like Pierce Brosnan, the movie actor, only much younger of course. But the point is he's real good-looking and very nice, too. He's always sincere when he says hello to me.

"How are you, Andi?" he says, but the way he says it makes me feel that he's really interested in my answer.

Personally, I think he could do a lot better than Beth. She's very bossy, even with him. She always insists on having everything her way, like what movie they're going to see, and where they should go to dinner. And she tells him that he's wearing the wrong colored belt. It doesn't match his shoes. Which I think is a dead giveaway she is going to try to run his life. She should just let him alone. And for sure she should let him decide on a movie or what belt to wear. But oh no, Beth has to have her way in everything.

Mr. Porter—Henry—our gardener is driving me over to Sunny Meadows. Even though school's out I have decided to continue being an Angel through the summer months. During the summer you only come on Saturdays. You can choose to take a rest from it if you want. But when I mentioned to Mrs. Sterling that I might not be coming over the summer months, she started crying. That pretty much settled it. I'm going to be there for the summer. But it's not so bad. Now I'm used to yelling as I read.

When I get to the Sterlings' room—it's at the end of the hall— Mr. Sterling is sick. One of the nurse's aides is taking his temperature and his blood pressure.

"Should I maybe come back later?" I ask.

The nurse's aide, whose name is Joyce, makes some notes on her clipboard and then says, "No, I'm sure Mrs. Sterling would enjoy some company. Mr. Sterling's a bit under the weather." She pats his hand. "You should be feeling better in no time."

"What's wrong with him?" I ask. I know he's eighty-something and I remember how my grandfather died when he got in his eighties.

"He's got a bit of a cold, is all," Joyce says and leaves the room.

I figure I could sit quietly and read to Mrs. Sterling and I won't have to shout, but she turns to me all teary-eyed—she's been very weepy lately—and asks if I'd mind putting some lotion on her back.

"I keep telling those jerks, but they're always in a hurry," she says.

I open the drawer next to her bed. Sure enough, there's a blue plastic bottle of hospital lotion and it doesn't look like any of it's gone. Mrs. Sterling slips her top off and sits there in her bra. She's very skinny and the bones on her neck stick right out at you and say hello. She's so thin I'm not even sure she needs a bra anymore. There's nothing there to fill it. She sits on the edge of the bed while I warm the lotion in my hands. When I feel it's just right I smooth some on her back.

"Oh, Andi," she says, "That's better than heaven."

Imagine thinking a little lotion on your back is better than heaven. But then her skin is very dry and cracked. The nurse's aides who bathe her must have noticed. You'd think they would have written on their clipboard: *Needs lotion ASAP!* I guess they're too busy to bother.

When I'm finished applying the lotion I help Mrs. Sterling with her blouse. She has trouble with the buttons.

"My daughter gave me this blouse," she says.

"I didn't know you had a daughter." I've never seen her visit.

"Oh, yes. We have three of them," she says proudly. "But they're very busy, you know. They come visit when they can. One lives too far away. She's in Maryland."

I have been coming to read to them every day after school for months and I've never seen one of them, not even once. Now my eyes are tearing up.

"Would you like me to read to you?"

Mrs. Sterling glances over at Mr. Sterling. He is sound asleep. His mouth is partly open and some spittle is dripping down his chin. I take a Kleenex from the box on his nightstand and dab at it. Mrs. Sterling smiles at me.

"You are a precious girl, Andi. Did you know that?"

If all it takes for one to be considered precious is to wipe some spittle off a chin, I'm surprised that the entire world isn't full of precious people. How much work is wiping spittle? Exactly.

Mrs. Sterling says she's tired and thinks she'd like to take a little nap before lunch. I tuck the sheets around her and place her hands on top. She nods off in no time. I decide it would be nice to visit Nana Louise. My grandmother's getting very old, too. And you just never know how long old people will be around. I find her out in the dayroom sitting in one of the wicker chairs. It has extra padding in it and nearly swallows her up.

"Hello, Nana Louise," I say as cheerfully as I can.

She looks at me and smiles, but I can tell she has no idea who I am. I guess those days when she did are over for good, but I keep hoping.

"Hello," she says. "Is it time for lunch?"

She thinks I'm one of the aides. It must be my Angel badge. I look at my watch. It's almost noon, which means it is time for lunch. Plus, I can smell it. Cafeteria food here seeps up through the vents and mixes with the all the other odors floating around the corridors, old people sweat, and medicine, and disinfectant. It's not very appetizing.

I take Nana Louise's arm and help her up out of the chair.

"Yes," I say. "I'm here to take you to lunch."

"What a nice girl you are," she says.

I gently guide her down the hallway. "Would you like to go for a walk after lunch?" I say.

"I'm not sure," she says. "I'm expecting Walter, you know."

I'm not aware of any Walter in her life, past or present. My grandfather's name was Arthur, like my dad.

"Walter?" I say.

"Yes, dear, I'm sure he'll be here after lunch," she says and her eyes light up like stars.

Nana Louise has forgotten every one of us. So, who is this Walter guy? And why does she remember him? I ask the nurses and they say, "That's our janitor. She's very fond of him."

Now I know my grandmother has lost it. She's gone bonkers over the janitor.

Chapter Forty

Mrs. Hall is visiting with my mother when I get home from Sunny Meadows. She's Rodney's mother. Rodney still hasn't written lately and I'm sort of mad at him. Still, I'm very anxious to hear any news. I burst into the room right in the middle of their conversation.

"Where did they take him?" my mother says. Take him? Is he hurt? Is it bad? I want to rattle off questions like it's an inquisition. Did he lose any of his arms or legs? Is he blind? Can he come home for good?

I stop dead in my tracks and nearly knock a vase off the end table. My mouth is open but nothing is coming out of it.

"Well, first they treated him in the field, but then they quickly transferred him to a hospital aboard one of the navy's hospital ships." Mrs. Hall dabs at her eyes with a hankie. Her eyes are big blue lakes. Rodney has those eyes. Oh please let his eyes be okay. Please. Please. Please.

"But he's going to be alright." My mother is nodding her head like that will make it so.

"They're not sure about one hand." Mrs. Hall looks like she's about to cry.

"How bad is it?" I yell. "Tell me!"

"Andi, where are your manners?" My mother says. She turns to Mrs. Hall. "Please excuse her rudeness, Pamela. Normally, she's a perfectly lovely child."

Mrs. Hall nods her head. My mother takes hold of my arm and pulls me down on the sofa next to her.

"Mrs. Hall's son has been injured." No kidding.

"He's at the Naval Medical Center in Bethesda, Maryland for now," Mrs. Hall adds.

"W—w—will he be alright?" My teeth are rattling worse than a rattlesnake's tail.

"Hot shrapnel penetrated his hands. He has some pretty severe injuries, so they're not sure if he'll regain full use of them." Now she really starts crying.

My mother goes over to comfort her.

"Of course, he will," she says. "That's nonsense. They perform miracles nowadays. Why, they keep babies alive that weigh less than a pound."

What premature babies have to do with the severe injury of one's hands I have no idea. But it seems to comfort Mrs. Hall. She looks up and nods and smiles. My mother asks Rosa to bring some tea. I sit back deeper into the sofa and rest my head. So that's why Rodney hasn't written. He can't use his hands. I picture him with these huge bandages like boxing gloves covering him up to his elbows and burst out crying.

"Andi," Mrs. Hall said, "I didn't realize this would upset you so much. Do you know Rodney?"

I nod my head emphatically that I do. "We—we—were almost— you know sort of going together," I say softly.

My mother looks at me like I've taken leave of my senses.

"Why Andi," she says. "Where on earth did you get an idea like that?"—like it's impossible for Rodney to love me. "You're not even fourteen years old. Don't be silly." My mother sits down next to me and puts her arm around my shoulder. Mrs. Hall opens her pocketbook and pulls out one of those little photo albums people carry. She flips through it until she gets to one near the back.

"Here it is," she says and holds it up for my mother and me to see. "Her name is Sarah. Isn't she pretty? A beautiful girl. They've been engaged since Christmas."

I want to take that album and toss it in the fireplace. Instead I hold the album closer to get a good look at this Sarah. She has long blonde hair. She has on a sundress with thin straps and white eyelet lace at the bottom. Rodney has his arm around her and is pulling her closer to him. She's leaning in against him. She's very pretty. In fact she's prettier than Beth. I didn't think anyone could ever be prettier than Beth. It's not fair. I close the album and hand it back to Mrs. Hall.

"I guess I was wrong," I whisper. "Excuse me."

My entire future is over before it's even begun. I run to the bathroom that's next to the library. I make it just in time to be major sick. My life is over—absolutely, positively, totally over.

Chapter Forty-one

BRIDGET'S COME UP WITH the idea that we should head to the mall and then have a nice dinner out. Just the two of us.

"Let's go to Lenox. We can check out all the new stores and they have lots of places to eat. Henry can take us, right?"

She's trying hard to cheer me up.

I watch as she opens her closet door and starts tossing clothes on the bed. "We'll wear some really cool clothes and fix our hair and—"

"I'm not very hungry," I say.

"But you will be." She takes my arm and drags me off her bed. "Come on. It'll be fun." When Bridget gets in one of her moods to do something, there's just no turning her down. She'll have us out and about if she has to dress me herself.

I decide it's time for me to start living again. I can't pine for Rodney forever. I'm too young. Surely there'll be another love in my life.

"Of course," Bridget says. "Maybe even two, you never know."

Bridget—always the optimist. But it gives me hope. I tell her I'm going home to get dressed and for her to come over when she's ready. "I'll go find Henry."

My mother is reading a magazine and Rosa is waddling around in the kitchen, her favorite spot in the entire house. She could cook for an army and be perfectly happy. Henry is in the gazebo hanging flower baskets from the eaves.

"Can you take me and Bridget to the mall?"

He says it's what he lives for and grins. He hangs the last basket and wipes his hands on his coveralls. I tell him I'll be ready in an hour give or take. He'll go in and shower and put some Brut on. It's his favorite. "It doesn't take much to please Mr. Porter," my mother says and picks up a bottle at the drug store whenever she spots it. He lives in an apartment above the garage my father had remodeled especially for him. He's very happy there. He's very happy, period. "Life's too short not to be," he says. His wife died years ago. He's been alone ever since, well, except for us. "You're all the family a body needs," he says. I think of Henry being perfectly happy over nothing and then realize what a dope I am for being down in the dumps over Rodney. He's only one part of my life and he wasn't really even a part of it, after all. I just thought he was.

I hurry and get ready, sort of excited to be going. It'll be fun. My mother will give me her credit card and tell me to buy something nice, but not too much, she'll say. "Think of all the children who are wearing rags." My not buying too much won't change that, but she thinks it's somehow related.

"Your friend be here," Rosa calls up the stairs. I bound down the steps and wave to my mother. She smiles. She's happy to see me go. I've been moping around the house for days.

We climb in the car and Henry heads to Lenox Square. It's a great place to shop. It has three levels and there's even a fourth level for a small portion of it. It's got a Rich's and a Macy's and Neiman Marcus. But my favorite stores are those that carry makeup, which includes the department stores as they have every kind of makeup counter possible. Macy's has a counter for every brand. And most of them will give you a free makeover if you ask. Then you just buy a blush or something as a thank-you.

I tell Henry we'll meet him back at valet parking at eight. He nods his head and makes the okay signal. Bridget and I are off. It feels good to be out and about. I feel like skipping! It's amazing how well the human spirit can recover even from a major heartache. It's probably programmed in our genes. Otherwise everyone would kill themselves and before you know it, no more people. So, it's got to be in our genes to be happy after being sad. Which is a major relief—that day I puked in the toilet after finding out Rodney was engaged all along was the pits.

After three hours of scouring the stores, Bridget decides she wants to see the inside of the Ritz-Carlton. It's right across the street. "It's got to be really nice," she says. We wait for the "walk" light to change. "Look, they have a man to open the door in a fancy suit. Just like New York."

Once we're inside a young woman at the front desk asks if she can help us. I guess they don't want teenagers milling about doing nothing.

"We'd like to have dinner," Bridget says out of the blue. This is news to me. The young woman nods and points to the corridor straight ahead. The restaurant has been set up for afternoon tea. Servers are busy resetting the tables for dinner. Bridget walks right up to the maitre d'.

"Table for two, please," she says. He bows slightly and says, "Follow me." I guess teenagers aren't to amble aimlessly about the hotel, but they can have dinner. No problem. I'm anxious to see what's on the menu. It's a pretty cool place. The fireplace takes up one long wall and is bigger than a freight train. There are several other couples already seated at tables, but there are so many large plants and giant intricate vases that it's hard to get a look at them. The maitre d' tucks us into a little corner near the window and says our waiter will be with us shortly. Sure enough, a guy in a fancy black suit with a bow tie is at our side in no time. He places our napkins on our laps and hands each of us an oversized menu. Everything's á la carte, which means the bill is going to be more than my mother counted on showing up on her credit card. I'm starting to have second thoughts about staying to eat. I ask the waiter where the restrooms are. Maybe we can sneak out.

"We'll need some time to make our selections," I say. He leaves and I motion for Bridget to follow me.

"What?" she says.

"Let's get out of here," I say. "He'll think we've gone to the restroom. By the time he realizes we're taking a long time, we'll be long gone."

I get up and grab her arm and head toward the side door that leads to the restrooms. Bridget giggles and follows. We turn the corner and are twenty feet from the door. There's a small table tucked in an alcove. It's set with beautiful crystal and china. The couple before us is raising their glasses like in a toast. They're sitting right next to each other instead of across from one another. They put their heads together and kiss. It's a long passionate kiss, complete with tongues. Gross! Bridget coughs loudly. I want to smack her.

The couple stops kissing and turns their heads in our direction. I nearly jump out of my clothes. It's my father. And right next to him—nearly sitting on his lap—is Donna.

Chapter Forty-two

MOSTLY BRIDGET AND I are in shock. Of course we knew my father and her stepmother were still doing it with each other, but we didn't think of them as having a relationship as in going to dinner and stuff like that. When my father realizes that I saw them, he excuses himself to Donna and takes my arm and walks me outside the restaurant into the lobby and down the hall to a quiet spot. He says, "What are you doing here, Andi?" I'm thinking maybe that should be my question, but I'm too afraid to ask it. I tell him we were at the mall and how we happened to come over, perfectly innocent.

"We weren't spying on you. That's the truth."

"Well," he says, "the important thing is that you understand my having dinner with Donna is not something your mother should be privy to."

Privy. He's always using words in sentences that if you used them alone I would have a hard time understanding, but when they're in the middle of a sentence they're perfectly clear—my mother is not to be told I saw him mixing tongues with Donna.

"She's still fragile in her recovery," he adds.

I nod my head and spot Bridget standing at the end of the hall. Donna is nowhere in sight. I guess she's leaving this mess up to my father.

"You are to go home and disregard whatever it is you think you saw. Is that clear?"

Now he's holding my arm much more firmly than when he walked me out of the restaurant. I look him straight in the eyes. "I'm not telling

Mother," I say. "I don't want to be the one to break her heart." There, I said it. I hope it leaves him with a lot of guilt. He looks worried that I'm not telling the truth. If he's so intent on being with Donna, why doesn't he just tell my mother himself? That's the question.

My father lets go of my arm. I motion for Bridget to come over. She walks down the hall like she's on a tightrope forty feet above the ground. "Hello, Mr. St. James," she says when she gets to us, like it's a perfectly normal afternoon and we happened to bump into each other. My father nods his head, then turns to me.

"I think you two should go home. Is Henry picking you up?"

Then I realize it's after eight and we told him we'd meet him at the valet parking at eight sharp.

"We need to go," I say. "Henry's been waiting for twenty minutes."

My father does what my mother always does. He brushes the hair out of my eyes. There's a look of concern on his face.

"Don't worry," I say. "I'm not stupid. I know what's at stake here."

"I hope you do, Andi." He turns and walks away. He probably told the maître d' to bring the check yesterday and he and Donna got out of there. Bridget and I walk across the street to valet parking. Sure enough, Henry's waiting for us. He's his normal cheerful self.

"Here's my girls," he says. "I thought some space aliens got you."

We don't even smile. We climb in the car and sit like zombies for the entire ride back home.

"You don't look like my happy girls," Henry says, knowing something's up, so he's trying to make light of it. But not even his good nature can jar us out of our funk.

"It's getting worse," Bridget says.

I'm thinking the exact same thing. It's written all over my face.

Chapter Forty-three

SOMETIMES LIFE IS ON a roll. And not necessarily a good one. Sometimes it just goes downhill. Today is a perfect example. I go to Sunny Meadows expecting to see Mr. Sterling sitting up in bed yelling for someone to repeat what they said and I walk in the room and he isn't even there. Mrs. Sterling is sitting on the edge of her bed and her face is all red. The kind of red where you've been crying for a long time and it leaves blotches all around your face and your eyes stay puffy. I know something bad is coming. I'm afraid to ask. And worse, I don't know what to say or how to start a conversation. "Would you like me to read to you without Mr. Sterling?" would be really stupid. And "Hello, Mrs. Sterling" seems so cold and distant. Really I just want to put my arms around her thin shoulders and tell her everything is going to be alright, but of course it isn't and I'm right. Mr. Sterling is dead. Joyce comes in. "He died last night in his sleep," she whispers. Which is a nice way to go, if you have to go and it's your time to go, but I can hardly tell Mrs. Sterling that. I search my entire brain and can't think of one gentle thing to say that might help her.

"I'm so sorry, Mrs. Sterling," I blurt out. And then I lean over and give her a hug. And that's all it takes. She starts wailing like a baby who wants something, but not a bottle, and who knows what it is?

"I didn't know I'd miss the old fart," she says between sobs. I just pat her back and stand there and don't say a word. It seems to work. She calms down and dries her eyes.

"He was eighty-nine years old," she says. "That's a lot of years."

"My grandfather was eighty-five when he died," I say and wince. I just said the "D" word and I was trying to avoid it. Trying to just talk around it, but it's hard.

"Would you like me to maybe do your hair for you?" I ask. She's a real mess. She keeps a cosmetic bag in the drawer of the nightstand. "Maybe put some makeup on. How about that?" I say. "Would that make you feel any better?" I don't know what else to do for her.

"Why not?" she says. "No sense my going to pot because Howard decides to haul off and leave."

I once read part of this book on death my father had when his father died. It said there are stages to recovery when a person you love dies. One of them is denial, and one is anger, and there were some others I can't remember before the final one which I do remember was acceptance.

"Just like the old goat," Mrs. Sterling adds.

She's obviously in the anger stage. Maybe she's skipping denial.

I open the nightstand drawer and pull out her cosmetics bag. It has pink stripes and is heavily soiled. There are finger marks all over the outside, smudges of lipstick, three different shades of foundation and traces of purple eye shadow. Maybe I could buy her a new one and next time I come I could transfer everything into it. Mostly all the makeup inside is old and half used-up, but she seems perfectly happy with it, so maybe a new bag would be all she needs. I take out the foundation and she tips her head up. Her face is still caked with tear marks. There are fresh washcloths in the bathroom.

"Let's make like we're doing a real facial."

I go into the bathroom and wring one of the washcloths out with cool water and gently wash her face. She leans her head back and sighs.

"We'll have you looking good in no time," I say brightly.

She holds her face up and closes her eyes tightly like a small child afraid of getting soap in their eyes. I ring the washcloth out three times and keep washing until all traces of the tear marks are gone. Next I start with her foundation. It's the type that comes in a tube and goes on pretty smoothly, but she has so many wrinkles it starts to collect in the folds. I dab some powder over the top of it and smooth them out as best I can. Her face has more lines than a Shakespeare play, but if I don't hold the mirror too close, maybe she won't notice. When I'm satisfied I've done the best I can with her foundation and powder, I'm ready to dab on some blush. She uses the kind that comes in a little pot, rouge my mother calls it. Mrs. Sterling's is bright red and much too bright for her skin tone. I end up using too much and she looks like a clown. I mix a little foundation on top of it.

"That's better," I say. When I get her lipstick in place, I reach for her hairbrush. She keeps that in her cosmetics bag, too. If there's one thing Mrs. Sterling still has in her old age, is a full head of hair. I brush it carefully off her face. There's a little blue hair clip sitting on the nightstand. I pull some strands of her hair off to the side and clip it in place. It's not really the kind of clip a woman her age would normally wear. It's more like the kind you see second-graders wear, but it's all we have. I hand her the mirror. And then remember to pull it back away from her a bit.

"What do you think?"

She studies her reflection carefully, then, sets the mirror on the nightstand.

"I think you should definitely try a different line of work when you grow up."

"But you look lovely," I say, and straighten the collar of her blouse.

"In that case, I think you'd best get your eyes examined, too."

I put my arm around her and she leans in against me and we have a good laugh. Before long her laughter turns to tears. The makeup I tried so hard to put in place comes sliding off her face. What a mess. And now I'm crying right along with her.

"Hear that Howard?" she yells into the air. "You ain't even gone a day and already we miss your sorry deaf ass!"

Chapter Forty-four

I GOT UP WHILE it was still dark outside and couldn't get back to sleep no matter how much I turned around under the covers. Now I'm on my knees in front of my window watching the sun rise. It's nice that my bedroom faces east. The sun is just peeking over the horizon and it glows like it's wearing a halo and you just know there's a God when you see it and it's like he's winking at you. And that got me thinking, I wonder how many other people are watching this very same sunrise, right this very minute. Did they have trouble sleeping, too? Did some of them set their alarm clocks the night before and say, "I think I'll just watch the sunrise tomorrow." How about that? So they set their clocks for six a.m. and here we are. It'd be nice if we were all lined up in a row, watching the sun climb over the horizon together. We'd probably, every one of us, just suck in our breath and let out a big sigh. It's that beautiful. It takes the air right out of your lungs. But you have to be here at just the right second, because the sun peeks out at you one second and the next instant it's full in your face.

The reason I couldn't sleep is because my mother is drinking again. But she is not drinking out in the open like she used to. She is doing it on the sly. She probably thinks this way none of us will notice, not me or Beth or Rosa or even Henry. This is silly thinking. When she is drinking she gives herself away in a number of ways. To begin with, she will slur her words a bit, depending upon how much she's consumed. And when she walks she has a way of making her way carefully through a room, balancing herself against the furniture along the way, like a toddler. It is very pathetic. I want to tell her outright that I know she is drinking and ask why she has stopped attending her meetings. I don't believe she is calling her sponsor anymore either. At least I don't hear her on the phone like I used to every afternoon.

Beth is not aware of what's going on as she's at school. She might not notice even if she were home. She's preoccupied with herself. The wedding is getting closer, so I don't blame her for this. But I am tempted to talk to her about the situation. If our mother keeps up her drinking she might end up a complete drunk by the actual wedding day and what kind of mother-of-the-bride will that make?

Rosa knows for sure about the drinking. I know this because my mother hides the empty wine bottles in the kitchen trash can under newspapers. They clink together when she asks Henry to empty it. They look at each other and shake their heads. When I am there to witness this they look away when my eyes meets theirs. It's like they want to keep this knowledge from me, but it is no good and they know it. I stare blankly back at them, with tears in my eyes, which is a dead giveaway that I know what's going on.

Rosa asks if she can fix me something good to eat. I shake my head. Henry asks if I'd like him to take me someplace. They are trying so hard to make my world work right. I love them all the more for this, but there is nothing they can do. It is up to my mother to change the situation. Her Alcoholics Anonymous book is still on her bedside table. I sneak it into my room and start to read. Maybe there is information that will help me find a way to convince her that she needs to get back on her program. An early chapter explains that the founder of the organization discovered that the only way he was going to remain sober was to help carry his message to another alcoholic. If this is the only way to recover, my mother is in worse shape than I thought. She is not in contact with any other alcoholics presently, so she is hardly in the position to help them stay sober in order to stay sober herself. I turn the pages and keep searching for something that can help me help my mother. I discover that she must reach her bottom before she will be once again willing to get help. And the bottom is different for each and every drinker. Who's to know where hers is? The book also says that she must place herself in the hands of a higher power. That's a start. I could get her to Mass every day. Going on Sunday is obviously not enough. I go find Henry. He is more than happy to drive us over to St. Lucy's. I take the Alcoholics Anonymous book back to my mother's room to place it on her nightstand. My mother is on her bed sleeping. Her mouth is open and an empty bottle of wine is on the floor—so much for hiding her drinking. But this is good. The book says those that hide it are in complete denial, which makes it much harder for them to reach bottom.

In the morning I hear my mother on the phone with her sponsor. She is talking in AA language, which makes me happy. It could be a sign that she is ready to go back to being sober.

"I've picked up," my mother says.

I go into the library and quietly pick up the extension. Now I am an eavesdropper, but I forgive myself. My mother's life—all of our lives are on the line. Her sponsor's name is Alice. She has been in the program for over twenty years. She is telling my mother that there will be many tests along the way, but she can step up to them one day at a time.

Many tests, that's a scary thought.

"Just how many?" I blurt into the phone without thinking. When I realize what I've done I drop the handset back in the phone rest and wait for my mother to come looking for me. I know exactly what I will say to her. I will tell her that I love her and that I am worried and I want to help her get back on her program. She will look at me and smile and tell me everything will be alright, and not to worry one more minute. I close my eyes and wish this with all my might. No more tests. No more tests. No more tests.

My mother peeks her head into the library. She does not smile and tell me everything will be alright. She opens the door and says, "This is my battle, Andi. Not yours, sweetheart. There is really nothing you can do. It's up to me."

That's what I'm afraid of. It's up to her and I'm terrified she's not up to it. And I'm worried that any little thing could push her over the edge. Like finding out my father is having an affair, which is not really a little thing, it's a major thing. Surely that would push her over the edge. Then I realize, going over the edge would mean she's sure to hit her bottom. So, there is something I can do. I can help her hit her bottom. And I know just how to do it. I should have thought of it sooner. Now there's no time to waste.

Chapter Forty-five

I'VE BEEN WORKING ON my plan to help my mother, but right now I have to set it aside. We're having a memorial service at Sunny Meadows for Mr. Sterling. All the nurses set it up. Today is Thursday and the Director of Nursing has called in the minister who comes every Friday. The nurses have chairs set up in rows for the nursing home residents that can still sit in them without falling over. They put the wheel chairs in the back area, but I doubt those that will be sitting there can even see. They probably don't care. They probably don't know what this occasion is all about. They're looking all around like, *what is the deal here?*—and a couple of them that always act pretty strange are swatting at each other, like kids do in a car if you're on a long trip and they think the other person is too far over on their side.

There's a podium with a white cloth draped over the top that has a cross on it. Two of the nurses have put construction paper on the windows to make it look like stained glass, which I think is a very nice thing to do. But then I learned the elementary school kids were here yesterday making them for today. Still, they used them, so I have to give the nurses credit for doing that.

Of course the setting is not a real chapel, but it's nice the nurses tried to make it look like one. They're being very nice today, which makes me want to ask them why they weren't so nice to Mr. Sterling while he was still alive. I'm sure he would have appreciated it. But no, they were always telling him to be quiet, or ordering him to eat and standing over him to make sure he shoveled in all the peas on his plate and I know for a fact he hated peas, so he shouldn't have had to eat them. They could have given him corn. He really liked corn.

Mrs. Sterling is sitting in the first chair in the front row. I think she's kind of enjoying herself—like it's her day. All the people that have their faculties start walking up to her after the minister says what a great man Mr. Sterling was—but you tell me how he knows, I never saw him once in their room—and they all pat her on the back and then they lean over and say things to her.

"Our prayers are with you, Mavis." And Joyce says, "He was a fine man, now, wasn't he?" That's the only nice thing she's ever said about him. It's a shame that he's dead and will never hear it. Joyce is the one who always made him eat the peas.

Right now, I'm sort of used to Mr. Sterling being dead. I've read to Mavis every day since. It's much better reading to people when you don't have to shout. Still, it would be nice if he was still alive. They could die together. I picture them reaching across their beds and holding hands and Mr. Sterling saying, "See you on the other side, Mavey." That's what he always called her, Mavey. And Mrs. Sterling would have said, "Beat your ass there, Buddy." She always called him Buddy, which I thought was really cute. She curses a lot, I'll give her that. But it always made Mr. Sterling laugh, right out loud. But he never cursed that I know of.

After the service, I concentrate on baby Joshua. He's home with Amy from the hospital and is doing really good. He's still not the size he should be for a baby his age. He's in the twentieth percentile, which Amy says means eighty percent of all babies his age are bigger than him. "But that can change," she adds. So, we'll see. He's two months old now and looks all around, so I think he can see things clearly. Sometimes I think he has a little smile on his face, but my mother insists it's gas. It looks like a little smile if you ask me.

Beth came home this past weekend and took over the place.

She's getting everything all set for the rehearsal dinner, which they are having at the Ritz-Carlton. I nearly choked when she picked that place. The last time I was there wasn't so hot with my Dad and Donna sucking each other's faces. When Beth announced that she and Parker had made the arrangements, I watched my father's face to see if he had a reaction, but he didn't.

"That's good," he said. He lives this double life, but he can keep it completely off his face.

My mother and I are busy packing for the cruise. She took me shopping and I got some really cool clothes to wear, deck pants and middy tops and plenty of bathing suits. My mother insists you need to wear a different one each day, like anybody cares. So now I have six of them, but I like the blue striped one best of all, so I'll probably end up wearing that every day. I put everything in the suitcase in the order that my mother instructs. It makes her happy, but if it were left to me, I would just dump them all into the suitcase in a heap and sit on the case to close it.

Bridget and I are excited. We're hoping that there will be plenty of boys. The ship brochure says they have all these teen things to do, so we're counting on not only girls being around.

"Just think," Bridget says. She's doing my hair in a French braid and it looks totally great. "We could actually be meeting our future husbands. You just never know. And then, years later, people ask how you met and you say, 'Oh, on this cruise ship I went on.'"

"I don't know about that," I tell her. "It'll be nice just to meet some cute boys. They don't have to be the ones we're going to marry."

At dinner, my mother explains that Rodney is coming over with his mother after dinner. Normally this would have my heart pounding like it was a drum. But I've gotten used to the idea that there no longer will be a me-and-Rodney future, so it's a big letdown.

"His fiancée is coming with him," my mother adds. She puts a serving of mashed potatoes on my plate, which I really don't want.

I want to make sure my hips stay as skinny as they are right now for the cruise, so I've been cutting out starch totally. If I do meet a cute boy I want to look great. "Isn't that nice?" she says. "Andi, are you listening?"

I nod my head that I am. Actually, I don't really want to meet her, so I must still have some feelings for Rodney or why would I care?

"You remember," my mother says. "Her name is Sarah."

Just rub it in, will you. I nod again, but my lips are twisted up in a smirk. I don't know why he wants to come over and introduce his fiancée to us anyway. It's not like we're family. But it will be nice to see if he has full use of his hands. I'm still sort of mad at him for not loving me back when I loved him. And I still fantasize about him. I picture him seeing me again and then realizing, *Oh my God, I love Andi!* Wouldn't that be cool? Except for telling Sarah. She's probably a very nice girl. There is no sense in both of us having a broken heart from Rodney. Besides, I'm sure that's not going to happen, but I think about it for a while and it's really romantic. Like something on a soap opera. Where the camera zeroes in on one of the actors and you can hear the words in their head and they've just made a major discovery, like Rodney really loving me for instance, and then the music starts playing really loud, and then they cut to a commercial. I always love those parts, even if I haven't been watching the show on a regular basis and have no way of knowing what's really going on.

When we're done with dinner, my mother says not to wander off. "They'll be here soon," she says.

I go upstairs and flop on my bed and look through the latest *People* magazine. I like to know what's going on with my favorite, Tom Cruise, or maybe Meg Ryan. I like her a lot, too. I trust *People* magazine to tell the truth. All those other magazines have a lot of lies in them. I'm fairly sure of this because they get sued a lot.

Ten minutes later I hear the door chimes. It must be them, Rodney and Sarah and Rodney's mother. I lean over the banister.

Rosa goes to answer the door. Then I remember I haven't even brushed my teeth and what if I have spinach caught in one of them? I run into my bathroom. My French braid still looks perfect. I could kiss Bridget. I didn't even know Rodney was coming and she does my hair and it looks so great.

I have on a cotton shift and sandals and my legs are very brown. I put some lip gloss on and some blush. I can't believe how good I look. Something's been happening to my face lately. It's looking more and more like Beth's. It's a small miracle.

Rodney and Sarah are sitting next to each other on the sofa. Rodney jumps up when I walk into the room.

"Andi," he says all friendly-like.

Now I'm feeling very self conscious. I don't know what to say. "Hi!" is all that comes out. I notice his hands. He doesn't have any bandages on. I'm glad he's all better, even though he doesn't love me.

Rosa has a large tray with iced tea and pastries. Sarah takes a glass but nothing else. She takes a sip and sets it down on a coaster on the end table, then turns back to Rodney.

"This is Sarah, Andi. Sarah, meet Andi. She was a great help to me when my grandmother died."

I really want to hate her or something. She took Rodney away before I even had a chance, but then I remember she met him first. They've been engaged since Christmas, so hating her would be totally unfair. I'm not sure if I'm supposed to shake her hand, so I nod and smile and turn to Rodney's mother.

"Hello, Mrs. Hall," I say. "It's nice to see you again."

I know that will make my mother very happy. I'm doing everything right. I go over and take the chair next to the sofa where Sarah's sitting. For some reason being around her makes me very nervous, like maybe she can tell I once had a thing for Rodney and in a way I still do. When he said my name when I came into the room I was hoping he'd get that look on his face that I imagined where he realizes he's in love with me. Of course, he didn't and I admit to being disappointed even though I knew in my heart it wouldn't happen.

Rosa holds the tray of iced tea out for me to take a glass, which I do, and then for some stupid reason I reach to pick up a pastry, before I remember I'm not eating any starches or sweets 'til after the cruise. When I pick up the glass, it slips and I lurch forward to try and get a grip on it, which makes it worse. The glass tips sideways and hits the side of my hand and the tea ends up all over me and Sarah. It's very cold and she nearly jumps a foot. I'm too much in shock to feel it.

Rosa sets the tray down and runs into the kitchen. She'll bring back enough paper towels to sop up the ocean. Rosa's good for emergencies. In the interim, my mother jumps up.

"Oh goodness," she says. "Are you okay, dear?" she asks and gives me a look that says, *what is with you tonight?*

I'm so embarrassed. It's bad enough that Rodney doesn't love me one bit like I loved him, but now he knows what a big klutz I am. Sarah is dabbing at her clothes with her hands and grinning.

"Andi," she says, "Do you have anything dry I can put on?" Now she's laughing. She stands up and loops her arm through mine. "Excuse us, y'all," she drawls. "We girls get a chance to make a second entrance. Don't go away!"

And to think that I was so prepared not to like her, that I'd be so unhappy that she was ending up with Rodney. Now I see she's perfect for him and a really nice person, too. Every once in a while, out of the blue, life just stands up in your face and says, *gotcha.*

Chapter Forty-six

MY PLAN TO HELP my mother concerns an idea I had way back when I first found out about my father and Donna. I thought of writing notes to my mother from Donna to let her in on what was going on. I decided against it when I realized I would be ruining the wedding plans, and Amy was in the hospital in danger of having the baby too early, plus I didn't want to hurt my mother, so I changed my mind. Now, I'm thinking it would be good to have a letter or two of this nature as a back-up plan in case my mother starts drinking again. Really make her hit her bottom. She's not drinking right now, but one never knows. It's good to always be prepared, an adult thing to do. I decide to write several letters and take out some stationery Beth has in her desk drawer. The first one I compose is one from Mrs. Decker. She is the one who has a face that looks just like her Doberman's. A letter from her makes the most sense because she is always walking up and down the street with that dog, sometimes scaring the daylights out of people who happening to be walking, too. I don't know this Doberman's name, but he looks like he could swallow your leg with one bite. She got this dog when Mr. Decker died, so the dog is most likely for protection and probably pretty ferocious given the right circumstances. I always stay out of his way.

I start thinking about how to compose the letter and what words Mrs. Decker would choose to use and decide to keep it very simple.

Dear Margaret, [I'm fairly certain she would use my mother's first name. I have seen them conversing from time to time when Mrs. Decker was outside without her dog.]

This is not an easy note to write, but I feel you should know what is going on with your husband. He is having sex with the young neighbor next door to you. [I cross out "having sex" and start over.] *He is having a sexual relationship with the young neighbor next door to you. I am sorry to be the bearer of this news. Sincerely, your concerned neighbor* [I cross out "your concerned neighbor" and write "one of your concerned neighbors"].

I decide not to actually put Mrs. Decker's name on the note in case my mother should take the letter over to Mrs. Decker and confront her. This way it could be a note from any number of neighbors. How my mother will figure they know this information to be factual is the next question. But I don't have an answer for that and will have to rely on the fact that my mother will be so overcome with grief that she will not question how they know, just that they know. After all, it's common knowledge on soap operas that the wife is always the last to know, and soap operas are designed after real life. I'm fairly sure of that.

The next one I write is from the viewpoint of Mrs. Anderson, who is in her eighties and is known for being a nosey neighbor if ever there was one. She once reported that she saw Beth smoking a cigarette when Beth was still in high school, and Beth got grounded until she convinced my father she would never smoke again. She hasn't that I know of. Mrs. Anderson is the neighbor who weighs at least three hundred pounds. She rarely leaves her house so it is possible that she knows everything that goes on in this neighborhood and what time of day any and all events occurs as well. I oftentimes see her peeking out of her plantation shutters. And her backyard is adjacent to Bridget's pool house, so she could easily have heard all the groaning that goes on in there.

So a note from Mrs. Anderson would not be questioned. Plus I can actually sign her name. She is old enough that she might not remember whether she wrote the note or not if my mother should approach the subject with her. This note is right to the point:

> *Dear Margaret,*
> *I am sorry to inform you that your husband is having an affair with your neighbor. I'll let you decide which one.*
>   *Helen Anderson*

I decide to write one last note from an anonymous neighbor who doesn't really exist. Since I've made this person up I decide the note should be formal.

> *Dear Mrs. St. James,*
> *Your husband is being unfaithful. You may wish to visit your next-door neighbor's pool house to confirm this. Wednesday evenings are the best time. Yours truly, A concerned neighbor.*

I'm finished. I reread them to make sure that each one sounds different. It's the best I can do. I put them in my top dresser drawer. They will be there when I need them. Days go by and I see no need to use them. My mother is back on her program in earnest and seems to be doing very well. She amazes me. Eventually I don't think about those letters anymore, which is a very sorry thing, because I should have burned those letters the minute I wrote them.

❖❖❖

Rosa is sick and my mother is actually doing the laundry. She's putting my undies in my top dresser drawer. That's where I keep the letters stashed along with the one I wrote to Donna. They're under my panties, except I'm fresh out of panties. That's why my mother decided to tackle the laundry.

I'm about to walk into my room. The door is partway open and my mother has one of the letters in her hands. I watch as she opens each and every one. I'm not sure what to do. Maybe I could tell her it was an English assignment. We were to make up the biggest lie possible and write all about it. That might work. Before I can decide my mother glances at the door and sees that I'm standing there. She quickly folds up the letter in her hand, places it on top of the others and puts them back in the drawer like she's never even seen them. And what do I do? I stand there and pretend I haven't seen a thing, either.

"How's the laundry going?" I say and walk into my room very casual-like, but my insides are actually doing the tango. I plop down on my bed. My mother turns to me and says, "Fine. That was the last load." She fluffs the back of her hair. "I certainly hope Rosa gets better soon. I'm completely worn-out." She puts a pleasant look on her face, but it's the kind of pleasant one she always uses when she's trying to make people think she's fine when she's not. Fine, the very word reminds me of her program literature which it says stands for Frustrated, Insecure, Neurotic, and Emotional. She presses her lips together in a closed-mouth smile and her eyebrows go up a little bit and her eyes open wide—that kind of look. I know that look.

"I think I'll take a nap," she says. She walks out of my room but leaves the door open and I can easily see she's not headed down the hall to her bedroom. I watch as she goes downstairs. I lean over the banister. She's headed toward the kitchen. I sneak down the stairs and slide behind the column that separates the drawing room from the wet-bar. She isn't headed to the kitchen after all. She stops at the cabinet next to the wet-bar sink and takes out a bottle of wine. It's only half full, but it's been sitting there since the day she last stopped drinking. She said it would remind her of how pathetic she can be. My mother takes a glass down from the wine rack above her. She pours a full glass and downs it in three swallows. She pours another. My mother is drinking again and it's my fault. And it's Donna's fault for enticing my father to begin with. This makes it my father's fault for ever getting involved with her regardless of what she did. We're all guilty—every one of us.

"What are you going to do?" Bridget says.

Telling Bridget was supposed to make me feel better, but it doesn't. I'm as miserable as ever. I want to stick my head in the washing machine while it's still on the spin cycle. Have it smack me around good. How could I be so stupid? I should have burned those letters. Instead, I kept them tucked away like I did my prized artwork when I was in the first grade.

"There isn't anything I can do," I groan and flop backward onto my bed spread-eagle. "My mother hasn't said a word. It's like it never happened. Weird."

"Maybe not," Bridget says. "Maybe she's doing what lots of grown-ups do. They ignore stuff. Like that will make it go away. My father does it all the time."

"He does?"

"Sure. Like when he took me out of Westwood Academy. He acted like I'd never even been there in the first place. And when my grades were so bad afterwards, he hired a tutor and said, 'Looks like you're definitely doing better,' and my grades didn't get better for a long time."

"Double weird."

"No, denial!" Bridget says and pops up into a sitting position. "She's having a major case of it."

"But why?" I say.

"Probably because then it won't hurt so much."

I go to the dresser drawer and retrieve the letters. "Here." I hand Bridget the one from Mrs. Decker. "Help me tear them up."

We sit over the wastebasket and tear them into pieces the size of confetti. I dump the contents of the wastebasket into a paper sack. We go over to Bridget's and she tosses the mess into her trash can.

I'm going to be like my mother and pretend they were never there to begin with.

Chapter Forty-seven

THE DAY OF THE wedding rehearsal is here. Both families and all of the attendants are instructed by Beth to meet at St. Lucy's at seven o'clock. We're here early and Beth is greeting everyone as they arrive like she's already in the reception line. She has Parker standing next to her and he's busy shaking hands. Kind of silly, but I get in line and shake along with the rest of them.

They're having a solemn high Mass at noon tomorrow. There will be a priest and a deacon and a sub-deacon—they're actually priests, too, but they take on a different role for this type of Mass. There will be a lot more chanting and singing going on than a regular Mass. And they'll use incense. To begin with, in the sacristy, all the priests wash their hands. There will be two acolytes to assist them with their vesting, which is a big deal. Thankfully, I won't be one of the acolytes. I'm excused because I'm in the wedding, which is a relief because I think it was my turn to serve again. Anyway when the deacon and the sub-deacon put their stuff on they must follow all these rituals and recite certain prayers each time they put on another piece of clothing. First, comes the amice, which is a rectangular cloth of linen with long strings for tying and it's kissed, because it's embroidered with a cross, and then it's placed on top of the head while reciting one of the other prayers. Then it's tied around the shoulders on top of the cassock. Next this long linen tunic with sleeves, which is called the alb, is put on and then the cincture, this long cloth cord is tied around the waist. The sub-deacon completes his vesting by putting the maniple on his left arm. The maniple is an embroidered piece of fabric folded in half with a cross in the middle. He already has his tunic on, which has short sleeves. The deacon places his stole, a long narrow embroidered piece of cloth—which is similar to the maniple, except it's longer—over his left shoulder and binds it in place at his right hip with a girdle, an elastic cloth. He then puts on his maniple and his dalmatic, which is similar to the tunicle. Talk about complicated. Now you know what I was doing every Saturday at altar class. Very boring and confusing. The priest celebrant does the same except that he crosses his stole in front of him at the waist. And after the maniple he puts on a cope, a long, heavy embroidered cape. The Catholics are heavy into embroidery. After the Gospel and homily, the priest, assisted by the acolytes, removes the cope and puts on a chasuble, similar to the tunicle, but without sleeves and usually with an embroidered cross on the back. After the dismissal and before processing out, he'll take off the chasuble and put the cope back on. It's like they play musical chasuble with celestial music.

There's no telling why they go through this ritual, but they take it seriously and you will not see one smile the whole time they're doing it. They also wear a biretta while they're sitting. This is a four-cornered hat with a pom-pom on top in the center and three fins on top around the edges. They're plain black for the priests and deacons, but if anyone special shows up for a Mass, say a monsignor or a bishop, they're purple with red trim, or sometimes black with red trim. Archbishops are purple and cardinals are scarlet. There are so many different types of masses and so many orders for these priests to follow that it's no wonder they're not allowed to get married and have a family. When would they see them?

Father O'Malley explains the procession to Beth and Parker. He'll be the main priest tomorrow at the wedding. I don't know the other priests' names. They're from a different parish. Father O'Malley makes it clear that only after the other priests have all filed in will the wedding march begin and the bridesmaids may proceed to the altar. Beth insists we are to proceed slowly making sure to stop and bring our feet together after each step and take a slight pause before proceeding with another step. When we attempt this it looks like we all have sprained ankles.

"Andi," Beth explains, "It's right foot first, left foot up to meet your right foot, then left foot next, and bring your right foot up to meet your left foot and then right foot again. Can you do that, please?"

If I tell her no, maybe she'll kick me out of the wedding, which would make me perfectly happy. But it would destroy my mother. I smile and say, "Sure. Watch this."

I do it perfectly. It still looks all jerky. I think we should just take our time and walk down the aisle and forget the feet meeting feet part.

With the rehearsal out of the way we head over to the Ritz-Carlton for dinner. It is a major feast. This is the best part so far. The entire banquet room is lit up like Camelot. All of the tables have candles and white roses in the center. There are twenty-four people in their wedding party, not to mention Parker's parents and brother and sister and then me and my parents, so it's quite a crowd. Dinner is four courses. The first course is an avocado and shrimp appetizer, after which they serve us lobster bisque, followed by Cornish game hens that are the cutest things, accompanied by garlic mashed potatoes and string beans almondine. For dessert there is a raspberry torte with fresh whipped cream. It looks like a work of art. Naturally there's champagne, but I notice my mother is back to drinking apple juice, so maybe she's gotten over the letters. Better yet, maybe she's forgotten all about them. All in all, it's a very nice evening. Beth looks quite beautiful, like always, but happier than I've ever seen her. Tomorrow's the wedding, supposedly the best day of her life, but if she knew what was going to happen she'd excuse herself and go to the bathroom and kill herself, or at least puke. That's another reason it's best we never know what's in our future. No sense upchucking a perfectly wonderful dinner.

Chapter Forty-eight

PICTURE THE WORST THING happening at a wedding. That's Beth's wedding. Everyone's in their place, exactly where they're supposed to be. The flowers are like a garden from heaven. They're everywhere. The priests are doing all their chanting and rituals right on schedule. Father O'Malley steps to the front of the altar and bows, and then turns to Parker. He places Parker's right hand in Beth's left hand, then turns to Beth and says, "Repeat after me."

"I, Elizabeth Amelia St. James, take you, Parker Chandler Barrett, to be my lawfully wedded husband, to have and to hold from this day forward, for better or worse, for richer, for poorer, in sickness and in health, to love and to cherish, from this day forward until death do us part."

Personally, I think they should have come up with something more original for their wedding vows, but Beth insisted on keeping it completely traditional, right down to "Here Comes the Bride." But that's not the point. I'm getting to that.

So Beth repeats every word without skipping a beat and places the ring on Parker's left hand.

Father O'Malley turns to Parker and tells him to repeat after him. Parker looks like he's about to fall on the floor. His face is whiter than milk. Parker, says, "I, Parker Chandler Barrett, take you, Elizabeth Amelia St. James, to be my lawfully wedded wife, to have and to hold from this day forward, for better or for worse, for richer, for poorer, in sickness and in health, to love and to cherish, from this day forward until death do us part."

Father O'Malley is about to tell him to place the ring on Beth's finger and Parker jumps in and says, "Wait!"

No one in the church moves or makes a sound. If someone dropped a feather you would be able to hear it. Everyone has their eyes riveted on Parker who has a peculiar look on his face that says he would rather be at an inquisition than standing at the altar.

"I can't, I mean I don't. That is, I'm not ready," Parker blurts out and turns to Beth. He mouths what looks to be an "I'm sorry" and darts behind the altar and out the door that leads to the priests' dressing area. My mother starts sobbing. My father stands up and turns to all of our guests with his mouth open. Beth drops to the floor like she's been hit with a stun gun. I lean over and gather her in my arms as best I can.

"It's going to be okay," I say. Even though I don't think for one minute it will be. Everything's a mess. Plus, they have a gazillion wedding gifts stacked up at home. I'm wondering what's she going to do with them. And then, out of the blue, Beth opens her eyes at me and smiles and says, "Oh, Andi, I'm so relieved."

You figure that one out.

It's been six weeks since Beth's wedding fiasco, but you would never know it even bothers her. It's like she doesn't even care that she never got married. But it's bothering my mother. She's nipping at the bottle again. I can smell it on her breath. And she has stopped going to meetings. My father doesn't notice, yet. He's too busy adding up all the wedding bills and trying to figure out if he can write it off his taxes. My mother had Rosa move all the wedding gifts to the front parlor. It looks like a department store gift registry. There's china and crystal and every electronic gadget you can think of—actually, some really neat stuff.

I invite Beth to come down to Table Grace and help pack the food boxes. Then I get a great idea.

"Why don't you donate some of your clothes to the boutique? Wouldn't that be cool?"

Beth gets this look on her face like she's been smacked in the head and has finally come to her senses.

"Perfect," she says. "I'm getting rid of anything I've ever worn for the last four years. Why not? I don't need those clothes."

She dashes up the staircase to her bedroom and starts tossing most of the contents of her closet onto the bed. The boutique will have enough cool stuff to outfit an entire school if she keeps this up. But I'm not complaining. Our stock was getting kind of low. Of course, not everyone is Beth's size, but we'll worry about larger sizes later and take everything we can get.

I ask Henry to drive us down to Table Grace. The trunk is loaded. Beth eagerly climbs into the front seat. She's getting back her old spunk. I'm happy for her. Being jilted at the altar after planning the wedding of the year has to rank right up there with all time worst moments.

"Hey, let's stop next door," I say. "I'll ask Bridget to come. She can help us tag all the clothes."

Henry does a U-turn and pulls into their driveway. Donna is out in the front yard wearing a skimpy halter top and short-shorts. She has a figure like Demi Moore, I'll give her that. She looks up when I get out of the car. There's a smudge of dirt on her face and she brushes her hair out of her eyes and smiles. She looks like something out of a magazine ad for Pike's Nursery.

"Hi, Andi," she calls brightly.

Why does she have to be so nice? It's hard to hate her. I nod and wave. "Is Bridget home?"

She points to the house and nods her head. I ring the bell and hear Bridget bounding down the stairs. Her golden retriever Rudy barks like the house is being invaded, but actually he's a very friendly dog and will lick you like an ice cream cone if you let him.

Bridget tells Donna she's going down to Table Grace and will be back in time for dinner.

"Can you walk Rudy?" she asks, not waiting for an answer, and climbs into the car.

Beth is amazed that there are so many people standing in line waiting for their box of groceries. "Where do they all come from?" she asks, finding it hard to believe that there are lots of people whose circumstances reduce them to accepting charity. She's been living on another planet where money grows on trees. But she joins right in and is happily sorting and handing out boxes along with the rest of us. I watch as she smiles and pats the wrist of a small woman with three straggly children clustered around her, two girls and a boy.

"Lemme see," the little boy says. He stands on tiptoes and peeks into the box.

"I put extra macaroni and cheese in for you," Beth says. "Do you like macaroni?" This boy's face lights up like a lamp. It pinches at my heart to see Beth so loving and happy to be helping. Maybe I've judged her wrong all these years. Maybe there's a streak of goodness in all of us and it just has to have an opportunity to come out and say, *Hey, I've been here all along! Look at me!*

When we get home Beth takes my arm and pulls me into the parlor.

"You know what I'm going to do?" she says. Her eyes are positively dancing in her head. "I'm going to auction all of the wedding gifts!" Mother has been after her to get busy and send them back. "And I'm giving all the money to Table Grace. Isn't this just the greatest idea?"

I have to admit it is.

"It's worth almost getting married over," Beth says and she's grinning from ear to ear.

Chapter Forty-nine

THE LADY IN CHARGE of Table Grace calls the newspaper when she finds out that Beth is auctioning her wedding gifts and giving them the money. The following day a reporter shows up at our door and gives my mother a nervous breakdown.

"Why in the world would you want everyone in Atlanta to know what's happened?" she says to Beth.

Beth stares at my mother and says, "Absolutely everyone we know in the states of Alabama, Georgia, Tennessee, and South Carolina knows what happened. They witnessed it first-hand. Why does it matter how many strangers will know?"

Which is a very good question.

Beth lets the reporter in and shows her to the parlor where all the gifts are stacked from floor to ceiling. This photographer the reporter brought with her starts snapping away with his camera. He's like seven feet tall. It's a good thing our ceilings are extra-high.

"I'm Natalie Carson," the reporter says, "*Atlanta Journal-Constitution*." She hands her a business card and holds out her hand for Beth to shake. Beth takes the card and shakes her hand, before extending one arm to the sofa.

"So what can I tell you?" Beth asks as they sit down. The sofa rests in an alcove surrounded by windows two stories high. The parlor is large and round. It's located on the right side of our house, with a turret roof that my mother fell in love with the moment she laid eyes on it.

"Tell me everything!" Ms. Carson says.

Beth looks at her like she's been told she's been crowned Miss Universe. She scoots up to the edge of the sofa.

"How are you doing?"

"Well," Beth says, "actually, I'm doing great." She gives a little half-laugh. It's obvious she is enjoying herself. She tosses her head and her hair sweeps to one side. "Of course when it happened, I wanted to die of shame."

"Are you still in love with the runaway groom?"

"Oh, let's talk about something else, okay?" Beth clears her throat and waits for the next question.

Ms. Carson asks how it came about that she decided to auction off her wedding gifts and how she plans to go about it.

Beth explains all about Table Grace and her visit to help pack food boxes. She mentions all the little children hanging onto their mothers with their tiny faces so hopeful.

"I hired a company who specializes in auctions," Beth explains. "They're taking care of everything."

Beth is very organized. Maybe it's good she's becoming a philanthropist. A person could do worse things with her life.

My mother is up and down with this drinking business, but for now, she has stopped. At least, I don't see her going to the liquor cabinet and she is no longer stumbling around the house. She's also taken an interest in gardening.

"Would you like to help me, Andi?" she says.

I think that I better, to be supportive. "Sure," I say. "What are we planting?"

"Herbs," she says and flashes a smile that could melt the sun. Rosa loves herbs and shops every other day for them so they'll always be fresh for whatever she's cooking. I think of her happily plucking from the garden everything she needs and get a little excited about my mother's idea.

Of course, I have no understanding of herbs and how we are to go about planting them and unfortunately neither does my mother. We go find Henry.

Henry gives us a crash course on herb gardening. There's more to it than I counted on. Henry says what we're looking for is culinary herbs.

"Perfect in the kitchen," he says. "Sage, thyme, marjoram, basil. You can do it."

I'm not so sure.

He goes on to explain that there are a variety of herbs to consider, annuals, biennials, and perennials. "The annuals bloom one season and die—anise, basil, dill." His voice trails off. "Biennials live two seasons but they only bloom the second season—caraway, parsley. Perennials bloom every season once you get 'em going. You can have chives, fennel, thyme."

"All right," my mother says. "How do we start?"

"Well, you need to decide the size of the garden. That'll depend on the variety you want," Henry says. He takes off his straw hat and wipes the sweat off his brow with the back of his arm.

"And you need to consider drainage and soil fertility. Drainage is the most important. If it doesn't drain properly you won't have a crop."

My mother is nodding her head, taking in every word. She's wearing a straw hat, too, with a wide brim, along with cotton blue jeans turned up at the ankles and a crisp white man-style shirt with the sleeves rolled up. She has on rubber mules. I try to imagine her on her hands and knees weeding through her herbs, plucking the fragrant leaves from their stems and placing them in a basket looped over her arm. The sun would be shining brightly. I see her turn and wave to me as I leave to go to Bridget's. There she is, my mother, sober and active and obsessed with her garden. It makes a little dent in my heart and rests there snug and warm. Even so, I've completely lost interest in this project. It sounds way too complicated. I was thinking that you just stick the seeds in the ground, put some water on them and let them grow.

"Well," my mother says and brushes her hands together like she's already been digging in the dirt. "It's something to think about. What do you think, Andi?" She turns to me. In an instant I realize I'm supposed to rescue her.

"I—I—I—" I'm not sure what to say. "We could read some books on it and then decide if we'd like it. How about that?"

"That's a splendid idea," my mother says and turns and walks back into the house through the portico.

I'm pretty sure she's lost interest in starting an herb garden, too. It's strange, but there's a bit of sadness that gathers in the pit of my stomach. I think of my mother and me producing a sumptuous crop of herbs for Rosa to use for all our meals. I see us together, digging in the dirt, laughing and harvesting our crop. The thought of it works its way into my chest and forces a big sigh out of my mouth. Then I realize it doesn't even have anything to do with the herbs. It's the thought of being together and her taking joy from being alive and being with me and being sober.

Chapter Fifty

IT'S A GOOD THING I didn't get into gardening. I'm on a major new project. St. Lucy's is hosting a babysitter's class complete with CPR training. I think of Joshua and immediately sign up. The classes will run every Friday afternoon for three weeks and then it will be time to leave for the cruise, so I'm going to be wall-to-wall with stuff to do. Saturday mornings I still have altar class and mostly hate it as much as always. But the sitter class sounds very exciting. After I sign up I get this handbook. It's filled with really cool information. Did you know that there are specific things to check on if babies are crying? Naturally, I know to first check and see if their diaper is wet, and maybe it's time for them to eat. But you are also to check to see if a thread from clothes is caught around their fingers or toes. I would never have thought about that.

I invite Bridget to join the class, too. She's not a Catholic, but you don't have to be to take the class. You just have to pay the fee. It's twenty-five dollars, which is a lot, but then you get the use of a life-like baby doll and diapers and clothes to practice on and you also get CPR training, so maybe it's really a bargain. They teach about taking care of older children too and cover things like leaving the house as orderly as you found it. The manual says the easiest way to do that is to not put things down, but put them away. It also says to stay awake until eleven or twelve unless you've been told otherwise. That's in case a baby or one of the kids wakes up and you need to be alert to hear them. Today we're practicing diapering a baby. Bridget is much better at this than me.

"How do you know how not to make it too tight?" I ask her. My diaper completely falls down to the doll's knees when I pick her up.

"Here," Bridget explains. "Just put two fingers on the tummy when you fold it over their stomach and then sort of pull it snug against your fingers and pin it in place."

I try that but my diaper still does not look as good as hers. Mine droops a bit on one side. I'm not concerned. Every baby I've been around has had on Pampers. They're a snap to put in place.

Next, we practice burping a baby. They say the best and easiest way for a beginner is to place the baby over your covered shoulder and gently pat the baby's back between the shoulder blades. I think most people know this, but our instructor insists we practice it. Her name is Mrs. Evans. She's like eighty years old. Where they found her do not ask me. I have no idea. It wasn't from Sunny Meadows nursing home, that's for sure. I've never seen her before, so she can't be from our parish either.

"Remember to burp the infant once or twice during a feeding and also afterwards," she says, holding one of the dolls up to demonstrate.

I have this part down pat and am anxious to move on to the next part, which is the CPR.

"Pay attention, now, girls," Mrs. Evans says. "This is critical."

Of course, she's right about that. If you come to a situation where you need to do CPR, basically you're in trouble to begin with, like did you let the baby crawl around on the floor and swallow a button, or something?

"The first thing you do is clear the airway," she explains. She has one of the baby dolls lying on its back with the head tilted backwards.

"For a baby or a very small child, place your mouth over the child's mouth and nose, making an airtight seal. For an older child, cover the child's mouth with your mouth, also making an airtight seal. Pinch the child's nose closed."

She looks up at us to see if we are paying attention. We are.

"You won't of course pinch a baby's or small child's nose closed, your mouth will be placed over it."

I think about when Joshua had a sneezing fit and snot was running from his nose. I prefer never to put my mouth over a child's nose.

"Now, give slow, gentle breaths into the child's mouth, one every three seconds. Pause after each breath to take in a replenishing, oxygen-rich breath."

Mrs. Evans leans over the doll and makes like she's breathing into its mouth. "Look to see that the chest rises when you blow a breath in. If the chest doesn't rise, the child's airway may be blocked. We'll go into that later."

Mrs. Evans sets the baby aside and clasps her hands together. "We will be having actual demonstrations when the Red Cross joins us for our next session. Any questions?"

Not one of us has any. Actually, I want to ask what happens if the baby throws up while you're breathing into its mouth. I'm thinking by the time you stop gagging over it, the baby will be a goner. I sit there and let the question rest in my brain. I hope I never have to even consider giving CPR, but decide that I will pay attention just in case I do. Maybe the Red Cross covers the part about throwing up. Maybe they'll explain during an emergency like this you will not even be aware a person has thrown up in your mouth. Your adrenaline is pumping so hard you don't even taste it. That would be a lot to expect. I think about all the paramedics and what they go through. They should get paid double.

Chapter Fifty-one

HENRY IS SICK. My mother wants to take him to the hospital, but oh no, he will have nothing to do with that. He says he's fine.

"I've felt a lot worse than this before," he says.

Beth brings him some of Rosa's chicken soup. She sits on the edge of the bed and spoon-feeds it to him and it is such a beautiful sight, sort of like watching a bird feed another bird. Not that Beth is a bird, but you know what I mean. It's just so tender it takes your breath away. I can hear Henry as he slurps a little off each tablespoon. He's so grateful. He pats Beth's hand and says, "It's very good," like she cooked it or something.

I want to do something for him, anything, so I fold the blankets next to the bed and put them on the chest next to the window. That doesn't seem like nearly enough compared to chicken soup so I tuck the sheets back in at the bottom of the bed and pat his feet. Henry smiles and it's more than worth it. Henry has been with us since before I can remember. He's like a grandfather.

"You have to get well," I say. My face is determined, like that will make it so.

I still think he should let my mother take him to the hospital, but that is still out of the question. I stand by his side and wonder if he is thinking of his wife. Her name was Millie and when he talks about her he always says her name like a little whisper on the wind, it comes out so softly. And I'm thinking that maybe he's thinking he wants to see her again, even though he has always said he's perfectly happy, maybe he hasn't been and he really wants to join her all along. It makes me very nervous.

"How are you feeling, Henry?" I say. He doesn't answer. He is sound asleep and looks just like an angel. Henry has that kind of face. Some people absolutely do.

Chapter Fifty-two

HENRY HAS RECOVERED, WHICH is a major relief as we're leaving for Cape Canaveral to go on the cruise. Vivian is coming with us. Beth has decided not to join us, even though my father thinks it's a good idea. There are no more rooms available in order to book a private one for her and she's not into sharing one with me and Bridget. What a relief. I prayed for ten hours that she would not want to go. Me and Bridget would have extra eyes watching us at all times and we really want to run off and be sort of wild. Not bad wild, but just sort of. We're going to be touring exotic islands. It just screams at you to let your hair down and go for it.

The one part that is upsetting is my father and Howard, Vivian's husband, are not going. I don't care about Howard, but I counted on my father going to reconnect with my mother. Say, another honeymoon for them, where he'd discover he wants nothing more to do with Donna and what was he thinking, he should have his head examined and my mother is all he will ever need for his entire life and he's so glad he found out. So right now that is not going to happen, but what really worries me is that he will be spending all of his time with Donna, because Rodger, Bridget's father, is in England and will be there for two more weeks. My father couldn't have planned this better if he planned it. And then I realize he did plan it.

"We can't let this ruin our trip," Bridget says. "Just ignore them. Let's make like they've never even met."

Right, like I'm going to be able to do that. But for sure, I don't want it to ruin our trip so I try to put it out of my mind. I get busy finishing my packing. First I hang my certificate I earned from my babysitter's class on the wall. My mother bought a plain black frame for it to rest in. I passed CPR and it says so right on the certificate. Passing was pretty amazing because the whole time I was thinking about snot and vomit and was having a hard time not gagging when it was my turn to demonstrate.

"Very good," Mrs. Evans said when I finished. A major relief is what it was.

It was exciting to finish the class but mostly because it would be time for the cruise and I have counted on this to be one of the best times of my life. I hope I haven't jinxed it or something. My mother comes into the room while I finish my packing and starts snooping about in my suitcase, supposedly to make sure I haven't forgotten anything. Actually, I've removed most of what she laid out for me to put in and have pilfered some really neat stuff from Beth who could care less, when before she would have screamed my head off if she so much as caught me in her room. Since she's become a philanthropist nothing fazes her anymore. It's a miracle. I should be on my knees.

"What's this?" my mother says and holds up a skimpy striped tank top of Beth's that I have wanted to wear since the first time she wore it.

"Ah, I sort of borrowed it from Beth."

"Andi, this is not appropriate for a child your age."

There you go—she thinks I'm a child and how do you answer that? There is no answer. It's useless. I watch as she fumbles through the rest of the clothes I've packed. She takes out half of what I've put in. I was going to look so hot.

"Where are all the new outfits I bought you?" she says.

She doesn't wait for me to answer. She goes to my closet and finds the missing items and carefully folds each and every single piece. She places them in my suitcase. She's ruining everything.

"There," she says, "That's better. Now you're all set."

Right! In ten minutes I've gone from being totally cool to totally dorky. If I do meet any boys, they probably won't even notice me.

"Thanks a lot," I say, trying to sound nice. Once she's gone I drag all the stuff back out and decide to mix and mingle a bunch of Beth's stuff with it. Maybe she won't notice once we're cruising.

Henry is taking us to the airport. He's back to being his normal wonderful self. He's poking about in the garden and he is doing the dearest thing! He's planting a complete herb garden. It has everything Rosa uses. She's out there with him now nearly jumping off the ground she's so excited. She's chattering away in Spanish, which Henry does not understand, but he smiles and shakes his head.

"No Español," he says.

Rosa starts chattering away in English, which I love to hear when she speaks it, because she leaves out words and it's so cute, like a toddler just learning to speak.

"Cilantro," she says, "Is good, no?"

Henry says yes he can plant cilantro.

"Epazote," Rosa says.

Henry repeats it like he hasn't heard right.

Rosa smoothes her skirt and lifts her head high. "Sí, *epazote*," she says and sticks her chin up in the air. "No gas, eat *epazote*. Is good."

Henry takes off his straw hat that has seen many better days from way back to who knows when, and says, "Epazote smells like gasoline. Not a good plan."

"No," Rosa says, "Smell like mint."

Henry is never one to argue. He nods and takes a tiny pencil out of his pocket like you get at a miniature golf course and writes something down. Rose nods like she is very pleased and continues with her list. She raises her hands and motions wildly. "*Mejorana*," she says and does her best to explain this spice. Henry is amazing. He understands and nods his head. "Marjoram!" he says and Rosa claps her hands. It's understood. They'll have marjoram.

"*Romero*," she says, which turns out is rosemary and "*Tomillo*," she says raising her voice at least an octave, which Henry decides is thyme. So there's our garden and my mother and I do not have to do anything but sit back and eat. That's my kind of garden. I can breathe in these spices already. I close my eyes and they grab my nose. I nearly sneeze.

Chapter Fifty-three

We're in Cozumel, the first stop on our cruise. I don't know who's more excited, me or Bridget. We keep dancing around in circles taking everything in. Right now we're on a tour of the city. My mother insisted on it.

"To understand the history and get a feel for the culture," she says.

Not that I'm interested in that. I'm just soaking up the sun and marveling how beautiful it is here. The water is the most amazing shade of blue. "Azure," my mother says. It's hard to believe how white the sand is on the beaches. I picked up a handful. It slipped through my fingers like the grains were made of silk.

Our tour guide is a young local girl of Spanish descent. She has dark honey skin and jet black hair. She's petite with large white, even teeth. She's wearing her hair in a braid that hangs down to her waist and has on a colorful cotton skirt with a white blouse that keeps slipping off one shoulder.

"My name is Maria Contreras," she says. "Welcome to Cozumel." She spreads her arms out in the air and smiles. "Cozumel was a little fishing village until 1961," she explains, "when a Frenchman by the name of Jacques Cousteau declared us one of the most beautiful scuba diving areas in the world. We have dazzling coral reefs and a variety of tropical fish."

We learn that the people native to Cozumel are of Mayan descent. They ruled for two thousand before the Spanish explorers arrived in the fifteenth century.

"One of the more interesting sites here on the island is called San Gervacio. It was once a sacred site where Mayan women journeyed to worship the goddess Ixchel, the goddess of fertility."

So bring two teenagers here, will you. By the look on my mother's face I can see she's thrilled with this little bit of culture. It's no concern to me—I'm not planning on being pregnant. Besides, it's beginning to sound like a history lesson. I'm anxious for the tour to end so we can go snorkeling. We've got reservations on a glass-bottom boat in Chankanaab. It's a three-reef trip. Vivian and my mother are coming along to enjoy the scenery, but don't want to snorkel. Vivian's just had her hair done at the salon on the ship and my mother doesn't like fish or anything from the ocean touching her.

"We'll be there to make sure you have a great time," my mother explains. Actually, since Bridget and I are under eighteen we're required to have a parent or guardian accompany us, so they have to come along.

A man named Luis greets us as we board the catamaran. We're offered a soft drink and shown how to use the snorkeling equipment. It's a snap to learn. Nothing to it—put the mask on, bite down gently on the rubber mouthpiece, and slap on your fins. Bridget and I are eager to get into the water. The catamaran takes off and we head to the first reef on our tour. They have to drag me and Bridget out of the water when it's time to leave for the next stop. We're having so much fun. Luis spots a big fish and dives down to point it out. There are tons of fish here, thousands really. Every color imaginable—it's like a kaleidoscope. Luis dives into the middle. A swirl of fish fans out around him. There are angelfish and sergeant fish that swim within inches of you and six huge parrot fish that must weigh forty-five pounds each. We have a disposable underwater camera and Luis offers to takes picture of us. This could be the highlight of our trip, which is kind of sad seeing as we have six more days. Maybe we should have saved the best for last, but the ship has a certain route they follow. Next we head to Grand Cayman.

"There is good snorkel there, too," Luis explains, "but not good like ours!"

So maybe I'm right. This is the highlight of the trip. Now what do we have to look forward to? Even so, we are very happy with our trip. Everything is going as planned. The only problem is eventually we get into major trouble.

I wake up the next morning and know instantly I'm going to pay for all the sun I got snorkeling. My skin feels like it's been slapped all over with a sledgehammer dipped in hot pepper sauce. When I look in the mirror it's hard to believe I'm a regular person. I look like a tomato in pajamas. Bridget's not in any better shape. She moans when I roll her over.

"You awake?"

"I am now," she says. She leans over and the sheet scrapes against her back. "Ouch!" She strains her neck to get a good look at her shoulders.

"I think we overdid it," I say.

We go next door to wake my mother. She'll have some cure. She has an opinion on everything.

"Oh, dear," my mother says when she gets a good look at us. She calls our cabin steward and asks if he will please bring us a bottle of vinegar from the galley.

"One cup of vinegar in a tub of cool water is what you need," she explains. She takes the bottle of lotion she has packed in her suitcase and puts it in our little refrigerator which is the cutest thing.

"This will feel good when you get out of the tub."

I can't believe we're as burned as we are. We used a ton of sunscreen. Just goes to show how hot a tropical sun can be.

After we bathe, my mother applies the lotion first to me and then to Bridget. Vivian is busy getting a facial. Tonight is the first of two formals nights they have on the cruise. There's another one on Thursday. We will be dressed to the nines. My mother bought me a special dress that even I'm happy with. It has spaghetti straps and is made of the softest material. It's short and has an empire waist. Buttercup yellow, the tag said. It'll go great with my sunburn. And, I've got these strappy little sandals that lace up my ankles.

Bridget is wearing a navy blue strapless knit dress that also has an empire waist. Hers is a little sexier than mine, but I'm not complaining because I figured my mother would have me looking like Shirley Temple, so what she let me pick out has me tap dancing on the clouds.

For dinner they have several entrées to choose from like always, but tonight they have lobster and filet mignon on the menu as well. Bridget and I order a serving of each. You are allowed to do that. You simply say, "I believe I'll have both the lobster and the filet mignon." The waiter doesn't even blink. He writes down on his pad what you've ordered and asks you if that will be all. Amazing!

Chapter Fifty-four

OTHER THAN THE FOOD, the formal night was sort of boring. Bridget and I start to think that maybe the cruise is not so hot after all. We quickly change our mind the next night when we meet these two guys. It starts out very innocently, which is how a lot of things begin. Consider World War I. One day people just didn't up and start shooting at each other. The Archduke Franz Ferdinand was riding along in his carriage with the Duchess Sophie at his side, waving at his subjects and probably having a very nice day, and this guy Princip assassinates him. But that didn't immediately start the war. There were other things that happened. A lot of people think that Germany started the war, but I know for a fact Russia was the first to mobilize troops and Germany had no alternative but to defend itself. Of course then they became evil. My point is, it all started with a little carriage ride. As for the war with my mother, it starts out when me and Bridget decide to go to the teen center. My mother and Vivian are going to take in the evening show.

"Make sure you're back by ten, Andi," my mother says. "That's late enough for you to girls to be out wandering about."

So we head to the third floor. After we get a cold drink we start dancing with a group of other kids that are out on the floor in a big circle. Before long Bridget is swirling around and around to the music likes she's crazy and manages to land on her butt. I grab hold of her hand and end up flat on the floor next to her. These two guys come up laughing and asking if we're alright.

"Let me help you up," the tall one says.

"Thanks," I say and hold out my hand. My heart is pounding and it's not because I got thrown to the ground. This guy is gorgeous. He looks like Brad Pitt.

"What's your name?" he says.

"Andi," is all I can think of to say. I wanted to add something after that but my mind is a blank.

"Jason," he says and pulls me to my feet.

The other guy is helping Bridget up. He's not as tall, but sort of cute with a cowlick that stands up at the back of his head.

"That's Gavin," Jason says and jerks his head in Bridget's direction.

Bridget stands up and straightens her sweater. It was pulled up around her midriff.

"Hey, you want to go to the club upstairs? It's where the adults go," Jason says.

"They play some cool music and there's lights flashing everywhere," Gavin says.

"Sure," I say and look at Bridget. She just shrugs her shoulders and gives me a look like, "Why not?"

So it starts out without any trouble. It isn't until later that things get out of hand.

We follow them up to the fourth floor where a small adult lounge is. It's all very innocent. We each get a Coke, which you have to pay for, and Gavin and Jason treat us. It's like we're on a date. We start dancing and just goofing off and then Jason says his brother is at the disco on the third floor and why don't we go there and hang out. I don't see any problem with that. I mean, his brother must be an adult or what would he be doing in the disco, right?

We head down there, going past the casino on our way. There are people everywhere feeding the slot machines. Bells are ringing like crazy, so someone must be winning something, or maybe the machines do that to keep the gamblers excited and anxious to keep playing.

The disco is called White Heat. It has a floor that looks like glass and a ceiling that is one giant mirror. The walls are peppered with wall-to-wall television sets flashing the word White Heat on them. It makes me dizzy just looking at them.

Jason finds his brother. "Hey, Jerry," he calls out. "What's up?"

Jerry is every bit as good looking as Jason and a couple of inches taller. He has dark hair that hangs down on his forehead and dark blue eyes with longer eyelashes than an ad for Maybelline.

"How about getting us some drinks?" Jason says.

"How old are you girls?" Jerry says.

"Eighteen," Jason says.

"Almost nineteen," Bridget says. I stab her in the ribs with my elbow. "Well, we will be in a few years," she whispers to me.

Try four and five years respectively. I'm not much into the idea of alcohol, but don't want to be a dork, so I go along with it. Bad decision.

Jerry comes back one by one with drinks for each of us. I guess the bartenders are too busy to keep track of who orders what. What kind of nut orders four drinks in quick succession? Or maybe he asked different bartenders. There's about six of them bustling about. I take a sip of mine. It's something with orange juice in it and has a cherry and a slice of an orange with an umbrella resting on top. It doesn't even taste like it has anything in it other than maybe orange juice and Seven Up. It's good and I drink it down without any trouble. Jerry brings another round. That's when Jason takes this flask out of his jacket and spikes our drinks. I can really taste the alcohol now. It isn't long before the room shifts a bit before my eyes. Now there's two of everything and my stomach feels like it's on a roller coaster while my head is on a merry-go-round. Then the room starts to spin like it's a top. I hang on to Jason to keep from losing my balance. Bridget is giggling and carrying on with Gavin. He has his arm around her waist and she's wobbling back and forth like a whirling dervish on a stick.

"Whoooeeee," she says. "I better sit down."

Three rounds later I'm outside on the deck heaving my guts out over the railing. That is, I'm trying to keep it over the railing, but the wind keeps tossing back what I keep tossing up. Bridget joins in.

"I think I'm dying," she says.

"I hope I do," I answer.

Jason and Gavin bring us some towels they take from the pool deck and start wiping our faces. "Guess you two have had enough," Jason says. "Come on, you can lay down in our cabin 'til you feel better."

His cabin consists of adjoining suites with a queen bed in one room and twin beds in the other. Bridget and I sack out on the queen bed. Jason covers us up and says he'll be back to check on us later. I lean over the bed and tell him to make sure it's before ten. When later comes I'm not sure what time it is, but my head feels like it's twice the size it's ever been and the motion of the ship is making me sick all over again. Jason and Gavin are nowhere in sight. I consider getting up to go find our cabin, but the moment I get up all I can manage to do is head straight for the toilet. There's nothing left in me to throw up. Regardless, my body keeps on trying to toss up my insides.

"Dry heaves," Bridget says and joins me over the john.

"I'll never drink anything again as long as I live," she says. "Ever."

I want to agree with her, but the thought of trying to form words is too much of an assignment. All I really want is my mother. I drag myself back to the bed and pass out. Bridget must have followed. When I wake up again, it's morning. Bridget is sprawled on top of the bedspread beside me. Jerry is asleep on the sofa and Jason and Gavin are asleep in the twin beds. The door between the rooms is open. I peek in to see if they're awake. They're not.

I nudge Bridget. She opens her eyes like they're connected to strings that don't quite work. "Let's get out of here," I whisper.

Which is exactly what we do. It takes us forever to figure out where we are and where our own cabin is located. Finally we come to 7806. We know it when we get there. We run straight into the captain and his crew and my mother who are parked in front of the door to our suite. My mother spots us and sees the condition we're in, which isn't pretty. I don't remember hearing such screaming since my brother died.

Chapter Fifty-five

MY MOTHER HAS DECIDED two things. First, she's convinced I've been violated as in I'm no longer a virgin. I don't care how much alcohol I had, I would have remembered something like that, or wouldn't there be some evidence of it on my body in the morning? Exactly. But oh no, she's calling the ship's doctor and demanding an examination and I am having a complete hysterical nervous breakdown. The idea of a strange man poking around in my private spots has me wanting to jump overboard.

"I want these boys arrested," my mother says. "Immediately!"

The ship's captain explains that they are only sixteen years old. So they lied! There's actually no crime other than furnishing the alcohol, which technically they didn't. Jerry did. Jerry could be in some very serious trouble, but we don't mention him.

The second thing my mother has decided is that Bridget and I are not to go anywhere for the rest of the cruise without them. I don't blame her on that accord. If I were my mother I'd be having a hissy fit, too. Still, it will be the pits. Today we are in the Cayman Islands and are going horseback riding along the beach. Vivian is going, too. She loves horses. My mother's going to watch. Remember she doesn't like any type of animals or fish touching her. I can just picture her standing on the beach for two hours, melting under the sun—ridiculous. She should just stay on the ship and bite her nails.

I did not have to have an examination. My mother called my father and he said they would discuss it when we returned. I could just hug my father! I hate him for being with Donna, but I love him for not insisting I have an examination. Fortunately, my mother did not call Bridget's father. She decided to let my father handle the entire situation. Good plan. Bridget's father is out of the country anyway.

After we finish riding horses, my mother and I are in her cabin and get into a major battle. It starts when she tells me she is disappointed in my behavior and has decided no matter what my father's decision is that I am to be grounded for the rest of the summer. This flips me out. There are some really cool things I planned on doing. Like taking a canoe trip down the Chattahoochee with Bridget and her church group and maybe hanging out at this new teen center that just opened.

But my mother insists I will not see the light of day. There are to be no exceptions. This gets me upset. Can't a teenager make a mistake?

"It's not fair!" I say. "We were wrong, and we drank stuff we shouldn't have, but we got sick and we've been punished enough and you should understand. You were young once too, right?" I think I am making a great deal of sense. Does my mother think so? Absolutely not. She says, "Andi, this hurts me more than it does you."

That is absolutely it. I've heard that before and it is a bunch of crap. I tell her that she is a total loser.

"A loser!" I yell. My voice cracks when I want more than anything to sound fearless.

"Andréa, you are to go to your room right now," my mother says and her eyes are darts and I am the bull's-eye.

"No!" I say. "I know I've disappointed you. I was stupid, but grounding me for the rest of the summer isn't the answer!"

"Andi, I know what's best for you," she says.

"You do not!" I say. "You don't even know what's best for yourself." I'm in very deep water here, but I can't seem to get out of the boat.

"Excuse me?" my mother says and puts one hand on her hip.

I keep blubbering on. "You don't know anything. You're stupid."

I've lost all control. "You won't even face the fact that your husband is screwing Donna!"

I can't believe I just said that. My mother drops on the bed like a torpedo hit her in the heart.

Chapter Fifty-six

WE SPEND THE NEXT day at the pool on the ship. The sun and sand and wind have done their job. My body's limp as a rubber band. My head hits the pillow and I'm about to drift off when I hear my mother on the telephone. At first I'm thinking she's calling room service and then I hear by the tone of her voice it's not an ordinary call. "Andréa," she calls over her shoulder. "It's your father."

My mother has probably called my father and told him that I've told her about Donna and my stomach detaches itself from my intestines. My mother is standing in the door way between our rooms and holding the phone out to me.

"He needs to talk to you," she says. I walk over and take the handset out of her hands and swing my hair away from my face.

"Hi," I say weakly, then, decide I better tell him what I've done, so he doesn't think I'd try to keep it from him. "I'm sorry," I say, "I told mom about Donna, when I was all upset and now I can't take it back." There is dead silence on the line. "But I want to!" I add.

"I'm sorry to hear that," my father says. "I thought we had an agreement."

"Well, we did, but then—"

"Listen to me Andi," he says, interrupting me. I'm going to get the lecture of my life. "I'm not concerned about that right now." I'm thinking how can he not be?

"Something's happened and you and your mother need to fly home. The ship will be in Labadee by morning. I've made your travel arrangements. A jeep will meet you at the dock. From there you'll take a helicopter to Santo Domingo. You'll fly back to the States from there."

"What?" I don't understand. Why are we cutting our trip short? That's when I notice my mother is crying and I'm freaking out thinking something's happened to Beth and sure I've never always liked her, but lately she's been turning into a regular person you can do things with and it'd be just my luck that I never get a chance to make up for all my bad thoughts about her.

"Is it Beth?" I say, and my voice breaks down completely.

"No, no, no," my father says. "Beth is fine. She's here with me now."

"Then what—" I'm trying to imagine why he'd be phoning ship-to-shore and insisting we have to leave our cruise and fly home.

"It's Henry," my father says. "He's had a heart attack."

"But he's okay, right?" I say. There is a long silence that gives me the answer. "Daddy?" I say, feeling like I'm five years old again. I love Henry like you'd love a grandfather. "He's okay and he's just asking for us, right?"

"I'm sorry, Andi," my father says. "Rosa found him in the garden. He's gone."

I drop the phone and look over at my mother. She reaches for me, but my knees collapse and I plop onto the floor before she can grab me. Henry, dear sweet Henry, who always does something nice before you even ask him to, is gone.

Vivian and I are having a heart to heart. She's convinced I need one and I just love her so much that whatever she says is okay with me. She's sitting next to me on the long narrow couch they put in all of the suites and has her arm around me.

"Andi," she says, "You're being too hard on yourself."

She kisses the top of my head. I start blubbering. I tell her I've destroyed my mother's entire world.

"I told her what my father is doing with Donna."

"I know," she says, which doesn't surprise me. She and my mother are closer than lint on a sweater.

"Andi," she says, "you haven't spilled any beans. Your mother knew all along what your father was up to with Donna."

"Of course she did. She found my notes!" I bury my face in my hands. I'm so ashamed that Vivian will now know I was destroying my mother's world when all I really wanted to do was help her hit her bottom, like the AA book said was necessary in order for a person to recover.

"Silly girl," Vivian says. "Your mother knew you wrote those notes. You used Beth's stationery that I give her every year for her birthday. Your mother recognized it immediately."

"She did?"

Vivian squeezes my shoulder and nods.

"But she had to know what I was writing was true."

"She already knew, Andi. She was just very concerned that you knew and wondering how that could be. How did you know?"

Vivian peers into my eyes like the answers are resting in my pupils. I look away. I'm not going there. I shrug my shoulders and shake my head. Maybe she'll think I just had a hunch.

"Why didn't she say something to me? And why didn't she confront my father if she already knew? She never said anything to him that I know of." I stop and sniff and wait for her answer.

Vivian takes her hands and smoothes the sides of my hair. "If your mother had confronted your father he would have had to make a choice."

"So?"

"Your mother was afraid he wouldn't choose her. She still is. That's why she doesn't want him to know that she knows."

I'm getting dragged into some very grown-up stuff here. Now I really start sobbing. In addition to Henry being dead, I've already told my father I told my mother. So he knows that my mother knows, but my mother just doesn't know that he knows. What a mess. I need to tell Vivian. Somehow I know she'll make this all better; about Henry, too. There's just something about Vivian. When you're feeling down she can just smile at you and lift you up. It must have something to do with her spirit; it's so gentle and honest.

"I told my dad!" I say. "He knows I told my mother!" Now I'm wailing. Half of it's still about Henry. I feel awful, like my body's been hit by a baseball bat and is black and blue all over.

"Oh Andi," she says. She turns me around and wipes my tears with a tissue. "You poor little darlin'—what a weight to carry."

"And now what can I do?" I say, choking on my hiccups. "I've already told him."

"You do nothing," she says. "Now it's your mother's turn to step up to bat. It's as simple as that."

It doesn't sound so simple to me. Our lives are at stake.

"All games eventually need to be played to the end, Andi." She sits me up straight on the sofa and tucks her hand under my chin. "Winner take all."

Chapter Fifty-seven

I DON'T KNOW WHAT's going on with my mother and father. They're being very kind to each other. We're on our way to Henry's funeral. Beth is wearing her little black dress that she used to say everyone should have. Now I know why. I don't have a black dress. My mother says I should wear my navy blue one that has little squares on it. I hate that dress, but I'm too sad to argue.

My father drives us over to the funeral home, Evans and Matthews. It's an enormous older house that has many sections to it. It's quite beautiful and looks like a house that an old couple might still live in. The house has black shutters on all the windows and little flower boxes below each one. It doesn't look like the kind of place that would have dead bodies in every room. Whenever I see this house, I picture an old woman pouring iced tea on the front porch and saying, "More, my dear?"

But this is the house where they have Henry and he's not having any tea, that's for sure. They have him in the third room on the left with a little sign with his name out front. Henry Lewis. I run my hands over his name, wishing I could erase it. I don't want it posted here. I'd rather see it someplace else, like maybe in the newspaper for doing some kind deed, which would be just like him, or maybe in a garden book showing off his herb garden with Rosa standing right by his side smiling. I think of all the things Henry could still be doing and something grabs hold of my chest and won't let me breathe. I swallow hard and take my father's hand. He pats my shoulder and says it will be alright. Henry's in a better place, he says. That's a stupid thing to say. He's in a box. I just nod my head and squeeze my eyes shut and try to stop the tears.

It's a pretty nice box they have him in—I'll give Evans and Matthews that. It's lined in satin the color of cotton and Henry is dressed in the gray suit he always wore on Sunday when he drove us to church. He'd park the car and then come sit beside us. He's not Catholic but he never let that stop him. He'd lean down on the kneeler and wink at me. My mother loved having Henry join us. She thought she'd converted him. But in truth Henry was a Baptist. He said he stopped going to that church when he found out a bunch of them were hypocrites.

"How did you know?" I asked him.

He said it was written on their other face.

"Their other face?"

"Yes," he said. "The ones I ran into had two of them, one for church and one for the world."

I guess he thought the Catholics don't—have two faces that is—but if you ask me, they have too many opinions.

So now I'm staring at Henry and his face is frozen in place and I'm wondering why they call this a wake. Then I remember reading that centuries ago people were often buried alive and no one knew except when the graves were unearthed for some reason and they saw the claw marks, so the English—I believe it was the English—starting having viewings where they stayed up all night long and viewed the body to see if it would wake. And I'm standing here and picturing Henry sitting up and saying, "Hi Andi, why did they embalm me?" And I burst out laughing and I cannot stop laughing. I keep hearing Henry saying, "Andi? Andi? What's going on here?" My mother is about to faint. She has her hand on her neck and is taking deep breaths and my father has his arm around me and is saying, "Andi, stop it! What's wrong?"

Everything's wrong. Henry's dead. My father's having an affair with Donna. My mother knows. I lost the love of my life before I had a chance to have him as the love of my life, and I'm just feeling all-around miserable. And he asks what's wrong.

My father is moving out. His suitcases are already packed. They're in the front hallway. I'd love to go and just dump everything that's in them out on the floor. Throw a tantrum. Instead, I sit in the library, doing nothing. When I peek around the corner I notice my father is coming my way. I go back and sit down. He enters the room and scratches the back of his head, like maybe he's more at a loss as to what to say than I am.

"Andi," he says. He takes a seat next to me on the leather sofa. I've always loved this room. Now it will never be one of my favorite places again. I'll always remember it as the room my father sat in before he left us. That makes me cry. He puts his arm around me.

"Andi," he says again. "Your mother and I have decided this is for the best."

"Best for who?" I ask. My father hands me his handkerchief. Of course it smells of Herrera for Men which makes me cry all the harder.

"It's complicated, Andi," my father explains. "Your mother and I need some time away from each other to think things through. But I'm not leaving you. I'll be available whenever you want to see me."

"So, you're leaving Mom," I say. "Just like that, after all these years. Just break up our family. Throw everything away." I blow my nose into his handkerchief and hand it back to him. My father takes it and looks at it and then looks at me, but he doesn't say anything. He's usually never speechless, but he is right now. He must really be upset, too. He stuffs the handkerchief into his back pocket, which isn't something he would normally do. He'd drop it on the floor and let Rosa tend to it. Already he's acting like he doesn't live here.

"You're getting a divorce," I say. I want it to be a question but it comes out like a statement.

"That's—that's one of the things we'll need to discuss, your mother and I." He puts his arm around my shoulder. "When you're older, Andi, you'll understand that these things happen. People grow apart."

He takes hold of both my shoulders and turns me around to face him. "Right now, I'm more worried about you. Your mother told me you stayed out all night on the ship. Andi, do you have any idea what could have happened to you?"

"But nothing did," I say. "We just drank all this stuff and got sick and then just passed out and when we woke up we got out of there. They didn't even know we were gone. They were worse off than we were."

"I want you to make better choices in the future," he says. "We can't be there for you every waking moment. We can't lock you in your room. We want to have faith in you, to know that you'll be okay."

I'd like him to make better choices, too. I'd like him to stop seeing Donna and stay home where he belongs. But I nod my head like a good daughter and tell him I will make better choices. I've learned my lesson.

"Are you ever coming back, Daddy?"

"I don't know, Andi. That's why I'm going away—to find out."

My father leans over and kisses me on the cheek and pats my head. "Take care of your mother, okay? She's going to need you right now. She's not feeling well at all."

Right, like he could care.

Chapter Fifty-eight

BRIDGET'S BACK. SHE AND Vivian weren't happy to see us leave the cruise ship, but they managed to have a pretty good time regardless.

"The Parade of Chefs the last night was so cool," Bridget says. "They marched around the dining room waving hankies and the music was loud enough to blow the roof off."

She also got to feed the stingrays and windsurf in Labadee. And there was a beach party they went to on the north coast of Haiti.

"It was at Dragon's Breath Point," Bridget explains, "where all the pirates used to hide out. These guys cooked our food right in a pit on the beach."

We're in my bedroom playing Clue. I move my token into the library and then move Mr. Green and the rope in with me. "I say the crime was committed in the library by Mr. Green with the rope," I say, convinced I'm right. Bridget immediately produces Mr. Green's card and disproves my theory. She's won the last three times. It takes a good memory to win this game and the only thing my memory is good for lately is remembering my father has left my mother and I'm miserable.

Tonight we're going over to visit Amy and Jeffrey and baby Joshua. I'm really looking forward to that. The only thing is—my father won't be going with us. He's leased a furnished condominium near Lenox Mall. It's on the twentieth floor and has a view of the Atlanta skyline. All of the furniture is sleek and modern. It looks exactly like what a rich bachelor would have. It's really beautiful and I hate it. The furniture is stainless steel and black with chocolate-brown and white throw pillows. And there's large vases of fresh flowers in the entryway, which has an enormous mirror over a credenza with a sculpture of a horse resting on top. Double doors lead to the corridor outside his unit, where there are two elevators side-by-side that remind me of the ones they have in fancy hotels. And there's an elaborate sign outside the building that says, The Landing at Peachtree.

My father's three thousand square foot unit has three bedrooms. If he's just going away for a while to think, why did he take such a big place? Exactly. He's going to divorce my mother and is too much of a coward to tell me. Sometimes when I look at him now I want to stick pins in his face, but mostly I just want to throw my arms around his neck and beg him to come home for good.

Bridget taps my knee. I stop daydreaming and go back to the game. "I say Colonel Mustard did it in the kitchen with the knife," she says. I have nothing in my hand to prove otherwise. Bridget checks the envelope and sure enough it's Colonel Mustard in the kitchen with the knife. I don't know how she does it.

"You win," I say. "I've had enough. How about you? Want to get something to snack on?"

She nods her head and collects the game board pieces. I gather the cards and the board and put them back in the box and slide it under my bed. We head to the kitchen. Rosa is there making chicken enchiladas. My mouth starts to water. If it were possible I'd eat the air. It smells that good.

"Want to stay for dinner?" I say.

"I can't," Bridget says. "My dad's taking us out to eat. Donna has something important she wants to share with us, or so she says."

"God! Maybe she's going to tell your dad she's seeing my father."

Bridget shrugs her shoulders. "She's getting her real estate license. I think it's about that. She's all excited because she's going to work for Harry Norman Realtors."

"What for?"

"Don't ask me," Bridget says. "I have no idea." She looks at the clock on the wall next to the breakfast table and heads for the door. "I gotta go. I told my Dad I'd be back by five."

I'm bouncing Joshua on my knee and he is having the best time. He already has his two bottom front teeth and one coming in on top. He leans against me and starts chewing on one of my buttons.

"No no, Joshua," I say and gently pull it out of his mouth. "You could choke on that, you little monkey." I scoop him up in my arms and dance around the room with him.

"Careful, Andréa," my mother says. "He's not a doll."

She's sitting at the kitchen table and looking at a baby album Amy has put together. Jeffrey has a late class this evening. He's working days now in my father's law firm and going to school at night. My father is going to take him into the firm when he graduates from law school. But that's ages from now. He hasn't even gotten his undergraduate degree yet, but my father has it all planned out.

It suits me fine. It means they'll be staying in Atlanta and we'll get to watch Joshua grow up. I wonder if it hurts my mother to look at him. He looks like the pictures we have of Alex when he was a baby. If it does hurt her, you wouldn't know it. But then, maybe she's in so much pain over my father leaving that she's come to expect her life to be just one big pain after another. At least she's not drinking. She's going to her meetings again every day. Maybe that's what's holding her together, those meetings and the friends she's made there.

Chapter Fifty-nine

IT REALLY SURPRISES ME that my mother is staying sober. If anything could make you want to knock yourself out it would be the fact that your husband has left you for a younger woman. But, even though it surprises me, the fact that she is sober does not feel like something I can count on. It's too soon to tell.

Presently, I'm keeping busy by volunteering at the nursing home. So far they haven't assigned me any new people to visit. I just wander around and make sure everyone is okay wherever they're sitting. I ask them how they are and if I can get them anything. I'm waiting for one of them to say, "Sure, girlie, I'd like a gin and tonic." Like that would be coming right up. Most of them just stare at me. It's really sad. I don't want to live to be this old if all I do is sit in a wheelchair and drool.

Of course, I'm still visiting Mrs. Sterling, and she's back to being her feisty self. In fact she's making a play for the new man on the block.

"He's a looker," she says.

And she's right. He is very good looking. He still has all his hair and is tall and tan. His name is George and he's eighty-five years old, but you'd never know it. And he's in good shape. The first thing he asked when he got here was, "Where's the gym?"

They don't have one, but they let his son bring his weights and install them in a corner of the library. So now every female here that still has her faculties is camped out in the library every morning at eight a.m. to watch him do his stuff.

Regardless of Mavis's wrinkles, she is a fine-looking woman and she's the one that catches George's eye. Whenever I get here at lunch-time they're always sitting next to each other. Mrs. Sterling turns to me and says, "Hello, Andi. Guess how many push-ups George did today?" He does them while he's parked on his knees, but still that is really something. Most of the other men here are just sitting in wheelchairs or being wheeled to the hospital on a gurney.

George always turns to me and says, "There's our angel—the prettiest one in the bunch." He's a charmer, alright. He has Mavis wrapped around his finger. I still read to her, but George joins us and he has me reading poetry. Elizabeth Barrett Browning. I should get extra points in English for this. Today I'm reading "A Thought For a Lonely Death-Bed." Talk about depressing. Mavis asked for that one. But the ending is pretty:

> But stoop thyself to gather my life's rose,
> And smile away my mortal to divine.

Since Mr. Sterling is gone I picture George gathering her in his arms as she takes her last breath and it pinches a little corner of my heart.

George asks me to read "A Woman's Shortcomings." And Mavis laughs and says, "Don't look at me. I don't have any."

"This one is an ode to lasting love," George explains.

I get to the part that says,

> Unless you can swear "for life, for death!"
> Oh, fear to call it loving!

So George must be right. It is about lasting love. And Mavis did love Mr. Sterling to his death, so her being with George feels okay. Now they're holding hands and Mavis has never looked happier.

And she never says curse words around George. That part's nice. And when I read, I never have to shout at them.

Still, I miss Mr. Sterling. He had so much spunk. I can still hear him. He's yelling in my ear, "WHAT'D YOU SAY, GIRLIE?"

Beth has decided to go to law school and has applied to Emory so she can continue to live at home. This is making my father very happy. "You can join my law firm, once you graduate. Keep it in the family."

I hope he is not counting on me following in her footsteps. I have no desire to be a lawyer. Actually, I have no desire to be anything right now. Life is just too depressing at the moment to want to do anything.

Beth makes the announcement at dinner. She even taps her spoon against her water glass to call us to attention and waits for Rosa to join us.

Rosa puts her arms around Beth and kisses her on the cheek. "Is good," she says. "Make your father big happy, yes?" Rosa looks at me and nods her head.

Like I am interested if my father is big happy. He should be miserable for what he's done. My mother doesn't talk about him other than to say he's called and wants me to call him back, that sort of thing. But in my heart I know she is hurting. My mother has always been devoted to my father and that is not something that ends just because he leaves. This is why I am afraid that my mother will start drinking again. Eventually she will not be able to keep herself together. I tell myself it's a matter of time. That's another reason why I'm so depressed. Why can't I believe in her? Beth does. She says, "Mother is making great strides. She's stronger than you think."

But how does she know this? And how can she be so sure? The only thing I am sure of is that life is not ever going to be the same. My father has not come back and it doesn't look like he's going to.

Chapter Sixty

DONNA AND BRIDGET'S FATHER are getting divorced.

"When did this happen?" I ask.

"Last night. They had this big fight because my father wants us to move to England and Donna said it was out of the question and my father said he would decide where they live and she could live with it or leave and she said 'Fine, I'm leaving.'"

Bridget plops down on my bed and puts her hands under her head. "I always thought I'd be happy if Donna went away," Bridget says in a whisper, like she's talking to herself. "But now I'd rather she come back so we don't have to move to London."

This is definitely not good, Donna and her father getting a divorce. It means she's free to see my father whenever she wants and I was hoping he'd realized he'd made a big mistake in leaving and come home. I had it all planned out in my mind. He'd come in the door and throw his arms around my mother, beg her forgiveness, and tell her he simply can't live without her. He can't understand what he was thinking.

"Living without you—ridiculous," he would say and shake his head like he should have it examined.

"Does this mean you're moving to England?" My whole life is falling apart.

"Maybe not," Bridget says. She rolls over on her stomach and rests her head in her hands. "After Donna said she was leaving he got all apologetic and said they really didn't have to move to England.

He just thought it was a good idea, but if she didn't want to go, that was fine. He'd keep commuting."

"And what did Donna say?"

"She said she'd have to think about it. She wasn't sure she could trust him anymore." Bridget starts giggling. "Huh! She can't trust him. That's funny, don't you think?"

Actually, nothing's funny to me right now. My life keeps getting more and more complicated. "So then what?" I ask.

"I don't know. They saw me peeking around the corner, listening, and started pretending everything was alright. And I said, 'Are you guys getting a divorce?' And my father said, 'Don't be silly. We're just having a little discussion, is all.'"

"And what did Donna say?"

"Nothing, she just sat there with one hand to her forehead and the other one in the air like she was trying to get him to stop talking. They're getting a divorce is what I think."

"I hope you're wrong," I say.

"I thought it would make you happy having Donna out of the way."

"Well, it would, except my father's moved out, remember? Having Donna divorced is just going to make things worse."

"Gosh, I forgot all about that," Bridget says. "You don't think that's the real reason Donna wants a divorce do you?"

"Duh!"

How was my mother ever going to compete with Donna now?

I don't want Bridget to move to England. I don't want my father to have his own apartment. I don't want Donna getting a divorce. I don't want my mother to start drinking again.

Everything in my life right now revolves around what I don't want. I think of Henry and know exactly what he'd say.

"Well now, I know what you don't want, Andi, but what is it that you want?"

That sounds like such an easy question. But all I can think of is that I want to be happy—not some kind of ecstatic happy, just plain old regular happy. That's going to be hard to accomplish. Bridget just called. Donna moved out last night. They have no idea where she went. Let me tell you where I figure she went: to my father's apartment, that's where.

Bridget's father has gone into a major depression.

"He's moping around the house," she says. "And he's taking time out from work. He says he needs to decide what direction we're going in."

Mostly downhill. Donna is the cause of two families biting the dust.

"I don't want you to move to England," I say. "Maybe this is a good time to tell your father that's not a good option. He will never get Donna back if he's in England. How about that? Tell him that!"

"I don't want to remind him about Donna, right now," Bridget says. She looks out my window and has such a sad look on her face that I want to hug her. "He's having enough trouble trying not to think of her on his own."

"That's so sad."

"I know. He turned over all of her pictures. They're facing the wall."

I want to sneak into their house and turn them around and stick daggers in them. If Donna had never been born maybe both of our lives would be going along really good right now.

"Let's go over to my father's apartment," I say. "If we just pop in on him, we can see if she's there."

Bridget turns around from the window. Her face is whiter than cotton. "I know she left my father, but I don't want to think it was just so she could have yours."

Bridget starts crying. And that makes me start crying. We're a mess, the both of us, just a total mess.

I grab the box of Kleenex from the bathroom and hand her a tissue. I take one for myself and wipe my nose, then pull another from the box to dab at my eyes. "So, you want to go over there or not?"

Chapter Sixty-one

WE GET BETH TO drive us over to my dad's. She's off to take the prelaw exam. Last night we sat on her bed and pored over sample questions. They are very bizarre. Beth is not concerned by the sample questions. She just smiles and says they are not that difficult if you break them down to eliminate which ones could not possibly be the answer and you are left with the one that is. I can't believe Beth is going to take an actual exam with these types of questions. It lasts for like four hours. I would shoot myself. I left her to her studies and went to bed.

Now we're at my dad's. Beth pulls up in front of The Landing on Peachtree.

"Are you sure you don't want to come in and say hello?"

"I'm running late already. Get Daddy to take you home."

With that she's off. Bridget and I take the elevator to the twentieth floor and ring the doorbell.

"Andi," my father says. "What a surprise." He doesn't seem the least bit nervous, which makes me think that Donna's not here, after all.

He asks us to come in and offers us a cold drink. Bridget sits down on the sofa and surveys the room. It has that magnificent view of downtown Atlanta. Bridget gets up and goes over to the windows. They run the entire length of the living room.

"Far out!" she says.

I'm about to join her when who should walk into the room but Donna.

"I thought I heard someone," she says, like it's nothing out of the ordinary for her to be over at my father's place. Of course, we walked in on them at the Ritz so it's no secret their being together, but still.

"Andi," my father says. "Come sit down. This is as good a time as any for me to explain what's going on."

There's a lump in my throat as big as a watermelon. I sit at the edge of the sofa and fold my hands like I'm praying. I really don't want an explanation. I want this whole thing to go away.

Instead of sitting down my father stands beside Donna and puts his arm around her. Here it comes.

"Donna and I have fallen in love," he says.

What'd I tell you?

"It wasn't something we planned. It just happened. We want to be together. Spend our lives together."

I can't help myself. Tears start spilling down my face.

"Does this mean you're not coming home?" This is a stupid question.

"I'm afraid not, Andi. Donna and I are going to be married as soon as our divorces are final."

"But you said you were going away to think!" I jump up from the sofa. "That you just needed some time away—"

"Andi, don't make this any harder than it already is. I know what I said, but I don't need any more time to decide what I want in my life. Life's too short to compromise. When you're older, you'll understand."

If I've heard that once, I've heard that a zillion times. It's how parents blow you off.

"Girls," Donna says and tries to reach out and take our hands. "Once we're married and we're settled, we want you to come by anytime. You're always welcome."

Please—the divorces aren't even filed and she's planning for company—already thinking of dinner parties and who to invite.

202 Jackie Lee Miles

"I don't want to visit you!" I scream. "I want my father back!"

Bridget hasn't said a word. In a way I think she's happy that Donna will no longer be in her life, but what about her father? She should think about that. Right now I just want to get out of there. But I don't want my father driving us anywhere. I reach for the phone and call my mother.

"No, we'll just meet you down in front," I say, when she asks if she should come up and see how my father is doing.

I want to say, "Trust me, you don't want to know how he's doing." Instead I hang up the receiver and turn to my dad.

"I hope you're both very happy now that you've ruined our lives." I look straight at Donna. "My mother will probably never recover," I say. "It's your fault. You're a husband stealer and you already had one of your own. I hate you." Then I turn back to my father. "And I hate you, too! You've ruined everything."

Bridget grabs hold of my arm and pulls me toward the door.

"Come on, Andi," she says. "That's not going to help. It's not going to change anything."

Maybe not, but it made me feel better just saying it. I had a lot more where that came from, but Bridget opened the door and dragged me to the elevator.

I was right about Bridget's father. He's taking the news very hard. The worst part is he's decided to take the promotion in England. And he says they can't take Rudy, Bridget's dog. Bridget has had that dog like forever. This bit of news has Bridget in hysterics.

"I'll be getting a flat until I decide where we'll live," her father says. "Taking the dog is out of the question."

Bridget runs up to her room and I follow. She slams the door and throws herself on her bed.

"I hate him! And I'm not going to London. I'll run away!"

Which makes me scared because saying you'll run away is kind of like a person saying they're going to kill themselves. Many times they mean it.

"I know!" I say. "We'll keep the dog. Then you can come and visit. How about that?"

Bridget sits up and wipes the tears off her face. "That'd be better than letting strangers have him."

"When are you going?" I want to know how much time I have to convince my mother we just have to keep Rudy.

"I don't know," she says, "but soon."

Her father says they're leaving at the end of the month. Well, actually, Bridget's father is leaving at the end of the month. He's put the house up for sale and is having the furniture auctioned. Bridget is going to North Carolina to stay with her mother's sister Ellen, until her father gets settled in London. So, in addition to losing my father, I'm losing my best friend in the entire world.

"You can visit, Andi," my mother says, trying to comfort me. "Won't that be nice?"

"It's not the same," I wail. "Now we see each other every day."

"Can we have her dog?" I ask. My mother has never been a dog person, but if we keep Rudy, then Bridget can come here and visit and get a chance to see him, and then maybe later her father will let the dog come to London. They have a lot of dogs over there. The queen has like six or something. My mother says she'll think about the dog.

I know what I'm going through with Bridget leaving is nothing compared to what my mother's going through. My father came over last night and explained that he was filing for divorce, but would make sure everything remained the same at home.

"Of course, you can stay in the house," he says. "And you'll be well taken care of, Margaret. I'll pay all the bills. You'll have a generous settlement. I'll do everything I can to make this as easy as possible for you."

Right! Like there's anything he can do now that he's destroyed her entire world. What's going to become of my mother?

She's sitting on the sofa, not saying a word. She nods her head that she understands. Tears are rolling down her face, but she doesn't make a sound. I go over to her and put my arms around her.

"I'm sorry, Margaret," my father whispers. And then he leaves. Just walks out the door and leaves! Only then does my mother break down. She starts wailing like the world has ended. My poor mother—in a way, her world has ended. At least the one she's always known. I think of what Vivian said on the ship, "Winner take all."

My mother should get a good attorney and take my dad to the cleaners.

Chapter Sixty-two

NEXT WEEK IS MY birthday. My mother says we'll have a birthday party and I can invite all my friends. What for? Bridget won't be here. But then I realize I've got to let my life go on. There's no other choice. I tell my mother a party would be fun. I'll invite Allison Whitley, you remember, the girl I met who volunteers at the nursing home who has the regular family with the real nice kitchen and the two younger brothers. And Joey and David—I can invite them, too. They were a lot of fun at the Sadie Hawkins dance even if they did laugh at me all the way home. They told jokes that were pretty funny and had no problem with the dancing part.

I help my mother decorate the terrace level of the house. Most people call it a basement, but there are windows and doors down there so I can understand my mother not wanting to call it that. I'm sort of excited. I'll be fourteen—I'm almost full grown. I have to start acting mature and that means handling the divorce. Beth says, "Andi, grown-ups get divorced all the time. It's sad, of course, but there's nothing you can do but accept it. That's the key."

That's what I'm trying to do. In between I'm working on not hating my father. So the party's a good diversion.

I haven't had a real party since I was ten. The week before the party drags on. Each day inches forward, longer than a ball of yarn. Everything is ready. The cake's ordered, the decorations are up, and there are plenty of snacks lined up in the pantry. Finally, I wake up on August 8 and here it is. It's my birthday. I'm fourteen years old!

But it's a major disappointment. I don't feel any different than I did the day before. Nothing happened when I was thirteen either, but I counted on it being different when I turned fourteen.

At the party, everyone seems to be having a pretty good time. David and Joey are off in a corner telling jokes and you can hear laughter every other minute. I'm talking to Allison Whitley. She tells me her father has lung cancer. What do you say to that?

"Will he be okay?" I ask. My eyes are big as grapefruits.

I hope it's not terminal.

"We don't know. But he never smoked, ever," she says.

That makes me wonder how he got lung cancer. And then I remember he cooked those delicious hamburgers on the grill. I hope that's not what caused it. All the cooking out he did and the fumes from the charcoal and all. I try to change the subject.

"Should we put some music on?"

Everything seems to be going real well. The food's great, the music's good. Everyone is laughing and talking and some are even dancing. Then my father walks in and ruins everything.

"Anyone seen my little girl?" he says. He still thinks of me as his little girl. He has a large package in his hand. If it's a Barbie Doll House I'll kill him. "There she is," he says. He walks toward me and holds out the package.

I'm about ready to open it, when I hear a commotion on the staircase leading downstairs to where we're all gathered. It's my mother. She has Rudy on a leash and is leading him into the room. He licks happily at any hand extended to him. He's such a great dog.

"Happy Birthday, Andi," my mother says gaily and hands me his leash. It's the best birthday present ever. I can't wait to tell Bridget. And I'll let her know I'm only keeping him until she can convince her dad they need him back.

❖❖❖

My father stays upstairs with my mother until the party is over. He stands by the door while everyone leaves and says good-bye and pats some of them on the back, like he still lives here. If he still did, it would make me very happy, since I rarely saw him when he did. But the fact that he's divorcing my mother and then comes over and plays host, has me very upset.

My mother seems so happy to see him, like maybe she's going to win him back or something. That upsets me even more. It's not going to happen.

"Andi," my mother says once everyone has left. "Your father would like to take you to dinner. Isn't that nice?"

I'd rather have my nails torn off. I stand there and don't say anything.

"I think it's a good idea for you two to spend some time together, don't you, Andi?" my mother adds. She gives me a big smile.

I don't want to make her more unhappy than I know she already is, so I agree it would be nice. If lies were pimples, I'd have a serious case of acne.

My father opens the door. I get in the front seat of his car and he pulls away. My mother is standing in the window of the library at the front of the house. She smiles and waves. All I can think of is what she'll do when we're gone. Probably lie on her bed and wail like a baby who's way beyond needing a diaper change.

Chapter Sixty-three

I GET A LETTER from Bridget. She's been gone for exactly two weeks. Finally I have her address. I tear open the envelope praying that by some miracle she is coming back to Atlanta. Maybe her father hates his promotion, or better yet hates London.

Dear Andi,

Charlotte is the pits. Not that there's anything wrong with the city. It's my Aunt Ellen. She is driving me bananas. She's some kind of history nut and insists I need to learn all about Charlotte, like I could care that it's known as The Hornet's Nest, or the reason why. Which in case you're interested, is because this British General was driven out of this place during the American Revolution and he wrote that Charlotte was a hornet's nest of rebellion. Where am I ever going to use that fact? I don't plan on being on Jeopardy. This city is also known as the City of Churches. Take one guess why. It's also where Billy Graham was born. Every morning at breakfast I get a quiz from my Aunt Ellen. "What is Charlotte the historic seat of?" she asks. Ashley, that's my cousin, doesn't wait for me to answer, even though this time I know it. It's the seat of Southern Presbyterianism. Ashley just butts right in and gives the answer which makes my Aunt Ellen light up like a match. Ashley's twelve years old and has never had a sister. So guess who's nominated? She hangs all over me. Worse, she is a Camp Fire Girl and now my Aunt Ellen insists I have to join, too. Ashley's been in it since she was a Blue Bird, which is what they call the younger ones. Each year the organization does something different to further their cause. This year they introduced the second phase of "Teens in Action." That part's kind of cool. You learn all about serving your community. But the uniform's awful. I told my aunt I really don't want to wear it. She said, "Nonsense. A uniform creates a sense of belonging. You're going to be part of something important." This means I have no choice in the matter.

They've been letting boys join for a while so now it's known as Camp Fire USA. Our group doesn't have any boys. What does that tell you?

One nice thing is we get snow here. Last year they got four inches. But I probably won't be here then. At least I hope not, but if I am at least I'll get to see snow.

That's all for now. Are you doing okay? Do you see your Dad and Donna? If my Dad had never married her none of this stuff would be happening. Who would have thought that saying "I do," especially when she didn't, would change entire lives?

Bridget

I put the pages back in the envelope. I need to show them to my mother, so she can see how unhappy Bridget is. Then maybe she could come and stay with us until her father gets settled and maybe it would take him years to get settled and me and Bridget could finish growing up together. There are so many maybes.

❖ ❖ ❖

Tonight my father is taking me to dinner again. You'd think he could think of something else to do for once. I'm only going because my mother wants me to. I have three outfits laid out on the bed and I can't decide which one I want to wear. It really shouldn't matter, but I'm thinking maybe my clothes could make a statement like all the fashion magazines refer to. My clothes could jump out and say you're a low-down dirty rat and you'll be sorry.

I decide on a black skirt with two T-shirts worn one over the other, a white one underneath and a pink and black paisley one worn on top. It's the new look—layered. I just got my hair cut and it's clean and shiny. All I need is some gloss and mascara and I'm ready. I look in the mirror. Beth stares back at me. I blink. It's hard to believe but I look more and more like her with each passing month. A year ago I never thought I'd grow up looking so good. It's a miracle.

"Well, don't you look nice," my mother says. I shrug my shoulders. I guess the statement I wanted to make is a lost cause. The door chimes ring. My father's right on time. Rosa opens the door. I can hear her chattering away.

"So good see you," she says.

My father walks into the library like he owns the place and then I realize he does. It won't really be my mother's 'til after the divorce, which won't be long. Turns out you can get a divorce in Georgia quicker than you can get a dentist appointment.

"Hello, Andi," my father says. "Margaret." He nods his head at my mother and offers a slight smile. My mother doesn't smile back, but she doesn't frown either. She just stands there looking like an animal that's jumped in front of a car. I'm thinking it still isn't real to her, my father not being here, my father divorcing her, my father getting ready to marry Donna.

There's a lump in my throat as big as Texas.

"All set?" he says.

I don't bother to answer. I sling my purse over my shoulder and head for the door.

"Have a nice time," my mother calls out.

I climb into the front seat of the car. My father pulls out of the circular driveway. "I have a reservation at Chima Brazilian Steakhouse," he says.

Whatever.

"You'll like it. They serve sixteen meats tableside and have the largest salad bar in Buckhead."

The thought of food starts to dissolve the lump in my throat. I realize I didn't have lunch and I'm starving. At least I'll get a good meal.

"All of the artwork on the walls comes from Brazil as do most of the furnishings," my father explains. "It's a very impressive place. You can tell your friends about it."

He is so out of it. My best friend is hundreds of miles away all because of him and he expects me to chatter away about what restaurant I've been to.

"Bridget's in North Carolina," I say. "There's no one to tell."

"Surely she's not your only friend," my father says as he pulls into the restaurant parking lot. "What about all your friends at your party?"

I just nod my head. No sense getting into it. He comes around and opens the door of the car for me. He places his hand in the small of my back and escorts me to the front door of the entrance. His hand feels warm. It makes me feel safe. I want to turn and throw my arms around his neck and beg him to come back to us. The very thought of it makes me catch my breath.

"Here we are," he says and reaches for the door.

The maître d' greets us. My father steps forward, "Reservation for St. James. Party of three," he says.

Party of three—he's so used to having my mother with us when we dine out. Tears gather in the corner of my eyes remembering just how many times we've done that and will never do it again.

I follow the maître d'. The dining room is enormous. It could easily seat three hundred people. Even so it feels warm and cozy. The lights are low and the tables are placed close together. There are crisp white tablecloths and candles. The salad bars are islands located on one side of the room. On the other side is a wall of windows to the kitchen where you can see the meat being cooked rotisserie-style. The meat is brought in by gauchos who wear Brazilian cowboy outfits, including tall boots, black pants, a white shirt and a red scarf. They're constantly in motion. They're carrying skewers of meat and stopping at tables here and there to cut slices of meat directly onto the customers' plates. My father is right. It really is an interesting place.

We've reached our table. At first it's hard to see in the dim lighting that someone is already sitting at it. Party of three—I should have known. I'll give you one guess who is already at our table.

"Hello, Andi," Donna says. "How nice to see you!" She's trying to be so sweet. I turn to my father.

"You didn't tell me Donna would be here." I'm being a brat but I can't help myself. If I act nice I'll feel like I'm being disloyal to my mother.

"We wanted to surprise you," my father says. "We have some exciting news."

Nothing they say can be exciting for me. My whole life is one big mess and they're all smiles. Plus Donna looks especially beautiful. She has on a white eyelet sundress and a simple silver chain around her neck with a heart edged in diamonds. It looks very simple, but elegant, and I wonder if it's a gift from my father. Of course, my mother is also very attractive and elegant, but Donna is a lot younger and it makes me mad. My father's fifty-three. He has to be old enough to be her father, which is totally disgusting, even if they do this in Hollywood all the time. Atlanta is not Hollywood.

Menus are placed in front of us. Our gaucho explains that we may select the all-you-can-eat meat option at $48.50, which includes continuous service from the gauchos along with the salad bar.

"Or you may select to fill your plates only from the salad bar for $28.50," he says, and hands us a menu that has the full selection of meats available.

"We'll each have the full selection," my father says.

Good. At least it will cost him plenty and I won't eat a bite. If I'm going to be a brat I might as well be a big one. I'm going to cut up the meat and scatter it all over my plate. I'll mush it around with my fork. Let them see what a mess I've become. Let them know they've totally ruined my life.

But when our gaucho brings our first order—filet mignon—I remember how hungry I am, that is, my stomach remembers. I'm drooling. I can hardly cut up the pieces fast enough. Our server brings side dishes of fried bananas, and tasty fried polenta with Parmesan cheese and mashed potatoes that melt in your mouth, along with a huge basket of cheese bread fresh from the oven. It's no use. I'll have to find some other way to be a brat. Right now I eat like I've never seen food before. They place a medallion by the side of our plates. If one side is up, the gaucho appears again with a large selection of meat to choose from. If the other side is up they pass you by. They don't pass me by. The next go around I choose the leg of lamb. It's smothered in spices and is heaven on a stick.

Chapter Sixty-four

I've DECIDED THAT I am going to bury myself in the other parts of my life and pretend my father and Donna don't even exist—though I must admit this is going to be difficult to do. Already they are entangling me in their plans. The good news they had at dinner is they have decided to get married in Mallorca and would like me to go with them for the ceremony and to stay for a few days afterwards to tour the island. Then I can fly back and they will continue their honeymoon.

"I've never heard of Mallorca," I say, making a face.

"Certainly you've heard of that. It's a beautiful island off the coast of Spain. You'll have a very good time," he insists, and pats my hand.

"There's a magnificent fourteenth-century Gothic cathedral in nearby Palma," Donna says. Her eyes sparkle like sequins. "That's where we want to be married. It'll be a trip of a lifetime, Andi. You're going to have the best time."

It's hard to have a good time when your mother is sitting home newly divorced and all alone.

"I can't go," I say. "It would be hard on my mother." I stare into her eyes and try to put out the sparkle.

"Nonsense," my father says. "She and Vivian are planning a trip to the south of France. I've already talked with her about it."

The south of France? When did that come about? It's amazing you can live in the same house with a person and not know anything that is going on in their life.

I have to admit that I've never seen my father happier than he is when he's with Donna. They're very attentive to each other. Every once in a while my father will brush his hand against the side of her face. It's a very small gesture, sure, but it is so tender it makes my heart sit up and pinch itself.

"Well, I'll talk to mom."

My father pays the check and we leave the restaurant. Donna puts her arm around me on the way out the door and says she looks forward to many more nice evenings out. "You're always welcome, Andi," she says. "Don't forget that." And she squeezes my hand. She's being so nice it's hard to hate her.

"Andi," my mother says when I get home. "Come sit with me." She pats the sofa and scoots over to make room for me.

I take a seat next to her. She puts her arm around my shoulder. "I thought it would be good for us to talk about what's happened. Are you doing alright?"

I don't know what to say. I want to tell her I'm miserable and my life is a total mess and I won't ever forgive my father. But I'm afraid that would make her feel even worse than she already does. But if I say I'm fine, that seems like I don't care at all what she's going through. I just can't win. I decide to tell her exactly how I feel and see what happens. I hope she won't start crying. I haven't seen her do that in days, so I'm hoping she's got the crying part out of her system.

"Well, I'm not really okay," I say. "I never counted on you and Daddy getting a divorce—even when I found out about Donna. I just thought he'd get, you know, over it and come back to his senses, and be real sorry over it and spend his life making it up to you, to us."

"Mostly that only happens in fairy tales." My mother turns

toward me and takes my hand in hers. "Tell me what's going on with you and your father. Are you able to forgive him?"

"Never!" I nearly jump up off the sofa. "I think I hate him! I definitely want to hate Donna, but she's being very nice and—"

"Andi, Andi," my mother whispers my name. "I know this will be hard, but let me tell you something. You don't hate your father. You're angry with him. There's a difference."

This makes me start to cry, because she's right. I don't really hate my father. I want him to come home. I want things like they were before, even if he wasn't always so nice to my mother.

"The thing is, Andi," my mother explains, "when we love someone—really love them—we want them to be happy." She takes her hanky and dabs at my eyes. "Your father was no longer happy with me. I've had to face that. And when he met Donna, obviously she made him happy again and he wasn't willing to give that happiness up." She turns and puts her arm around me again and pulls me close. "I'll always love your father, Andi. At least I think I will, but if I'm not what he wants in life than being with him would not bring me much joy, now would it? Don't you want me to have joy? You wouldn't want him to stay with me and just pretend he wants to be here, would you?"

I look at my mother and tears are running down my face. I don't want her to know it, but that's exactly what I want. I want him to come home and pretend my mother is all he ever wants in life and keep pretending until he no longer has to. Keep pretending until he no longer needs to. Until he falls in love with her all over again.

Chapter Sixty-five

JOSHUA IS GROWING FASTER than a patch of weeds. He's catching up with other babies his age and starting to pull himself up around furniture. He laughs and jabbers and gobbles up the baby food they give him. And he's the cutest little guy. He looks like a miniature Alex. He has the same curly blonde hair and big brown eyes.

Tonight is extra exciting because I get to babysit all by myself for the very first time. My mother has four tickets to the theater and thought it would be nice for Jeffrey and Amy to have a night out. Let me rephrase that. A man my mother met at one of her meetings has four tickets to the theater and asked my mother if she'd like to go and bring some friends. Normally, this would upset me. It's sort of like a date. But considering that my father is getting married and has no plans to come home, I'm excited for my mother. She claims it isn't a date. But he is picking her up and taking her to the theater. That sounds very much like a date to me. His name is Vincent Armstrong. Let me correct myself. His full name is Dr. Vincent Armstrong. He's a pediatrician. My mother's first date and it's with a doctor. He has his own practice. That should show my father. The only thing is my mother met him at an AA meeting. Bummer.

"Is he an alcoholic?"

"A recovering alcoholic," my mother says. "He's been in the program for over ten years."

"And he's stayed sober all that time?" I ask.

My mother nods her head.

"Why does that program work so well?"

"That's a bit complicated," my mother explains, "but the important thing is it works for people who believe in God and it works for people who don't believe in God."

"So it works for everyone?"

"Perhaps not for people who believe they are God," she says.

Babysitting is a little more complicated than I figured it would be. Joshua is having a crying jag. I've checked his diaper, I've checked to see if any of his clothes are pinching him like they taught us in class. I've tried to feed him, and I've played peek-a-boo for twenty minutes. No dice. He just keeps crying. I'm about ready to call the theater when I decide to try the television. I read babies and small children are not to watch it. Something about it intervenes with their creative processes, but I'm desperate. Being Saturday night, I can't find any cartoons on. Amy and Jeffrey only have basic cable. But I find a western, a rerun of *Bonanza*. There's a lot of shooting going on in this episode and horses are causing quite a ruckus, too. Joshua loves it. He immediately stops crying and starts laughing. Can you believe it? I've tried everything to make him happy and one episode of *Bonanza* and he's in baby heaven. I hope there's an episode two following episode one. We settle in on the sofa with him on my lap. He's chewing away on a teething ring I found in the freezer and his eyes are glued to the television. Then I realize that's what might be wrong. He's teething. Our instructor at the babysitting class says it can be very painful. Under those circumstances I personally don't feel that the distraction of television is a bad thing. He's not going to be doing anything creative anyway while he's in pain.

After *Bonanza*'s over, Joshua is happy to take a bottle. I change him one more time and rock him to sleep. I'm very pleased with myself. I've managed to soothe a teething baby and keep him well occupied 'til bedtime. If I were my instructor I'd give myself an A+ or maybe an A–. I did fall asleep before midnight and one of the rules was to stay awake until at least twelve o'clock in case the baby or children if that's the case need you.

I'm not sure how long I slept, but I got to meet my mother's date when they got back from the theater. Jeffrey picked me up before Dr. Armstrong ever got to our house, so I could get reacquainted with Joshua while Amy got ready, so I never got to see him before he picked my mother up.

After the theater, they all went to a restaurant for dessert and coffee, so obviously the doctor and my mother are getting along really good.

"Andi, this is Dr. Armstrong," my mother says. The doctor puts his hand out. He's rather nice looking. He doesn't have much hair, but he has blue eyes big as lakes.

"My daughter Andréa," my mother says very proudly, like I'm her greatest accomplishment. Leave it to my mother. She always thinks the best of me.

I'm too sleepy to make much of an impression. I nod my head and try to smile, but my eyes are not fully open. I look like I'd been on a bender, which is probably not a good image to portray to a recovering alcoholic. My mother says alcoholics have three kinds of behavior: compulsive, impulsive, and when they are drinking, repulsive.

I'll try to make a better impression next time. I hope there will be one for my mother's sake. It would be nice for her to get interested in someone else, since my father is no longer interested in her.

Chapter Sixty-six

School starts in two weeks. I'm kind of excited. This will be my second year of high school, but it's a new school just opening, so everyone will be sort of brand new and just wandering around trying to find the rooms they're supposed to be in. And that's exactly what I'll be doing, so at least I won't stand out and look stupid.

What's more exciting is that my mother has agreed to let me go to visit Bridget!

I leave in three days. And I get to stay three days. My mother said that is long enough for a visit or the hostess will feel that I've overextended my welcome. By hostess, she means Bridget's Aunt Ellen. Bridget would love for me to stay forever.

Beth received word that she has been accepted to law school at Emory. Her classes start next week. Right now she is visiting with a girlfriend from high school that she reconnected with over the summer. Her name is Adrienne. She's a missionary and is leaving for a place in the Congo called Zaire. Beth is in awe. My mother and I are, too. You can tell by looking at Adrienne that she is a tomboy and probably has been all her growing-up life. She's wearing a pale blue button-down shirt and white jeans with loafers and no socks. Surely where she is going she'll have to start wearing socks. Most likely there are snakes and lizards and all sorts of creepy-crawly things where she is headed. It doesn't seem to me like she and Beth would have much in common. Beth has always been what my father refers to as a girly-girl. They are a strange pair, these two, but seem to get along very well. The reason they got reacquainted is that Adrienne saw the article in the newspaper where Beth auctioned off all her wedding gifts and gave the money to charity. The next thing you know, Adrienne was on the phone telling Beth what a wonderful idea and they should get together and she had some exciting news, which is the fact she's a missionary. So there you have it. They're like best friends now and talk on the phone every day. Adrienne leaves next week. Zaire is not a good place to be going to. That part of the world is always cutting each other's heads off. I looked up Zaire at the library. The librarian was very helpful in pointing out articles of interest. Apparently Zaire's leader, President Mobutu, is very unpopular, and a lot of people want to oust him. But he doesn't care. He says he's not going anywhere. This is making a lot of people mad, especially parts of the military that have access to heavy artillery. There is one man who has been against Mobutu for twenty-two years. His name is Mr. Mungul Diaka. I can't pronounce it. He says the entire opposition has been fighting to remove President Mobutu. A lot of good it has done them. Mobutu is still in power. Mr. Mungul Diaka is also upset, he says, because the Western countries have stopped giving economic aid just when they need it the most.

One magazine article quoted him. "During twenty-six years your respective governments have supported Mobutu's regime. Now that the Zairian people are fighting to obtain democracy, the West leaves."

There's a picture of him next to the quote. He has his hand over his head and is raising his fist. He's pretty mad. Both sides are probably at a boiling point. I can't imagine why this friend of Beth's would want to travel to a place that is full of danger. What if they don't like her being over there? What if one side decides to cut off her head?

Adrienne is staying for dinner. While Rosa is busy in the kitchen preparing our meal, Beth and I are visiting with Adrienne in the library. She looks very ordinary—other than the fact she dresses sort of like a man. She has short brown hair, cut pixie-style and light blue eyes—but here she is ready to do an unbelievable thing, travel to a dangerous country to bring God's word.

"Aren't you scared?" I ask.

"I'll be working in the refugee camps and won't be in any immediate danger," she says. "There are over four hundred thousand refugees in need of help."

"I'm sure they have plenty of people over there doing their job. Couldn't you find another place to go to?" I say.

"Almost half of Zaire's population is under the age of fifteen," she says. "I need to be there to help these children."

Beth says it's an extraordinary thing to do and gets up off the sofa. She goes to the window in the library and looks out at our garden. It's always very peaceful there. Maybe she's thinking it's the last peaceful image her friend will ever see. Nothing against all those children under fifteen that need help, but I think someone older that's already had a life should help them. Adrienne is twenty-two years old, like Beth. Her real life has barely begun.

"You know, Andi," Adrienne says, "There's so much turmoil there and the birth rate is ridiculous. The fertility rate is estimated to be six-point-one children born per woman. We need to educate them in birth control. Someone has to do it. Why not me?"

I don't have a good answer for that question.

"So it's settled," she says. "I'm going. You can pray for me."

This girl is very determined. I doubt anyone could possibly change her mind. She's going to be an aid worker and a missionary in Zaire and that's that. This could be the last time we ever see her. I think of the meal Rosa is preparing. Sort of like a last supper.

I turn to Adrienne. "It really doesn't seem like a good place to be right now, is all."

"Oh, people go over there all the time and they're fine." She pats my hand and smiles brightly.

I'm not so sure. But it is not up to us to make decisions for other people. Otherwise I would definitely make the decision that my father would be returning to my mother.

When Adrienne leaves I turn to Beth. "Aren't you afraid for her?"

Beth gathers up two of her law school books that are sitting on my father's desk. She is using his desk now like it's hers. "A little," she says. "Most of all I'd admire her for her choices."

Beth sets the books down and comes over to me. She brushes the hair out of my eyes and cups my face in her hands.

"We all have to make choices, sweetie," she says. "Regardless of what has transpired in our life, the future is always up to us."

She makes it sound so easy, but I don't care right now that she does. She has never been so tender to me and it makes me want to cry. And I just want to hug her. I think of what she's gone through this past year and she never even complained. She just moved on. I guess she's truly grown-up. In a way that makes me very sad. I've lost my father and now I'll be losing Beth. She's bound to move away before long. Still, I'm a bit hopeful. Since there is a future out there for her, then maybe there is one out there for me.

My mother is going out again with Dr. Armstrong. He's picking her up at eight. They're having a quiet dinner and then, if they like, they might go see a movie.

"*The Crying Game* is playing at Cinema Eight," she says. "I'd love to see it."

The description in the paper sounds very depressing. "Why don't you see *Home Alone 2*," I say, "or how about *My Cousin Vinny*? Something funny."

My mother doesn't answer. She just smiles and nods her head.

I'm glad she's making new friends. I was worried that she'd start drinking again. I'm very proud of her. She goes to her meetings regularly and talks to Alice, her sponsor, every day. And now she's seeing Dr. Armstrong. Life is getting back to being just about perfect.

That means something's bound to happen to screw it up.

Chapter Sixty-seven

I'M FLYING BACK FROM Charlotte and there's a woman on the plane next to me that is too big to be sitting in one seat and part of me wants to say, "Excuse me, ma'am, but you're taking up half my seat," and there is another part that wants to just scrunch myself up and forget it. Like maybe she can't help it she's fat. Maybe she diets all the time and it's no use; it's in her genes or something to be fat, so that part of me wins out, the part that shuts up and smiles and doesn't say anything.

"Oh, look at the sky," she says, and leans over and nearly suffocates me. I look out the window and it takes your breath away, and I'm not sure if it's because the sky is so beautiful or if she has succeeded in crushing my lungs. Regardless, the view is breathtaking. It's like you're standing on top of heaven and all that's beneath you are white clouds cushioning all the angels.

Bridget and I had the best time. Well, we had the best time, other than the time we had to spend with her aunt's family who are really weird people. Her husband tells jokes all the time. The first night he said he had two new ones.

"What do you get if you cross an elephant with a kangaroo? Give up? Big holes in Australia."

Bridget and I are hoping he's done, but oh no, he has another.

"What do you get if you cross poison ivy with a four-leaf clover?" He doesn't even wait for us to guess. "A rash of good luck. Get it, a rash of good luck!"

"Oh, Edward," Bridget's Aunt Ellen says. "That's so funny! Ha ha ha," she goes.

But if you ask me it's really stupid. Bridget and I just sit there and roll our eyes. Adam starts laughing like a hyena. He's eight. That's one of Ashley's brothers. She has two. But he's really sort of cute, so he's not so bad. The other one is a mess. His name is Abner and he's twelve. He's mostly a jerk. He walks around the house sniffing his armpits. I'm serious. I saw him doing that twice.

"You didn't tell me you had two boy cousins," I tell Bridget.

"No," she whispers, "I never got past Ashley. It's pure hell."

Ashley is very annoying. She wanted to see what was in my suitcase so she just started unpacking it. Gross.

"Want to see my frog collection?" she says. Oh boy, that's exactly why I flew five hundred miles.

"Maybe later," I tell her. Bridget escorts her out the bedroom door and closes it.

Ashley knocks twice and opens it right back up. "Can I come in?"

Bridget has just shown her out of the room. Does that tell you what a problem this kid is, or what? Not that I'm not willing to give her a chance, but I only have three days. I'm not willing to waste them on Ashley, who cried at the airport because her mother wouldn't let her sit in the back seat with me and Bridget. And then at dinner she insisted that she sit between us and Bridget's Aunt Ellen said it would be okay. So, I'm thinking that Ashley's trying hard to muscle in on our time together, which makes me mad, because it's very limited. Plus, Bridget doesn't much like her either, so Ashley is hardly going to be on my good side. She whines a lot when she doesn't get her way. Bridget suggested instead of cooking that we go to McDonald's for dinner the next night.

"Pig out on some junk food for once. You're always cooking us nutritional meals so it probably won't hurt," Bridget points out.

And her Aunt Ellen says, "That's true."

And Ashley stomps her feet and says, "I want to go to Golden Krust!"

Golden Krust it is. Bridget's Aunt Ellen is always giving in to Ashley. At least the food's good. They have hamburger wraps filled with seasoned meat, sort of Jamaican style, and a lot of other stuff to choose from, like curly-Q fries and cheese nuggets. But the point is Ashley gets what Ashley wants and that part is annoying.

After dinner we play Sorry. Ashley cries whenever she's losing, which is almost every other throw of the dice. Finally Bridget says, "Look, either keep playing and be a good sport or just quit!"

Her Aunt Ellen comes into the room and says, "What's going on?" Bridget does her best to explain that Ashley is being a poor sport. Aunt Ellen says, "Well, she hasn't had much practice at this game. You need to give her a few extra turns until she gets the hang of it."

So you see what I mean about Ashley. Her mother is a big enabler for most everything that's wrong with her. But do you think she looks at it like that? Forget it, she thinks Ashley is perfect. This is the main reason I don't like Bridget's Aunt Ellen. She plays favorites. Now the boys, that's a different matter altogether. Take when they were brushing their teeth. Mostly they were just spitting on each other's head, but still they shouldn't have to go to bed and not watch television. That's just boy stuff, but Ellen comes up and sees what's going on and sends them straight to bed. Ashley could spit on her father and Ellen would say, "Don't worry, darling, it's just a phase." She'd kiss the top of Ashley's head and give her second helpings of pizza.

One of the things we did that was really fun was play miniature golf at this course that has waterfalls, Zuma Fun Center. Ashley had a meltdown every time she hit the ball. For the most part, she knocked it into the next hole. Well, not in the hole, but in the playing field for that hole. Her father tried to explain that she was swinging the club too hard, but do you think that helped? Take one guess. So the entire time the rest of us are having fun trying to get our ball into the hole with the least strokes possible—and not doing that good of a job of it I might add—Ashley is crying and carrying on that there's something wrong with her club or her ball.

"This isn't fair!" she says. "I can't play with this club."

"Let me see that club," Ellen says. She takes it from Ashley and gives it a good shake. "You know," she says, "I think Ashley's right. It's out of balance or something." She hands the club back to Ashley. "Just do the best you can, honey, and don't worry about the score. We won't count the ones that go over par by more than two. How's that?"

It must be fine, because Ashley doesn't complain for the rest of the game. But you can see that her mother is the big problem here, and all that means in the future is big trouble. Like maybe Ashley is turning into a serial killer. When she's fully grown, I can hear her mother, "Are you sure darling? You just have to kill her? Well, okay, then, sweetie, chop away, but I'm just going to pretend I didn't see it, okay?"

We could be talking lethal injection here. But Bridget's Aunt Ellen doesn't see it that way. Bottom line, Ashley's a pain and her mother is useless. The boys aren't so bad. In fact, they're doing fine on miniature golf. Actually, they're not playing that well, but it doesn't bother them, they just keep swinging and laughing and their father marks down the number of swings they take and we move on to the next hole, which is how the game should be played, without any complaints.

We hit the bumper cars next. Abner is tall enough to operate one on his own, but Adam rides with me. Bridget and Ashley ride in another, which is too bad. I really want to crash into Ashley, which means I'll get Bridget at the same time. It turns out I don't have to worry about that. Abner is very good at bumper cars. I spend all my time just trying to stay away from him, but he always manages to bash right into us. Adam thinks it's hysterical, but the truth is my neck is starting to hurt and my hands are numb from hanging on to the wheel so tight. I'm glad when our time is up. We got half an hour. The batting cage is our last stop. Bridget and I missed a lot of the balls pitched at us, but managed to slam a few good ones. It's kind of addictive. The more times you swing the more times you want to. We had a great time. Except for the part where Ashley missed all the balls pitched to her and had another meltdown—which, of course, did not surprise me. Ashley spent the whole day being Ashley, but the boys were real good sports and lots of fun to be around. It's like they came from a different family.

Chapter Sixty-eight

My mother and Dr. Armstrong pick me up at the airport. He is driving a convertible that has a cute little seat in back barely big enough to hold me. The car is bright red and he has the top down. My mother's hair looks like a bird's nest. Soon my own hair is sailing behind me like a flag flying in the wind. But who cares? It's totally exhilarating. I want to call out, "Faster, faster."

Dr. Armstrong's wife died of cancer when his children were still at home. My mother says it's when he started drinking and almost lost his practice.

"Is that when he joined AA?" I ask.

My mother nods her head. "It saved his life."

Not to mention those of his children. He has three. They're all grown. Two boys and one girl. They came over last weekend so we could all get acquainted. Still, my mother insists it's nothing. She is not getting serious.

"He's moving a bit too fast," she insists. "I'm going to have to let him know I'm not interested in a relationship at this time."

If this is the case, she better get busy and tell him. He acts like they're going together. He's always draping his arm around her shoulder. Then he winks and smiles like they have a special secret. Maybe they do. Maybe they're sleeping together even though my mother insists she's not interested in pursuing a relationship. Maybe it's just a sex thing for her. After all, they're grown-ups, so that's to be expected, the sex part. So much has changed—my father marrying

Donna, Bridget living in another state, Henry dead, Beth happy and busy with law school, my mother maybe having a lover. Life just keeps sending curve balls with no warning.

My mother has a few curve balls of her own. She's decided not to go to the south of France with Vivian. "I need to concentrate on my program," she says.

Dr. Armstrong slows down for a bend in the road. He turns around and yells, "You doing okay, Andi?" What little hair he has on top is zigzagging in the wind.

He's a very nice man. I think about him being left to care for his children when his wife died from cancer. No wonder he started drinking. There's a girl, Libby, at school whose mother has some kind of terminal illness. She's in my gym class and overnight she's changed from being happy-go-lucky to being so sad it hurts to look at her face. Mr. Larsen, the gym teacher tries to be extra nice to her. He gives her lots of help on the parallel bars and pats her back a lot. Mr. Larson wears baggie cardigans and puts his hand in his pockets a lot so the pockets are all stretched out and they look like they still have his hands tucked in them, even when his hands are actually by his side. He calls everyone kiddo. When Libby misses the ball three times during volleyball he says, "Listen, kiddo, come up under the ball. Go up to meet it. And then go up under it. Okay, kiddo?"

You really can't be mad at that, when a teacher calls you kiddo when he's correcting you.

But I can be plenty mad at my father. He's turned all of our lives upside down. He's coming over tonight to pick me up. He has something important he wants to tell me. Maybe he and Donna eloped. Maybe they're not going to Mallorca after all, which would be fine with me. I don't really want to go anyway.

I'm watching out the window and spot his car as it pulls into the driveway. Donna is in the passenger seat. My father toots and I grab my sweater. Most likely he'll head to a restaurant and some of them have the air conditioner on too low. It's like standing in a grocery store in front of the frozen foods.

My father waves and grins and gets out and opens the door to the back seat. I climb in and nod at Donna.

"Hello, Andi," she says. "How was your trip?"

We spend a few minutes going over the details and then my father clears his throat and says, "How about we head over to Chopstix?"

What did I tell you?—another restaurant. But it's okay with me. They didn't serve lunch on the plane except in first class and I'm hungry.

Chopstix is an upscale Chinese restaurant. Inside, the walls are lined with mirrors and there are these velvet banquette benches all along the walls with fancy table settings placed in front of them, sort of what you'd expect in New York. And the food is good, too. A little fancy, but very tasty.

Once we're seated and the waiter has taken our order my father gets a very serious look on his face. Here it comes. He's going to tell me to say hello to my new stepmother.

"Andi," he says and folds his hands in front of him and leans them against his dinner plate. Donna sits quietly by. She has a half-smile on her face. The kind when you want to look friendly, but not silly. She's wearing a black pantsuit that has a square neckline. It's very attractive on her. It looks like something Audrey Hepburn would have worn. Bridget and I watched her biography on television the last night of my visit, while Ashley and the boys went to bed. Donna's wearing a strand of pearls. Definitely an Audrey Hepburn look. I bet my father gave those to her. He was always big on pearls when it came to my mother.

I look up at my father and wait to hear whatever he has to say. Not that I'm anxious to hear it. Lately, whatever he has to say has been bad news for me. And I notice he seems very nervous which is making me even more nervous. Maybe this is not about them being married at all. Maybe he has a terminal disease. A lump gathers in my throat. I realize that no matter what he's done with Donna, I still love him and want him around.

"Andi," he says again.

"What is it?" I lean in closer to the table.

And then he just blurts it out.

"Donna and I are going to have a baby. We're going to be married in a private ceremony this Saturday." He sits quietly, waiting for my reaction.

I don't have one. I'm in shock. My shoulders slump. I hadn't counted on this and I don't know what to think. Mostly I think I'm mad. I'm breathing deeply and there's a familiar anger gathering in my chest like when Alex died. The kind of anger where you know you can't do anything about it and you want to and you want to blame someone but you don't know who to blame, except this time I do know. I blame my father. Donna didn't get pregnant all by herself. My father's a skunk. It's bad enough that he leaves my mother and decides to marry Donna. Now he's starting a brand new family. He probably won't care about me anymore. I'm being replaced.

I get up from the table and head to the restroom as fast as I can. The napkin on my lap flutters to the floor. Normally, I would lean over and pick it up and place it back on the table. It's the proper thing to do, but at the moment I no longer care what's proper, so I ignore it and continue on to the ladies' room. I hope it's empty so I can sit in a stall with no one around. I don't want anyone to witness how badly I'm falling apart.

Chapter Sixty-nine

AT LEAST SCHOOL IS going okay. I got most of the classes I wanted and just one that I didn't, geometry. I hate math. But the teacher, Mr. Blakely, jokes around a lot and tries hard to make angles and variables interesting. He lists the equations we're to solve on the chalkboard and puts smiley faces next to where the answer should be.

Something else nice happened. I met a girl who just moved here from Texas. We hit it off right away. Her name is Julia. She has long dark hair and eyes as big as pancakes. She has this habit of saying, "Well, wouldn't you know?" She nods her head when she says it and you realize she's really listening to you. Like, when I told her my father left my mother and didn't give us any real warning. She said, "Well, wouldn't you know?"

Don't ask me why I told her such a personal thing. I'd just met her, but there's something about her that makes you want to confide in her. She loops her arm through mine and says her parents are divorced, too.

"I live with my mother and my stepfather," she says. "And he's a jerk, wouldn't you know?"

Now I sort of have a new best friend. Not that she'll really take Bridget's place but I figure there's no problem with making new friendships. I hope Bridget is making some, too. It doesn't look like her father is coming back for her anytime soon, so it would help for her to have a good support system with friends to lean on.

Julia and I are going to the mall on Sunday. It'll have to be after

Mass. But that's okay. The mall doesn't open on Sunday until noon. And they've opened an indoor skating rink. We're going to give it a try.

"Think we'll meet any cool guys?" she says and her eyebrows go up and down.

I tell her about what happened to me and Bridget on the cruise ship and she giggles. "You're lucky you're not grounded for life. My mother would have put me in a convent."

I tell her about the Angels program at the nursing home and ask her if she'd like to help out.

"I've signed up again," I say. "At first I didn't think I would like it. But then I had this great old couple I would read to and it kind of grows on you. Want to give it a try?"

She says, "Why not?" And then I realize she could be part of Table Grace, too and help out at the boutique. "You don't get any extra credit at school or anything," I explain, "but it really makes you feel good inside. Wait 'til you see the look on some of the girls' faces when they get complete outfits! One girl broke down and cried, she was so happy."

"Wouldn't you know?" Julia says. "I've only been here two weeks and I have a full schedule already."

She grins and loops her arm through mine again and we head to the lunchroom. She picks out a table loaded with boys. "Hey, want some company?" she says. They shrug their shoulders. They scoot over a bit and we sit down. Julia doesn't waste any time. In five minutes she manages to get all of their names and what classes they're taking.

Julia and I don't get on the bus. We decide to walk home. We're not supposed to do that, but it's a beautiful fall day and we don't care that we're breaking the rules. At least, Julia doesn't and that makes me extra brave.

We're having what my mother calls an early fall. The trees are showing their colors early. They're dripping in shades of orange and yellow and red. When we get to my house the lawn is peppered with leaves. We no longer have a gardener. Now that Henry's gone, my mother can't bear to replace him. She hires a service instead. They come once a week and do their thing. The truck is now parked in our circular driveway. It's towing a long trailer with all sorts of equipment dumped in the back. *Personal Touch Lawn Care* is etched on the panel of the pick-up. There's a stocky man in khakis blowing the leaves on our front yard. He's gathered them into a big pile off to the side of the house. Julia looks at me and winks. She sets her book bag down and makes a run for the pile. I watch as she throws herself into the stack. She gathers up as many of the leaves as both her hands can hold and throws them over her head. They rain down on her, sticking to her hair and her sweater. It looks like too much fun not to join her and I make a mad dash for the pile. By now the nicely stacked pile is a total mess. I run through the leaves and plop down beside her. The mass of leaves is like a blanket of giant cornflakes beneath us. We roll around and around. We're being totally stupid, but we don't care. The man blowing the leaves stops and scratches his head. I don't think he knows what to think of us. The front door opens. It's my mother. Rudy bounds out the open door.

"Andi?" my mother calls as Rudy comes over to join us. Dogs know instinctively what to do with a pile of fresh fallen leaves. Rudy happily rolls over and over beside us. His tongue is long and lazy, lolling out of his mouth.

"Here, boy!" I say and gather him in my arms. His coat of hair is covered with broken bits of leaves and twigs. He barks twice, and leaps from my arms. He runs in circles around us. He's having a grand time. Julia and I stand up and brush at the leaves covering our clothing. She is laughing and stomping at the leaves still under her feet.

I can't help but laugh at the sight before us myself. The neatly blown pile of leaves is no longer a neatly blown pile of leaves. The lawn man is still standing with his blower still blowing. My mother is at the front door shaking her head. It's a glorious day. We've made a big mess. But it's so much fun. Rudy is in dog heaven. If only life could always be so carefree.

Chapter Seventy

JULIA IS TALKING NON-STOP about her father.

"I was supposed to go to Texas this summer and visit, but now I'm not going."

She is major mad. "What happened?"

"The same thing that happened last year. He calls out of the blue and says something's come up."

We're sitting next to each other on the bus. It's not our regular one. This one goes right by Sunny Meadows Nursing Home. We have permission to ride it on Tuesdays so we can join the other Angels. Today we get our assignments of who we'll be reading to. I'm kind of excited. I miss the Sterlings. Of course, I'll never see Mr. Sterling again; not in this lifetime, but I had counted on seeing Mrs. Sterling. But she is moving to Maryland to be with her daughter, and boy, is she putting up a fuss. She doesn't want to leave George. George doesn't look like it's going to bother him much. About eighty percent of the women at this nursing home are vying for him. Mrs. Sterling is having a fit.

"Don't worry," I tell her. "There are probably plenty of men in Maryland. They have a population in the millions. I'm sure of it." That seems to quiet her. Right now I'm more worried about Julia. She's very upset and that's not like her.

"What came up that you can't go?"

"Who knows?" she says. "Something stupid, like he has to take these classes this summer for his job and Betty can't handle having company without him being around. Like I'm company! I'm supposed to be family."

"Betty's—"

"The stepmother from hell."

Julia brushes at the tears in her eyes. "I should have known I wouldn't be going. It's been like this ever since they had kids."

"You mean there's more than one?" I think of my dad and Donna and wonder if they're planning on a large family.

"Four."

"Four kids?"

Julia twists her lips together and grunts. "They have a set of twins, twelve months old. And two little girls, three and four. My dad says that's why I can't come. Betty has her hands full."

"But you could help out," I point out.

"Right. Like that's going to happen."

I'm not used to seeing Julia so down and I'm not sure what to say. She's usually so happy.

"Here's the problem," she explains. "When he first got remarried they told me how I'd always be a part of their family. Then they had the first baby, a little girl and I got to visit, but then she got real sick and they said I couldn't come until she got better. Only she didn't get better. She got worse and she had to have these surgeries. Something to do with her heart. And then Betty got pregnant again, but the baby they already had, Suzie, got better after her surgeries, so I was supposed to go visit, but Betty wasn't feeling well. She was sick all during the pregnancy, so I didn't get to visit at all that year. And then after the baby was born, it was another girl, Katie. My father said we needed to wait 'til things calmed down and he sent me all these pictures of them instead. And my Dad looked really happy, you know?"

Julia crosses her arms and leans against the seat. She's sitting next to the window and traces her finger on the pane.

"Then she gets pregnant again and it's with twins, and my dad said it was just too much for her with two toddlers and the pregnancy, so he'd come see me, but he never did."

"So you haven't seen him in four years?"

"Once," she said. "He came here after Easter."

"But I thought you just moved here? Didn't you see him when you were in Texas?"

"Oh, we moved to Augusta when I was ten, right after my mother got remarried. Then this year my step-father got transferred here."

"So, you've only seen your father once since you were ten?"

Julia nods her head.

I'm feeling really bad for her and then I remember this could be me in no time at all. I think of Donna and all her reassurances that I'll always be welcome and now I'm not so sure.

"My dad and his new wife are having a baby."

"Well, I hope you have better luck," she says. "But mostly they never care about you anymore once they start a new family."

A lump is growing in my chest.

"It's that way for a lot of kids, Andi. I'm not the only one." She says this with a great deal of conviction and shakes her head.

The lump in my chest has moved up to my throat. I'm having trouble swallowing.

"I should have just cut him out of my life before he ever had a chance to do it to me," she says and leans her head against the window.

The bus goes over a pothole and Julia's head bangs against the pane. She puts her head in her hands and rocks back and forth.

"Julia? Are you alright?" I pat her back and feel her chest moving up and down and realize she's crying. She's buried her head in her arms so no one will see, but I don't think it's because she bumped her head.

❖ ❖ ❖

Julia and I get our reading assignments. When Julia receives hers, she suggests that they form a book club.

"Then we can pick a book a month to read from."

She's all smiles, her father forgotten for the moment.

"That might work," Mrs. Garrett says. She's the woman who put the Angels group together. "We could try it. Let me see if I can find a small group of ladies who are interested."

"Well, men can come, too," Julia says.

"There are about two men left in this whole place," I tell her.

"Oh, well, all women is okay, too," she adds.

Mrs. Garrett heads off in search of those interested. She's all excited. "Actually, this could work out very well," she says over her shoulder. "We're short on volunteers this year."

I'm going to be reading to Katherine Wilcox, a retired librarian. It's making me a bit nervous. She's bound to correct any of my mispronunciations. It'll be like being in school. Ms. Wilcox is sitting in a rocking chair next to her bed. She's a small woman with wisps of gray hair that are sticking out in all directions like a halo. Don't they groom these poor ladies anymore?

"Hello," I say politely. "I'm Andi and I came to read to you. Would you like that?"

Before she has a chance to answer, Nurse Gabby comes in and barks, "Say hello to Andi, Katherine!" She says it so loudly, I'm afraid I have another deaf person. Katherine nearly jumps out of the rocker. Obviously she hears very well and Gabby has scared her half to death with her bellowing. I take one of her hands—Katherine's, not Gabby's. Her skin is pale and so thin it's like the veins peppering the back of her hand are sitting out on top. I place her hand back in her lap and smile at her as brightly as I can. Something about her just makes me want to do my best. She has hazel eyes with bits of yellow flecks in the center. I picture her as a young woman and imagine those little flecks sparkling like bits of gold. It doesn't take much to see that she was once a great beauty.

"Well," Gabby says, again much too loudly. "Guess I'll leave you two to get acquainted." She turns and mouths at me, *call me if you need me.* Now, why would I need Gabby? I'm perfectly able to read to Ms. Wilcox all on my own and read in a voice that doesn't scare her off her chair.

I've brought along two books I checked out from the library that afternoon at school, *Little Women* and *Jane Eyre.* I decide to open with *Little Women* and see how it goes. I start at the beginning and get to my favorite part in Chapter Three. Jo is at the party at Mrs. Gardiner's house and is hiding in the alcove and discovers Laurie, Mrs. Gardiner's grandson, who is hiding there, too. They begin talking and get along very well and he asks her to dance. They go into the hallway to dance where no one will see them. I love this part. It's kind of romantic. Ms. Wilcox has a distant look in her eyes. Maybe she is remembering one of her beaus from long ago. One of the reasons I chose the books I brought is because they are very old and the residents here are very old and I figured maybe they would bring back nice memories of when they were young and reading them for the very first time.

"Read it again," Ms. Wilcox says and smiles.

I was right. These are the perfect books to read from. I'm about to start over when there is a knock at the door.

"May I join you?"

There's a tall, overly thin elderly man standing in the door way. He has on a long cardigan sweater that is buttoned up one button off and baggy pants full of wrinkles. Don't they ever iron their clothes around here either? He's wearing glasses. He still has a head full of hair. It's neatly combed over to one side. He smells of Old Spice and has a grin like Kevin Costner, slightly lopsided and very charming.

"Hello," I say. "I'm Andi. It's alright with me if it's alright with Ms. Wilcox."

Katherine doesn't say anything. She still has that faraway look in her eyes.

"Katherine won't mind, I'm sure. Isn't that right?" he says and takes the chair next to the bed. "I'm Joseph Stewart," he says and holds out one hand.

"It's nice to have you, Mr. Stewart," I say on my best behavior.

"Call me Joe," he says. "I'd like that."

"Joe."

He shakes my hand. I like him already. He's warm and friendly and listens to every word I read like he's hearing it for the very first time. Later I find he lives in the room across the hall.

"I'm very fond of Katherine," he says when he shows me his room. "She isn't herself anymore, I'm afraid."

I look at him with a question mark stamped on my face.

"Her memory," he explains. "She's not the same. She got a bad case of the flu this winter and it's been downhill from there."

He has a very sad look in his eyes. "She's my girlfriend," he adds.

I think he's blushing.

"That is, she was, many years ago before the war. She was Katherine Burroughs then."

Joe explains he was taken captive by the Japanese. "I was one of the six hundred and fifty Americans forced to march to Bataan," he says. "When the war ended, I came back to the States. But Katherine had gotten married." He lets out a deep sigh.

"She didn't wait for you?"

"I suspect she thought I was dead. We lost a lot of men on that march."

"So you married someone else, too?"

Joe shakes his head no. "I waited for Katherine, instead," he says.

"But she was married," I said.

"Yes, but I presumed he wouldn't live forever!" he says brightly. "I was right," he said. "He died last year and I followed her here. We had a lovely year together, yes we did."

"Until the flu," I say sadly.

"Yes, until the flu. But don't be sad, young lady. I'm counting on her being back to herself in no time."

I smile softly at him. He seems so convinced.

"And your reading to us will be lovely until she is."

"Until she is," I repeat and shake his hand. He shakes warmly and firmly, such a lovely man. I hope Katherine can remember him. Maybe I won't read *Little Women* after all. Maybe I'll read *Jane Eyre*. It's such a powerful love story. Maybe it will remind her that she has one of her very own.

Chapter Seventy-one

THANKSGIVING IS ONLY DAYS away. It makes me sad to think about it. It's the first one without my dad. Last year was the first one without Alex. We got through that one, which gives me a little spot of hope in my chest. Maybe this one won't be as bad as I think it will be, but then I remember how my father always carves the turkey and pretends like he doesn't know how to do it and makes a game out of it. Rosa will probably carve it in the kitchen and just bring out slices on a fancy plate. Half the fun of the turkey is gone when you do that. I like seeing the knife slide through slice after slice until the breast bone is bare and the wishbone stares right up at you, coaxing you to pull it out and make a wish. Maybe I'll help Rosa carve it. She won't mind. She'll say, "Ms. Andi, do like this." And she'll hand me the knife and step back and put her hands on her hips which are round and soft as pillows. Maybe Beth will want to carve it. She's good at taking over whatever needs to be done. Her studies are going well. She's at the top of her class and is very preoccupied with remaining there. When I told her my dad and Donna were having a baby she barely blinked her eyes.

"That's to be expected," she said. "Donna's very young. She's bound to want a family."

Nothing seems to bother Beth anymore. She spends all of her time when she's not studying writing letters to Adrienne. There's a flurry of them going back and forth. You'd think they were long-lost lovers. Beth is at the mailbox every hour checking to see if another one has arrived for her. I'm sure she's not even aware that Thanksgiving is almost here. I tell my mother I'm not looking forward to it and can we skip it altogether.

"Tell you what, Andi," she says and tucks a strand of my hair behind one ear. "Let's pick a nice restaurant and go out to eat. It'll be just the three of us. We'll start a new tradition."

I shrug my shoulders. Whatever. My mother starts chattering away that I can pick the restaurant. The paper is loaded with ads for fanciful feasts at all of the hotels around Atlanta. I nod my head and go outside. The temperature has dropped and the wind is blowing hard. The sky is blank. There's not one cloud floating around. It's a dreary day that matches my mood. I settle into the glider on the back patio and rock back and forth, scraping my feet along the stone pavers. I'm feeling very depressed. It's Thanksgiving week, and I'm not the least bit thankful. I'm not even the least bit hopeful. Everything that once was safely tucked in place is no longer tucked in place. Life has completely turned itself upside down on me. Then out of the blue, I think of what Nana Louise used to tell me when she could remember things.

"Just because the sun's not out, doesn't mean it's not shining."

I never understood what she meant, but her words were so kind when she said them that I always felt better just hearing them. Maybe there's other ways for the sun to shine, like in our hearts. Or maybe we can work to help the sun shine for others. I think of Table Grace and get a terrific idea for Thanksgiving. They're holding a Thanksgiving banquet for all the people that come to get their groceries every week. My mother and I can volunteer to help serve! We can stand in back of the food line and dish out helpings of mashed potatoes and gravy and stuffing and cornbread and sweet potato casserole. All of the little children will be standing in line, anxiously waiting for their plate to be filled to the brim. It makes my heart jump just thinking about it. I can't wait to tell my mother what I've decided we should do for

Thanksgiving. I head to the portico door and what do you know? The sun just peeks out at me, right out of the blue. Sometimes it's like God just looks down at you and winks.

Dr. Armstrong has invited me and my mother to come to his home Thanksgiving night for dessert. His grown children and his two grandchildren will be there. When we finish serving at Table Grace, my mother goes into the restroom to freshen up. Her face is perspiring and her cheeks are flushed, but I think she looks wonderful. She's wearing a simple brown knit dress. Her hair is pulled back at the nape of her neck and fastened with a tortoise-shell barrette. Some strands have fallen free and rest softly at the side of her face. She has one of the white aprons they gave us still tied around her waist. It's filled with gravy stains and cranberry juice. My mother didn't stop working for three hours. She served plate after plate and smiled warmly at each person standing before her. I served the rolls. Later my mother and another volunteer cut the pies and put the individual servings on paper plates. They loaded them onto large serving platters and bustled around the room to pass them out. There were blueberry, and apple, and cherry, and pumpkin. I served up the ice cream.

Four hundred people showed up to eat. It's amazing how many people are in need of the kindness of others. My mother wipes her hands on her apron. She smiles at me across the room and winks. She's glad we came. Satisfaction climbs into my lap and curls up like a kitten.

We say good-bye and get into my mother's Mercedes.

"That was wonderful," she says, and slips the key into the ignition. "I'm very proud of you, Andi, for thinking of it."

I snap my seatbelt into place, pleased with myself as well. My mother pats my hand and backs out of the parking lot. She's happy, happier than I've seen her in a very long time. I'm sure she feels good about herself for helping others who have so little, while she has so much.

Maybe my father didn't ruin everything, after all. Maybe he just put a few dents in it.

Chapter Seventy-two

I'M LYING ON MY bed staring at the ceiling and listening to WYOU, my favorite radio station and Skipper McCoy, my favorite disk jockey. This is that oldie-goldie radio station I discovered way back and still love. But tonight he is playing very sad songs, one after the other and it's starting to get to me and I don't even have a boyfriend that's breaking my heart, so I'm thinking that those that do are probably ready to slit their wrists. Skipper has on Connie Francis. She's singing "My Heart Has a Mind of Its Own." It's beautiful, but very sad. Next he plays Dion and the Belmonts. They're singing "A Lover's Prayer." It could break a heart made out of steel. I curl up and hug my pillow and pretend I'm in love with Rodney again, and he's left me for the second time and what do you know? Real tears come to my eyes. That's how powerful this song is.

Rudy is lying next to me. His head is resting in his paws and he looks so forlorn, like maybe I'm not supposed to be listening to this station. Petula Clark is singing "Kiss Me Good-bye." These are really old songs, but they have the same effect they'd have if they were still popular. I'm sure of it. So maybe Rudy is right and dogs have this inner sense about more things than we know. Now the station is back to Connie Francis and she's singing "I'm Breaking in a Brand New Broken Heart." Oh, boy. The rest of the program is all the same, songs to make you cry, even though the program tonight is called *Good-bye*, and they should be playing good-bye songs, so what is the matter with them anyway?

Skipper McCoy is leaving to go to another radio station, somewhere in Chicago. Guess he wants to break everyone's heart before
he goes, so they'll remember him. Good luck. Everyone has probably
killed themselves already, at least the ones that have a broken heart.
I'm okay, but then no one's broken mine since Rodney and that's
been a while, but I'm not sure about all the others out there. I'm
about to pick up the phone and call the station to let them know
they should lighten up, even if Skipper is going away. But then I hear
Petula Clark singing "Downtown" and it sounds very upbeat and I
figure maybe someone else already called in. Skipper is singing in the
background, sounding very happy, so he must be glad to be going
to Chicago.

"Downtown! Downtown!" he sings into the microphone, and he
has a really good voice. Then he plays Frank Sinatra. Frank is singing
Chicago, and Skipper starts singing "Chicago, Chicago, my kind of
town." Then the music just sort of disappears and he says, "Now,
remember, folks, if you get in the Chicago area be sure and switch to
WLMU on your dial. Talk to you soon!" Then you hear him again,
over Frank Sinatra, "Chicago, my kind of town!"

Next a commercial comes on and the program's over. I really like
Skipper McCoy. I wonder if they've hired somebody good to take
his place. I plop back on my pillow and think about the decision
I've made. I've decided not to have anything to do with my father
anymore. It will be much better this way. Why let him be the one
to cut me off, like Julia's father did to her? I'm trying to figure out a
way to tell my mother. This is the type of thing that will upset her.
Knowing my mother, she'll just want us to carry on like always and
pretend everything's okay, when everything pretty much sucks when
it comes to my dad.

I haven't thought of any good way to bring the subject up when
my mother pops her head into my room.

"Rosa has dinner ready, Andi," she says. She has one of her house dresses on and an apron around her waist, which means she was in the kitchen helping out, when I know for a fact Rosa would prefer otherwise. My mother's not much of a cook and she tends to get in the way. She fusses with the salad greens, like they haven't been torn into the right bite size pieces, or she picks up a knife and starts rechopping the herbs that Rosa is ready to put into the pot. I've seen my mother do this and when she does Rosa's eyes are twice their normal size.

My mother is sitting at the dining room table when I get downstairs and her apron is nowhere in sight. So at least she won't be serving. The last time she did she slopped sauce all over the dining room tablecloth. She insisted on changing it before we could continue and dinner was mostly cold by the time it was finally on the table. Which was okay, but my father made a big deal out of it. That was when he was still here. I wanted him to put his arms around my mother and nuzzle her neck like they do in the old movies my mother and I watch together sometimes and tell her how wonderful she is to try and serve him. It never happened. He sighed and got an irritated look on his face and never even got up to help her clear the dishes so she could change the tablecloth. He just pushed back from the table, put his napkin on his lap and waited like it was a major inconvenience. My mother just smiled and fussed with the linens and said, "We'll be ready in no time."

I stew over the memory and feel happy that I've made the decision to not see my father anymore. He's a crumb-bum. Now, I just need to find a way to tell my mother, without upsetting her too much.

Just like I figured, my mother is not happy with my decision. She motions for me to follow her into the library. I watch as she opens the blinds and lets the morning light pour in. It's Saturday. Rosa is busy in another room. I can hear the vacuum cleaner humming away.

"Andi," my mother says. She fusses with the back of her hair. She does this when she's not certain what to say. Her hair is pulled up into a soft curve and fastened with a barrette. While she fusses with it, some of it falls out of place. She looks so beautiful, like a commercial where the model pulls her hair pin out of place and her hair cascades all around her shoulders. Not that all of my mother's hair has done that, but I can easily picture that happening with my mother's hair, if she keeps fussing with it. I look at her and wonder how my father could possibly ever fall out of love with her. She's perfect. I watch her mouth as it forms words. Her lips are perfect, too.

"Don't make up your mind so soon about your father," she says. "It takes time to—to—well, to adjust. Eventually, this situation will become more familiar to you and—"

"They're having a baby!" I blurt out. "It'll never be familiar. We're supposed to be a family and he just goes and starts another one."

I tell her all about Julia and what happened to her and explain that I never want that to happen to me and she must let me decide. My mother sits back and sighs. Her face is pale, but her cheeks are flush like I've slapped her.

"Andi," she whispers. "Just give it some time."

I nod my head like I'm agreeing with her, but I'm not. I've given my father all the time I plan to. It's over. He can go on with his life and I'll go on with mine. I lean over and hug my mother. She smiles. She thinks I'm mulling it over. If only she knew.

Chapter Seventy-three

I AM HAVING BRUNCH at the Ritz-Carlton with my mother, Beth, and Dr. Armstrong. All three of his children are with us, along with his two grandchildren, Zachary and Elizabeth. Elizabeth is four and Zachary is one. He's just started walking and is toddling all over the place. I get to watch them and I'm having a very good time. Elizabeth has a little purse she carries around. She's sitting on my lap. Zachary is back in the high chair the maître d' brought to the table.

"What do you keep in your purse?" I ask Elizabeth.

She opens the clasp and pulls out a plastic baggie with photos inside. I watch as she pulls them free from the plastic.

"This is my friend, Charlie," she says. "We take ballet together. See?" She puts the picture almost under my nose.

I lower it to take a good look. Charlie is a pretty blonde-haired girl and at least a foot taller than Elizabeth.

"How old is Charlie?"

"She's four, like me," Elizabeth says, proudly.

"Goodness, she's a big four," I say.

Elizabeth takes the picture back and stares at it carefully. Her brow is wrinkled and her lips are pursed together tightly. "Well, next year when I'm five," she says. "I'll be a big four, too!"

I laugh and give her a hug. Children are wonderful. They really do say the darndest things.

"My hamster died," she says. "I liked him a lot and I hugged him too hard and his tongue came out and he died."

There is a very sad look on her face. I glance at her mother, who shakes her head, as if she is saying, "Don't go there."

"But I'm getting another one," Elizabeth adds. "I'll just hug him sort of hard. That should be okay, right?"

I'm not sure how hard to hug a hamster. "Maybe just hug him gently," I say.

She looks at me like the word gently is not in her vocabulary.

"What I mean is, don't hug him hard at all. Hug him soft."

"Okay," she says and settles down into my lap. "I'll just hug him a little." She lets out a deep sigh. Her mother smiles at me like I'm doing everything right and really I'm not doing anything at all but listening.

Beth invited Adrienne to join us. She's home from Zaire for a short visit to raise more funds at her church. When Adrienne arrived at our house the day she returned, Beth came bounding down the steps when the door chimes rang. I was on my way to answer it myself. Beth flung the door open and threw her arms around her, which wasn't so unusual because they're friends after all and Beth has not seen her for a while. But then Beth leaned in and kissed her right on the mouth! I wasn't sure what to do. Then it hit me. All of it. Why she ignored Parker all those months they were engaged. Why she was relieved not to be getting married. She was struggling all along with her sexuality and nobody knew. It made me very sad. Poor Beth. She's been suffering silently all this time.

I watched them walk into the entrance hall hand in hand. They looked like lovers. Then I realized, they are!

Later Beth explains her choice to my mother, who takes it all in stride, but I'm sure when my father finds out he will lose all his hair over it. I can just hear him. It makes me laugh right out loud.

"Andi," my mother says. "Goodness, what is it?"

"Nothing, I'm just happy," I say. And I am.

I think about all my father's attempts to see me and that makes me happy, too. It's good to be the one in charge. Each time he comes to the house, I tell my mother in no uncertain terms that I'm not going to even so much as talk to him. And I certainly am not going to go out to dinner with him. He sends me three long letters. They're under my mattress. I like to read them late at night over and over again. They all say the same thing. He misses me. He loves me. He wants me to be part of their family. He wants me to come and visit. Donna will be having the baby soon and I will be a big help to her. Wouldn't I like to give them a chance? Not on your life, I want to say, but I'm not speaking to him. I know that sounds very cruel, but I think of how he dumped us and how he treated my mother all those months when she was drinking and here she was just grieving over losing Alex and then I think of how he was sneaking around behind my mother's back when her heart was breaking for Alex and her knowing all along what he was up to and then I just go back to never wanting to see him again. Besides, if I started seeing him again, he would probably just get used to me being around. And he and Donna will probably have other babies, and I'd get lost in the shuffle. I can't bear the thought, so I just keep staying away.

When we get back from the brunch, my mother calls me to come down from my room. I run down the stairs thinking that she has a surprise for me. Sometimes she gets me a little gift, for no reason, really, and she wraps it up in fluffy pink paper. Halfway down the stairs I see that my father is at the bottom of the steps. Donna is right next to him. Her belly is huge. Then I remember, the baby is due next month, so it should be big. I stop on the step I'm on and freeze. What am I supposed to say to him?

"Andi," my father says. "Come down here right now."

Right. Like he is in charge of me. I don't move.

"Andi, this has gone on long enough. Now you come down here right now!"

I turn around and run back upstairs. My mother follows. I slam my door shut. At least my mother respects my privacy. She doesn't barge in. She knocks on the door. "Andi, sweetie, can I come in?"

Why not? Let me hear what she has to say.

"Alright," I say, and the door opens before I finish speaking.

My mother comes over to the bed and sits down next to me. "Oh, Andi," she says. "You're being so difficult and that is so unlike you."

I told you she always thinks the best of me. Basically, I think I've always have been difficult, but she's the only one who doesn't see it that way. I lie down on my bed and stare at the ceiling. It has this very interesting pattern. If you look really hard you can make out miniature stalactites. They're right there hanging from the ceiling. I count each and every point that's protruding. My eyes get lost and I lose track. I can hear my mother. She's trying to explain to me why I'm being difficult.

"Andi, they only want you to go to dinner. Would that be so much?"

I sit up straight on my bed and rub my eyes. I'm not sure if I can see straight any more. "I've already had dinner," I point out.

"Alright, supper," she says. "They want you to join them for supper."

"Well, they can forget it!" I say and plop back down on my bed.

My mother looks at me like she cannot believe that she's heard me. I sit back up and slam my fists at my sides. They hit the bed like they're made out of cotton.

"I can't stand it!" I say. "They've started a new life, they're having a new baby and I can't stand it."

My mother puts her arms around me and pulls me to her. "Andi, my sweet girl," she says, and turns me around and looks me straight in the eye. "If I can stand it, you can stand it."

❖ ❖ ❖

My mother is right, but there is one thing about trying to change your mind about something. It doesn't necessarily change your heart. I walk back down the staircase and confront my father again. Donna's belly is sticking out like a watermelon, but her cheeks really are glowing, just like I read in a magazine. I turn to my father and say, "I told you. I don't want to see you anymore. Please leave me alone."

I march back up the steps and walk right past my mother and go into my room and slam my door. Then I lie down on my bed and cry my eyes out. If you want to know the truth, I was hoping my father would march right up those stairs and yank me by the back of my head and say, "That's not good enough, Andi! You forgot one thing: I want to see you!"

He didn't.

Chapter Seventy-four

SPRING BREAK IS OVER and I go back to school assuming that it will be the same old same old. Then, out of the blue, my home room has a new boy and what do you know? He's the boy of my dreams. I know I thought Anthony was, and then later I thought Rodney was, but when you really meet the one you are meant for, it's like all the ones before are nothing. Nothing! Elliott Chambers. This is the one I am going to marry. He's everything. He has an English accent. His father's in the military, so he's been all over the world, well mainly China, and Germany, and England. Mostly he was raised in England. So I'm not sure if he ended up where he was born and is English or just sounds like he is. I love his accent. I'm convinced it's the way we should all be speaking English. Just like Princess Diana and Prince Charles, whose marriage—according to the papers—is on the rocks. What does that say for my mother and father? Royals can't even stay married. This should make me feel better, but it doesn't. I really like Diana and I love my mother. Both men in their lives have not lived up to what they said they would do in their wedding vows, stay married 'til death us do part. Men lie.

That gets me thinking that maybe Elliott will be the same way. I probably shouldn't get involved, but he's already paying a lot of attention to me and it's hard not to pay attention to that kind of attention. Just this morning he asked me if I'd like to go skating on Saturday.

"I can meet you there," he says.

"Okay," is all I manage.

He has light brown hair and blue eyes. There's a cut over one eye that's left a scar. I wonder if he gets into fights or something. Or maybe he's just clumsy and runs into things.

"What time?"

"What time?" I've lost my train of thought.

"Skating," he says, like where have I been?

"Oh—uh, maybe one o'clock," I answer, then, I remember I'll be at Sunny Meadows reading to Elizabeth. "It'll have to be three o'clock. I'm an Angel at Sunny Meadows. I have to read. That is, I volunteer to read. I'm not really an angel or anything like that. They just call us that." I'm babbling. I could kick myself, but my mouth won't shut up.

"An angel, huh?" He grins. "Well, the afternoon session ends at four. That would only give us an hour."

"Okay."

"No, I mean, maybe we should pick another Saturday."

"I have to read every Saturday."

He puts his hands in his pockets and just looks at me. What? I'm supposed to rearrange my life for him already?

"Maybe some other time," he says. He shrugs his shoulders and walks away.

We haven't even started this romance, and already things are getting complicated.

After school I decide to walk home. I know, I'm not supposed to, but who cares? I'm feeling really down anyway. Getting into trouble can't make me feel any worse that I already do. I look around to see if I can spot Julia. She takes the number eleven bus. It's already pulled away and mine is next in line. I turn around and walk away. I'm thinking about Elliott and how I could have helped things turn out differently so we'd be going skating after all. Maybe I should have said, "I'm supposed to be at Sunny Meadows Nursing Home—I'm a reader—but I probably could make arrangements. You know, change my day."

But then he would have thought I was too eager and all the stories in *Seventeen* say to be a little mysterious. Guys like the chase. They want what they think they can't have. If that is the case, Elliott doesn't get it. He walked away like, too bad for her. When he said *maybe some other time*, he didn't sound like he meant it. He could have been saying, see you around, and it would have come out the same way. No big deal here, girlie—I wasn't sure I wanted to go skating anyway.

If he was getting ready to like me, he probably will get over it, pronto. Maybe I could call him up and explain that we could go skating on Friday night instead. But I don't have his number and even if I did, it would be so pushy, me calling him. I could leave him a note with my name and telephone number on it and just write, "Hey, give me a call sometime." That might work.

I'm mulling that over when I look up and there's a mother pushing her baby in a stroller. There's a little girl about three hanging onto the handles. She's having trouble maneuvering the stroller in the right direction. The mother places her hands over the little girl and guides her along. The little girl smiles and says, "I can do it, Mommy."

That is so cute. A little butterfly just flutters inside me. Soon that will be Donna, pushing her baby along, maybe a toddler hanging on the handle and another one on the way. Suddenly it doesn't seem so cute anymore. Now what kind of person have I become that I don't find that cute? I'm not liking myself very much. I think back to when my father was still with us. I liked myself fine. He's turned me into a monster. He's dumped our life upside down and has changed my once-nice personality into a grumpy one.

We have a counselor at school, Mrs. Temple. Whenever I see

her in the hallways she has a smile on her face like she has a secret. I'll bet she has many. She's very well liked, so she probably keeps everything she's told to herself. I should go talk to her. Let her know what's happened to me. See if she can help me get back to being who I used to be. All you have to do is put a note in the box outside her office. Then your homeroom teacher quietly lets you know you have an appointment and you get out of study hall. But then everyone in class automatically knows, so it's not so discreet, even though the system was designed that way.

For once I don't care. What difference does it make what others think about me. I don't like myself enough anymore to care. The following morning I write my name on a piece of paper and slip it into Mrs. Temple's box outside her door. Andi St. James, homeroom 309. Urgent.

I cross off the word urgent and write sort of. In case she's real busy she can move me back or something, so she'll at least know I'm considerate, I'm not all bad.

Maybe there's hope for me.

Chapter Seventy-five

I'M BACK AT SUNNY Meadows Nursing home. Katherine has on a pink sweater over a flowered dress. She has just come from the beauty parlor. Her hair is set in little ringlets all around her face. It's a major improvement over the fluffy halo hairdo she wore last week. I tell her how nice she looks. She pats one side of her head with a shaky hand. It's so tender to see old people when they do something and their hands shake. It just makes you want to give them a hug or something. I pick up a new book I've brought along and she smiles.

"What are we reading, this week?" she asks sweetly.

I've decided to read James Fenimore Cooper's *The Last of the Mohicans*, because it's another really beautiful love story and I'm wild about the promise Hawkeye made, "You stay alive, no matter what occurs. I will find you! No matter how long it takes, no matter how far. I will find you."

I think of Joe and how he stayed alive on that long march where so many died. More or less, this book is for me and for Joe. Sadly, Katherine can't remember one chapter to the next, let alone what book we're reading. I just hold the book up for her to see. "It's *The Last of the Mohicans*, by James Fenimore Cooper. It's sort of a love story. Will this one be okay?"

She says the same thing she said last week. "Why, yes, that would be lovely."

She's such a lady. She leans back in her rocking chair and closes her eyes.

I start reading on my favorite part. Major Heyward is accusing Cora of defending Hawkeye because she loves him. And Cora says, "You are a man with a few admirable qualities, but taken as a whole I was wrong to have thought so highly of you."

I glance at Katherine. She still has her eyes closed and is slowly rocking back and forth in her rocker. I wonder if she's thinking about her long-lost love, about Joe, and remembering he got killed, only he didn't and she didn't find out until after she married Mr. Wilcox. In those days, one just didn't up and get a divorce, even if a long lost love came back on the scene. I picture Katherine pining away for Joe, all the while trying desperately to keep it from her poor husband, who probably loved her very much and would have been heartbroken if he'd known the truth. It almost makes a better story than Mr. Cooper's. I wish he were still alive. I would write to him and tell him I have a great idea for his next love story. It's bound to be a blockbuster, and all based on fact.

I keep reading, wondering where Joe is. I stop for a moment.

"Ms. Wilcox," I say. "Will Joe be joining us?"

"Who, dear?" she says and stops rocking.

"You know, Joe, your—your good friend—"

"No, I don't recall a Joe," she says, and goes back to her rocking.

So much for this love story—if James Cooper were alive he couldn't possibly write it. The ending is too sad.

Today it's raining cats and dogs. Well, that's what people say, but I don't get it. They might as well say it's raining forks and spoons or lamps and end tables. It doesn't make sense.

Rudy keeps running over to the library windows. It's like he's checking to see if the rain has stopped so he can go outside. He's very smart. Or maybe it's because he has to make a potty run, which I will eventually have to take him on, regardless of the rain. Rainy Saturdays are always so boring. I'm glad I have to be at Sunny Meadows this afternoon. It takes up most of the afternoon, getting ready, driving there, doing my reading, and then waiting for my mother to take me back home. Beth is busy studying as usual. My mother is busy fluffing throw pillows and straightening the various knick-knacks. Rosa has been dusting and they get moved out of place. If there is one thing about my mother she likes everything back where it started.

Rosa's going on vacation next week. In the spring she always goes to Mexico to visit her relatives. She brings us back all sorts of interesting things. One year I got a handmade pottery bowl that had all the colors of the rainbow in it. The pattern on the side was very intricate and I marveled at how someone's hands could just craft that out of a lump of clay. And then, since all of Rosa's relatives that I know about are very poor, I wondered how they fired it. Is there a store they go to or something? And what about the cost? Do they charge them a lot of money to do that? So, I really treasure that bowl. It's meant for the kitchen, but I keep it on my bedroom shelf and put all my favorite treasures in it. Right now that consists of a rabbit's foot good luck charm, the bow from the corsage I got from the Sadie Hawkins dance, a very good-looking gold button that belongs on something that I think I like, because when I look at it, I can almost remember, but then I can't, and it makes me sad or even anxious, so I'm saving it until I find out where it's missing from. Also, I have a hankie that my grandmother gave me that has my initials on it, with crocheted lace all around the edges. It doesn't seem like a lot, but treasures are hard to come by.

Bridget's letters would be there, too, but they don't fit, so I have them tucked in the top dresser drawer under my panties. I got another one yesterday and I'm worried about her. She sounds more depressed than ever. Her Aunt Ellen is still making her go to the Camp Fire meetings and her cousin Ashley is still mostly making her life miserable. Whenever Bridget invites someone over from school, Ashley insists on being included and her mother insists there is nothing wrong with it, when everybody knows teenagers need plenty of time by themselves with their friends. How can they even talk about boys they like with Ashley sitting there all big ears? The worst part, Bridget said, is that her father has decided that she should finish the school year and then maybe by the time school is set to begin next fall she will be in London. He's trying to get settled. He's been doing that for months. How long does it take?

Earlier he had said she could go over after Easter, but now he's changed his mind. Bridget's Aunt Ellen told him how disruptive it would be to take her out of school, which is probably true, but that doesn't make Bridget feel any better. Plus she's been away from her father for over six months, so it's kind of like she's lost her father, and she's already lost her mother. And she no longer has Rudy, don't forget that. Who wouldn't be depressed? It's Donna and my father's fault. I hate them. I fold Bridget's letter up and put it back in my drawer. Her last paragraph pinches my heart.

> *I wish we were together in my old room, just painting*
> *our toenails, like we used to. Do you remember that? You*
> *had yours all different colors. And mine were lime green.*

The rain hasn't stopped, or even slowed down a bit when it's time for my mother to take me to the nursing home. I take Rudy for a quick run, using my father's golf umbrella that's stashed in the garage. Rudy's quite a handful and runs me down the street. I can barely hang on and I almost lose the umbrella, he's pulling me that hard. He does that a lot when I take him out. When it's not raining he's off smelling something with so much determination you'd think he was being paid for it. Every once in a while he must find a scent that he particularly likes because he'll spend a lot of time at that spot before moving on. It'd be so neat to be able to feel what they feel, and smell what they smell at least once in our lifetime. But maybe not, because mostly he smells things that don't look like they'd smell all that good, and some of it is downright repulsive. Why do they sniff at each other's butts? Dogs are very lovable, but they're peculiar, too.

There's a man walking his little poodle across the street. Rudy takes one sniff and is off running. He bounds away so fast it's hard for me to keep up with him. I yank on his leash, but it does no good. He's off and running faster than ever and ends up yanking me. My feet slip out from under me. I land face down on the sidewalk where my forehead smashes into the wet concrete. Blood is pouring into my eyes and down my cheeks. Rudy turns back. In an instant he's at my side. He licks the blood off my face and whimpers. Dogs know when something's wrong. And something is definitely wrong. My head feels like it's been hit with a hammer. The man across the street gathers his little poodle into his arms and comes running toward me.

"Can you get my mother?" I say, holding my head with one hand. "I live in the big house on the corner." Blood has filled the palm of my hand. It drips down my arm and onto the sidewalk. "Please hurry."

He takes one look at me and goes back across the street. "Stay right there," he yells. "I'm calling an ambulance. Then I'll get your mother."

An ambulance! My face must be a mess. I'll probably never look like Beth again. I'm not sure what happened after that. Everything's a big blur. I do remember riding in the ambulance. And I definitely remember when they stabbed me with an IV needle. I almost climbed off the gurney.

"Steady now," the attendant said and patted my shoulder. "It's a bit of a nasty sting to get it in place, but you shouldn't feel a thing once I do."

"Do you know where my mother is?" I asked.

"I suspect right behind this ambulance," he said. "She was by your side when we got to you. You don't remember that?"

I shake my head.

"Well, you took a nasty bump on your head. Everything's bound to be a bit jumbled right now, but we'll have you to the hospital it no time and the doctors will have you all fixed up before you know it. Don't worry about a thing. Just lay back and enjoy the ride."

I close my eyes and try to relax. I don't want to think about what my face looks like. What if I am maimed for life? What boy will want me now? Then I remember Rudy.

"Did you see my dog? Did you?"

"I believe your mother left him with your neighbor."

"My neighbor?"

"The man with the poodle."

Right, the poodle—the very one that started this whole thing. Hopefully Rudy and the little guy are having a high old time of it getting acquainted. Something good ought to come out of this.

The doctor in the emergency room puts five stitches in my head, but insists on keeping me overnight for observation. By that time my mother has called my father. When he sees me with the bandages on my head he rushes over to my side.

"Andi sweetheart, are you alright?"

"She's going to be just fine," the intern says. "There's not much we can't fix around here."

My father isn't convinced. Concern is stamped all over his face. For a minute I forget how mad I am at him. I tell him what happened.

"Honey, you shouldn't be running the dog in the rain."

"Well, I wasn't meaning to run, but Rudy took off and I followed, and then he sort of got away from me."

The doctor explains that they are going to keep me overnight. "Just as a precaution," he says. "We'll take some X-rays and watch to make sure she's not bleeding from her ears."

"Bleeding from her ears?" my mother says, and looks like she might faint.

"Bleeding from the ears is indicative of a concussion, but don't worry," the doctor says. "Like I said, it's just a precaution."

"Mind if we stay with her?" my father asks.

"Not a problem."

My mother takes hold of my hand. "Would you like that, Andi?"

Actually I'd like my parents to get back together again. That nice young intern said there wasn't much they couldn't fix around here. I want to ask him if he can fix that.

Chapter Seventy-six

On Saturday I go back to Sunny Meadows. Joe is sitting in Katherine's room when I arrive. He gets out of the chair he's been resting in and gives me a big smile.

"Well, here she is," he says, "our very own angel."

Joe is holding Katherine's hand. And it is the sweetest thing, because she is letting him and her cheeks are flushed, which makes it look like she's blushing or something. Joe asks me about the bandage on my forehead and I give him the short version.

"Did they take X-rays?"

I nod my head that they certainly did. "They even kept me overnight," I say.

"That's good. Can't have anything happen to our girl," he says, and winks.

I take *The Last of the Mohicans* out of my satchel and start reading from where I left off. Joe takes Katherine's hand again. Ten minutes later he lets go and places his hand over his chest and leans inward against it. "Guess my lunch isn't agreeing with me," he says, but I decide at his age any ache or pain should be looked into and run to the nurses' station.

"Joe, I mean Mr. Stewart, is having a pain in his chest!"

Gabby runs down the hall and I'm amazed that she can move so fast. She's sort of fat and her legs aren't very long.

When we get back to the room, Joe is on the floor. There's a nasty bruise bubbling up on his forehead, so he must have fallen head first out of the chair. Katherine is down on the floor next to him and is cradling his head in her lap. Joe is just smiling up at her. For a minute I'm sure Katherine knows who he is! It makes my heart jump. Two orderlies arrive and place him on Katherine's bed. Gabby takes Katherine's hand and gently pulls her to her feet. She escorts her out of the room. Joe stretches out his hand toward her.

"Don't go, Katherine," he says. "Come back to me."

And that just does it. I start crying. I can hear an ambulance. It seems like hours before it pulls out in front. They dash Joe to the hospital. Katherine is standing in the hall and there are tears running down her face and she has her palms pressed against her cheeks. I knew it! She remembers.

And maybe Joe knew. Maybe he could tell by the way she held his hand and looked into his eyes. Maybe that is what is sustaining him now. On Sunday morning before Mass, I call the nursing home and ask to speak to Gabby. I want to know how Joe is doing.

"I'm sorry, Andi," she says. "Mr. Stewart never regained consciousness. He died this morning."

Now I'll never know if Joe really knew that Katherine remembered him. If in fact she did. But she must have. She was crying real tears when they wheeled him away.

My first session with Mrs. Temple goes like this. She motions for me to sit down. "Wherever you feel comfortable," she says.

My choices are a small burgundy recliner, a chair right next to her desk, but not too close, and a loveseat that looks like it has seen better days. That's another thing people say that doesn't make sense. How can a loveseat see anything, let alone better days? I choose the sofa.

"Where would you like to start?" she says. She has the kindest face. It's going to be easy to talk with her. I knew it. Sometimes you can just tell that about a person. There's something in their eyes or in their smile that makes you feel warm in the part of your stomach that could just as easily have butterflies.

I go back to the beginning when me and Bridget found out about my father and Donna in the pool house, but I leave out the part that we watched them over and over. I make it sound like we were just fiddling around and stumbled on them in the pool house when we walked by the window. I don't want her to think I'm a snoop before she even gets to know me, which probably I am, because we spied on them all sorts of times. Still.

I tell her the rest, about the divorce and my father getting married and having a new baby.

"Mostly, I hate myself," I say. "And I hate my father and I no longer see him, and that pretty much upsets my mother."

Mrs. Temple listens carefully to everything I say, without once interrupting. That's another reason why talking to a counselor can sometimes be better than trying to talk to your parents. Parents are always interrupting. They can't help it. It's part of their parenting routine. You try to tell them one thing and they are already onto the next. And they always want to know why. Mrs. Temple doesn't ask me why I'm feeling the way I do. She just nods her head and waits until I'm finished.

"I don't want to be this way," I add, "but I can't help myself. I've turned into a completely ugly, hateful person." That's when I tell her about the emergency ward and my father coming down and trying very hard to let me know he was very worried, but even so it didn't change my mind about him—that I don't trust him, he might be faking his concern. And I'm so scared that he is faking it.

"Well, Andi," she says, and puts down her pencil. She has been taking notes. I wonder what she's written. I hope that it's not that I'm a bad person. I want to think that maybe I'm still okay.

"You've had a lot on your plate this past year," she says. "Lots of changes." She leans over and picks some lint off her sweater by her elbow, then pats the sweater back into place. "And change is sort of like a death. There are many emotions we must deal with in any kind of death. What you're feeling isn't hate, Andi. It's anger. You're angry with your father for changing everything."

That's exactly what my mother said.

Mrs. Temple continues. "And you've had no say-so in the matter. You've lost all control. It makes you feel very vulnerable and that makes you angry. And that's perfectly understandable. What we have to do is to help you get past the anger and move towards acceptance."

"But how do I do that?" She is making it sound so easy. How can I just sit up and say, *I'm okay with all of this*. It's not that simple.

"To begin with let's take a look at why anger is such a normal reaction to what you're going through. We can't control what people do, and that leaves us feeling frustrated, and the frustration leads to the anger, which leads to more frustration, and so forth."

"Kind of like a gerbil on his wheel."

"Exactly, Andi. And the thing to do is stop the frustration and eventually come to grips with the anger. The best way to do that is to understand that you can't change your father's choices, but you are free to make choices of your own. And those choices will determine what happens in your life."

I nod my head, like I understand, but mostly I don't.

"You've chosen not to see your father. You want to punish him. He's changed the game plan. You decide not to see him, not to spend time with him. But he's not the only one you're punishing," she says.

"Well, there's my mother—"

I notice she is nodding her head. "Well, yes, there is that, but there's someone else you're punishing, too, Andi."

She takes her glasses off. "What if you choose to see your father and look forward to a new relationship. Perhaps one that's even closer than the one you had before. You did say he rarely came home when your parents were married. And now, look at all the times he's called or stopped by to try and see you. You're actually getting much more of his attention than you ever did before. And what about the emergency room? You shouldn't forget about that. Granted, all of his actions may be partially motivated by guilt. But that's another topic altogether. The important thing right now is he wants to see you! And you can make a choice of whether to see him or not. And that puts you back in control, Andi. And with some control, you'll feel much less frustration, which will lead to less anger. Basically, acceptance follows from there. It's just a matter of time. Make sense?"

I nod my head and think about Joe and his decision to wait for Katherine, even though she was already married by the time he came back from the war. He didn't put his life on hold. He didn't choose to pine away. He chose to have a good life. He flew airplanes, and took up sailing and climbed mountains. "Anything to feel free," he said. "I just didn't get married. On that long march to Bataan, I thought only of Katherine. I'd already married her in my heart by the time I returned to the States. Why marry someone else? I chose to keep loving her, if only from afar."

That is so sweet. But most important, he chose not to marry, to wait for her. It didn't turn out like he planned, no it did not, but still, it was his decision. And his last days were very happy. It was written all over his face. He was where he wanted to be. He was in Katherine's arms. And his choices had led him to her arms. There's that word again, choices.

Mrs. Temples clears her throat and folds her hands. She rests them gently on her desk. Then she turns toward the sofa where I am sitting and places her hands on her knees. Her fingernails are nicely manicured. She has pale pink polish on them. I like her hands. They are delicate hands, yet there is something about them; you can tell they are strong. They remind me of my mother's.

"Andi," she says, "you can choose to be happy, just as easily as you can decide to be sad. It's up to you."

Choose to be happy; decide to be sad. I never looked at it that way, but it seems reasonable.

"Just remember, your choices map your future." She is smiling at me now. "So choose carefully." She gets up and opens the door to her office and I realize my time is up.

"But don't be so hard on yourself once you choose, Andi," she says. "You can always change your mind."

Chapter Seventy-seven

BRIDGET'S AUNT ELLEN IS on the phone talking to my mother. It's the second call she's made tonight. The first one was to let us know that Bridget never came home from school today and there is clothing missing from her closet along with her overnight bag. The second call is so Bridget's aunt can talk to me. She thinks I know something and I'm keeping it from her. Bridget's aunt's full name is Ellen Buice, which rhymes with rice. Mrs. Buice is not pleasant to talk to. Her voice is very shrill. It sounds like a fingernail being dragged across a chalkboard. I can picture Bridget running away just to get away from that. But maybe she sounds that way because she is so upset.

"Mrs. Buice," I say. "I got a letter from Bridget last week, but she didn't say anything about leaving. Not one word. And I haven't heard from her since, honest to goodness, I haven't."

Wherever Bridget is, I hope she isn't hitchhiking. It's not safe. There are probably hundreds of serial killers out there roaming around just waiting for a victim like Bridget. Now I'm getting upset. Where could she be?

"If you hear anything at all," Mrs. Buice says, "anything, call us immediately. We're worried sick."

I assure her I will and hand the phone back to my mother.

"Alright then, yes, of course," she says and puts the handset back on the receiver.

My mother starts clearing the supper dishes from the table, while I start chewing my nails. The reason my mother is doing kitchen duty is because Rosa is still in Mexico and we are cooking for ourselves. That is, we're trying. I made macaroni and cheese out of a box and my mother mixed together a meatloaf that tasted okay, other than the dried ketchup sitting on top. That part was nasty.

"Try to stay off the telephone, tonight, Andi," my mother says, and fills the sink with dishwashing detergent. "I'm sure Bridget is going to try and get ahold of you."

I was going to dry, but decide I need to sit right next to the phone, just in case Bridget chickens out and only rings once. You know, maybe she thinks the police have tapped our phone or something. For three hours I sit there thinking scary thoughts about what could have happened to her. At ten o'clock I'm ready to give up when the phone rings. I yank the receiver off the hook.

"Hello? Hello?" I'm breathing so hard I sound like I've been running a marathon.

"Andi? What are you doing up so late?"

It's my father. I don't answer. I hand the phone to my mother who came running the minute the phone rang.

"We're trying to keep the line free," she says. "Can this wait until morning? I'm afraid Bridget's missing."

There's a slight pause. My mother is fidgeting with the cord. "Bridget Harman, the little girl that use to live next door, Andi's best friend. For Pete's sake, Arthur, Rodger Harman's daughter." My mother is totally exasperated. She hangs up the phone on him, but it rings again immediately.

"Arthur, goodness, we're trying to keep this line open— Bridget? Oh, Bridget, honey, everyone has been worried sick. Where are you, dear?"

I'm jumping up and down. "Is it Bridget? Is it?"

My mother motions for me to be quiet. I lean my ear against the handset. Yes! It's Bridget. I do a little dance right in the entrance hall. No serial killer got her!

"Oh, dear," my mother is saying. "Well, stay right there. We're on our way."

She places the handset back on the receiver and moves quickly to the guest closet and gets her coat. "Hurry," she says. "She's at the bus station. It's not safe. There are all sorts of people there who—who, well they prey on young girls getting off the buses. They sell them into prostitution." My mother shudders and hands me my jacket. "They get them hooked on drugs. All sorts of things." She grabs the car keys and buttons up her coat. "Goodness, why ever did she go there?"

Duh, probably because she had no car, and even if she had one, she doesn't know how to drive. So, a bus is a very good choice. How else would she get to Atlanta? Sometimes parents ask really dumb questions. I keep my answer to myself. Besides it wasn't a real question. It's what Alex used to refer to as a rhetorical question. It doesn't require an answer. I'm excited that we've found Bridget and gladly climb into my mother's Mercedes. Maybe she'll realize now how important it is that we adopt her. I mean it's not like her father wants her. He left her in North Carolina with a family that drove her crazy.

When we get to the bus station, Bridget is nowhere in sight. We panic and find a police officer and pour out our story.

"Oh yeah," he says. "We picked up a kid that looked to be twelve years old. They took her to juvenile."

"Did you get her name?" my mother asks.

"I'm sure it's on the report."

"Well, can you radio the station and find out if she's there. Her name is Bridget Harman and I don't want to leave here, only to find out later it was not her they took to—to—"

"Juvenile Hall," the officer prompts.

My mother puts her hand on her chest. For a minute I'm afraid she's going to have a heart attack or something.

"Please, it's important," she says.

"Alright, already," the officer says. He has a potbelly that is bigger than China and three chins to go with it. Somehow he manages to lean his head to the side and starts talking into a gadget clipped to his shoulder. "Roger," he says, and turns back to us.

"They got her there—Juvenile Detention Center over on Pryor Street. It's less than a mile."

My mother has no idea where it is, but she's a very determined woman and somehow I know she will find it. She thanks the cop and runs outside to the front of the bus terminal. There's a cab driver standing outside his cab. She has no problem enlisting his help. He knows exactly where it is.

"It ain't far, lady," he says. He takes his cap off and scratches the top of his head. He uses his hat as a pointer and says, "Take Forsyth Street here, go two blocks ahead and turn right on Trinity, then take a left on Central, then another left on Martin Luther King Drive. You'll go one block and you'll see Pryor. Take a left. You can't miss it."

My mother is frantically writing down his directions on an envelope she's pulled from her purse.

"Thank you, thank you," she says. She takes my shoulder and says, "Let's hurry before they take her someplace else."

"Have they arrested her?" I ask. I'm worried that they won't let her go.

"More like they've taken her into protective custody," my mother says. "It'll be all right. We'll call her aunt. She'll tell them to release her to us. Don't worry."

But I am worried. I can't help it. What if her aunt isn't home, or decides she wants to come and get Bridget herself? Or maybe she's calling Bridget's father and wants to wait until he gets here from London so he can pick her up. Always, always so many maybes.

Chapter Seventy-eight

BRIDGET AND I ARE in my bedroom, just like old times; just like she mentioned in her letter. My mother had no problem getting her out of juvenile. They have so many kids there, that they're glad to relinquish one. My mother had them speak with Bridget's aunt who authorized my mother to pick up Bridget and then my mother had to show her identification and sign a form. It was that simple. Bridget looked a bit rumpled from her journey. Her hair was all matted and her clothes looked like a bum had been wearing them for a week, but other than that she was fine. And not one person tried to pick her up, which I consider a small miracle. Even with her mussed up hair, Bridget is very attractive and she is definitely young, which is what my mother says child predators look for, so I guess there weren't any out that night.

Once again Bridget is braiding my hair into a French braid. She's waiting for a call from her father. Her Aunt Ellen says he is beside himself with worry and has already booked a flight back to Atlanta. My hair looks so cool. But I hate it when it turns out good and then you're not going anywhere. It's sort of a waste. Even if you take a picture of it, what good is it? You didn't go anywhere. Usually when you do, your hair looks really crummy. It's hair fate, which is never on your side.

"Maybe my father will let me stay here," Bridget says. "You never know." She stands back and puts her hands on her hips and checks out my hair. She walks around me and looks at it from all sides. I've already checked it out in the mirror, twice.

"It looks good," she says. "Do you like it?"

"I love it," I say. I have a smile on my face as wide as the Grand Canyon. But my hair could look terrible, and it wouldn't get any better than this, having Bridget here and just the two of us doing stuff like we used to.

"Hey, let's paint our toenails," I say, remembering her letter.

Bridget knows right where I keep the polish and retrieves it from the bathroom cabinet. I settle on one color, a dark brown, that's almost black.

"Cool," Bridget says. "Do mine with this color too."

I could just hug her.

We don't get to finish polishing her nails. Her father calls from London. My mother calls up the stairs, to hurry. He's on the line. Bridget picks up the phone in my room. I make like I'm going to leave her alone, but she motions me to sit down on the bed.

"Hi," she whispers into the mouthpiece. There's a long pause, then Bridget says, "I couldn't help myself, Dad. I've just been so miserable and I figured running away was better than slitting my wrists."

Good call! I give her a thumbs-up. Her father would have to be stupid to get mad at her after a comment like that. I grab hold of one of my pillows and hug it to my chest.

"Ask him," I whisper to Bridget. I nod my head frantically. Now is the best time to get him to understand she needs to stay here for a while.

"What I want to do is stay with Andi. Her mother says it's okay." Another pause. "Then when school's out we can see about summer. How about that?" Bridget lets out a deep sigh. She has a frown on her face. Her father is probably saying it's out of the question.

"And Rudy's here, too," she says. "Don't forget about that. I really feel good about being here with him. My depression is going away already."

Another brilliant call! Bridget nods her head several times into the phone, like her father can see her or something. "Okay," she says. "Okay, then—just a minute."

Bridget puts the phone down and goes to the banister. My mother is still parked at the bottom. "Mrs. St. James," Bridget says, "my father wants to talk to you."

Bridget returns to my bedroom and takes the pillow from me and buries her face in it. I pat her back and tell her it will be okay. We'll figure something out.

"Don't worry," I say. "It's going to be okay." Knowing it won't be.

Bridget puts down the pillow and bursts out laughing. "He said yes!" she says. "Yes! I can stay 'til the end of the school year." That's only a month, but still. Bridget starts dancing around the room. I jump up on the bed and start bouncing. I toss my other pillow at her and it smacks her in the head. She tosses it back, then jumps up on the bed to join me. We are being so silly, like a couple of twelve-year-olds, but we don't care. Bridget gets to stay. It's like heaven. It's like the angels have knocked on our heads and said, How about a little miracle tonight? How would you like that?

Sometimes there's just no second-guessing, parents.

❖ ❖ ❖

In the morning, we get another surprise. Donna had the baby in the middle of the night.

"Your father called, Andi," my mother says. Rosa is back and busy fixing breakfast.

My mother puts her hand on my shoulder. "It's a little boy. They're naming him Gavin Alexander. He weighed six pounds and seven ounces." She pats me on the back like this will make all of it okay.

I'm stunned. I knew the baby was coming, but all of a sudden, now that he's here, it's like it's real for the very first time.

"I—I—" I don't know what to say. "Are they all right?" I ask, wondering if I care and quickly deciding that yes, I do.

"They're fine. Your father wants you to come to the hospital, Andi. Would you like that?"

Rosa brings in a stack of pancakes and a pitcher of orange juice. Bridget takes the chair next to mine. She sits back in her chair and waits for someone to start eating. My mother gets up from the table. "I've already had my breakfast, so I'll leave you two girls to enjoy yours."

She dabs at her mouth and smiles and asks Rosa to bring her another cup of coffee in the sunroom. My mother is all smiles with everything lately because she had a long talk with Dr. Armstrong, explaining to him that she is not interested in their relationship going any further, and instead of him getting mad, he said he understood completely, that they should just take their time. There was no hurry and how about a movie Friday night. "We're just friends, Andi," she says. "And it's good to have lots of friends. It's helpful to my recovery."

She sounds so sure of herself in her recovery and this is a great relief. Now that the baby is actually here I don't want her falling off the deep end. I watch her go toward the sunroom. She seems very relaxed and not upset, like the baby is no big thing. She's accepting the situation and moving on. Something I have not been able to do.

Bridget digs into the stack of pancakes. "Are you going to go to the hospital?" she says.

"I don't know. I told my father I never want to see him again. I think I meant it." I pick up a pancake from the stack and slather some butter and syrup on it. Rosa's pancakes are to die for, but I'm no longer hungry. Bridget is devouring hers. She doesn't wait to finish her mouthful. "You should go," she mumbles. "It's a new little baby!"

I tell her about my friend Julia and what her father did to her.

"But your father may not be anything like her father. You said he's been trying to see you and calls and comes by all the time."

Bridget starts in on another pancake. She stops only to take two large sips of orange juice. She gulps too fast. Some of it slides down the front of her shirt. She licks it off. "And look at my dad. He's turning out to be pretty cool. Don't forget that!"

"I don't know—"

"I'd like to go," she says, "to see the baby. Just think, Andi. He's your little brother! I bet you never thought you'd have another one."

I think of Alexander and my face turns pale.

"No, no, not that he's going to take Alex's place," she says, and pats my arm. "But still, he's a little baby brother. He's never hurt anyone. Let's at least go see him."

It seems like an okay idea, and I am curious. It's not going to change my feelings about my father, I'm sure of that. But it wouldn't hurt to go see a little baby. It wouldn't kill me.

"Okay," I say, and put down my fork. I'll eat later. There's a lump in my throat, so food's out of the question. There's no way I can swallow right now.

Chapter Seventy-nine

WHEN MY MOTHER DROPS us off at the hospital, I go to the desk and ask where the nursery is. I'm going to go there and see the baby, and then I'm going to call my mother and ask her to come right back and pick me up. So I'm not sure why I'm even here, except I can't help myself. I do want to see the baby. It's not his fault all this is happening. It's not his fault his parents are disgusting.

The woman at the desk says the nursery is on the third floor. Bridget and I head to the elevators. There's a long wait and then finally one shows up. We stand back and let everyone get off. It takes a while. There is a lady in a wheelchair and an elderly man trying to maneuver it. I never know if I should offer to help or not. Sometimes they get offended. I step back and give him plenty of room. Once everyone is off, we dash in and head to the third floor. My heart is pounding. I wonder what the baby looks like. Will he remind me of Alex? Oh please, don't let him remind me of Alex. I'll be a goner, guaranteed.

Bridget runs out of the elevator the minute the door opens. She's racing down the hall like there's a fire. I want to tell her to wait up, but everybody around me is being very quiet. There's no way I can just yell out to her. I head toward the nursery. By now Bridget's rounded the corner and is nowhere in sight. Someone takes hold of my elbow. I whirl around thinking maybe we're not supposed to be here. I'm in for the shock of my life. It's my father.

"Andi," he says. Relief is stamped on his face like postage. He

takes a deep sigh. My name slips out of his mouth again. "Andi."
He whispers it reverently, like he used to whisper Beth's. A little
shiver ripples up my spine and hugs my neck. He slips an arm
around my shoulder.

"Oh, Andi," he says. "You came."

My father is elated to see me. He must be. His arm is warm as
fresh toast and his smile could dazzle the sun.

"Well, I—I—just thought, I—I—"

My father nods his head. "I'm just so glad you're here. Donna
will be too." His arm is still wrapped around my shoulder. He
proceeds to walk me down the hall.

"We're going to be a real family, again," he says. "It'll be different
than last time. You'll see."

I stop in my tracks. My father nearly trips over his feet.

"No!" I say. "Nothing's going to be better." Suddenly I am filled
with fear. I think of what Julia told me about her father and all of her
disappointment through the years.

"Everything is ruined." My voice cracks. I yank myself out of my
father's arms and will myself not to cry. "I don't want this! I don't
want you and mom to be divorced! I don't want you to be married
to Donna! I don't want you to have a new family! I don't like where
we're at!" Now I'm positively shouting.

Some of the nurses in the hallway have heard me and are
murmuring to themselves. My father takes one of my arms and pulls
me to him gently. He puts one finger up to his lips, motioning me
to keep it down.

"Sweetheart," he says, "Where we're at is all we've got. We need
to make the most of it. There are no more yesterdays, Andi, but there
are many, many tomorrows." He cups my face in both his hands.
"Let's not ruin today, okay? Today we have a new baby—a new little
life to bring some joy to." My father gently touches the bandage over
my stitches. He leans over and kisses the bandage. He is being so

tender. He takes hold of my hands and gently squeezes them with his fingers. Maybe he does care. But how can I be sure? What if he really doesn't? Maybe this is all an act. And maybe he'll forget about me later, like Julia's dad. How can I know? There's just no guarantee.

My father lets go of my hands and wraps his arms around me. He holds me tighter than I ever remember him holding me before. "I love you, Andi," he says. "I love you so much." He says the word "so" like it's five syllables long.

"Please be part of my new family, Andi. I need you."

I'm trying to answer, but I'm crying too hard to make any other sound but sobs.

"It's okay, baby," my father says. He pats my back and hands me his hankie. It smells like Herrera for Men. It smells exactly like him. Like always.

"It's going to be alright," he says. "Life's all about ups and downs, honey, but there are going to be many more high moments than low ones, I promise you that."

How does he know that? How could he possibly know that? But somewhere in the middle of my heart, I'm hoping it's true, that he does know. That he's been around enough to know it's true. And that makes me feel better and that makes me want to take a chance—to reconsider. I want my father back! And he's here. His arms are around me. He's patting my back and stroking my hair. And he's talking to me, really talking to me. His mind isn't a zillion miles away. He's right here. I think about what Mrs. Temple said about making choices, "Don't worry Andi, you can always change your mind." I want to change my mind. I do! I do!

"Come on, Andi," my father says. "Let's go see your little brother."

He takes my hand and together we walk down the hall. It's not a long hallway, but it feels like it takes miles for us to get to where we're going. I glance at the corridor in front of us and can see a sign flashing brightly: *Your future, Andi.* I blink my eyes and it's gone as quickly as it appeared. But I'm certain it was there. I could see it so clearly. *Your future, your future…*

Finally, we turn the corner and walk up to the glass window outside the nursery. I take a deep breath and step forward. My eyes are closed tightly. I open them slowly and stare intently through the glass window and there he is—my little brother, my own little brother. He's squirming and trying to fit his little fist into his mouth but he can't find it. He starts to cry. He's so beautiful, so absolutely, incredibly beautiful that I can't say anything. I just stand there in my father's arms and weep. And my father is holding me like he'll never let me go. And I just don't care that it might not be forever. I'm willing to take a chance. I need to take a chance. I have nothing to lose and everything to gain. So, I decide, right there in his arms, I am going to claim my father! Right now. Right this very minute. He is mine, mine, mine. But I am more than willing to share him. Oh, yes, I am happy to share him. I look at the baby and realize that there is enough love to reach around all of us and I start to cry harder. The baby is crying, and I am crying and I look up and my father is crying. But it is not sadness that surrounds us and encourages the tears to fall. It's all that we have before us. It would make an ocean weep.

Chapter Eighty

I THINK I'VE GROWN up overnight. I feel sort of like I know what life's finally about. It's not about having an amazing voice. It's about singing a song with the voice that you've got. It's not about having a gorgeous face. It's about being beautiful with the face you were born with. It's not about having a full house of cards. It's about playing your best with the cards you've been dealt. All that you've got—you have to make the most of it. That's what I've learned. It's a big part of all that's true. I'm convinced of it. I'm happy with it. I'm really happy with it.

And my mother's happy. And Bridget's happy. And Beth is totally happy. And my father's happy. Everybody's pretty happy. I'm weeding the herb garden Henry planted that keeps on keeping on. I'm just digging away and enjoying the harvest I'll bring Rosa. She'll clap her hands together and chatter away in Spanish. I look up at a sky so blue it could be an ocean—and out of this blue I consider something pretty profound. Maybe our own happiness isn't supposed to be the main priority in our life. Maybe we're supposed to bring happiness to someone else, and in the process we end up discovering our own. It's something to think about.

I picture Henry and Bridget and Rosa and Beth and my mother and my father and Nana Louise and the new baby and Amy and Joshua; basically all the people that I love. The sun warms the back of my neck. I get up and stretch and brush the dirt off my knees. My heart is so full up—all this goodness wandering around in the world.

Another person's happiness; it's definitely worth thinking about. The next time I'm sad, the next time my parents screw everything up, the next time some boy dumps on me, that's what I'm going to think about, someone else who might be even sadder than me and what I can do about it.

An Excerpt from

Cold Rock River

I WAS FIVE THAT spring Annie choked on a jelly bean. She was twenty months old; she wasn't supposed to have any. Mama made that quite clear. Sadly, I wasn't a child that minded well, so I gave Annie one anyway. I figured she ought to taste how good they were. I figured wrong.

Annie choked *bad* on that jelly bean, and her face turned blue. And Mama wasn't home. She'd gone to Calhoun to sell her prized jams; sold twelve jars of her double-lemon marmalade. Imagine that; there's Mama, waving folks over to get a sample of her jam—selling her heart out—and *all the while* Annie's choking to death.

My pa slapped Annie on her back; smacked her hard with the side of his hand, right between her shoulder blades. Pa had hands the size of skillets. He smacked her twice, but it didn't do any good— might of made it worse. Annie stopped making those sucking sounds like she did when her face turned colors, and her body went limp and her pretty blue eyes just rolled up and disappeared right inside her cute little head.

My older sisters, Rebecca and Clarissa—twin girls Mama had two years before she had me—got on their knees and prayed like preachers. They asked God not to take Annie from us. I didn't get on my knees. I watched Pa beat on Annie instead. It was more interesting. I didn't have anything against praying, mind you. We did it all the time in Sunday school and I knew most of the prayers they taught by heart, except for *The Lord's Prayer*, and I was working on that.

"She can't die," I said. "She's in *our* family." It made perfect sense to me at the time.

"Oh hush, you ninny," Rebecca said. "You don't know nothing."

"Help us pray, Adie," Clarissa said.

I wasn't worried. I knew Annie couldn't die. Bad things like that only happened to strangers. The proof arrived daily in the newspaper Pa buried his face in. Mama had hers in the Bible or a cookbook, the hands on the clock determining which one. While she stirred the pot and touted miracles, he turned the pages and spouted mayhem.

"She can't *die*," I shouted, stomping my feet, trying to get their attention.

Rebecca and Clarissa kept praying, and Pa kept pounding—his eyes big as mixing bowls. I started wailing. Pa dangled Annie upside down by her feet and ran with her like that all the way next door to Miz Patterson's. She wasn't home. She'd gone to Clarkston to see her grandbabies. She went every Friday; stayed the whole day—took me with her sometimes. She and her daughter Delores would sit on the front porch and sip iced tea and rock themselves dizzy while they watched Delores's kids—mostly boys—wrestle on the dirt ground that used to have grass. I wanted to tell Pa, but he ran out the door before I had a chance to. I chased after him but couldn't catch up; he was running two-forty.

"Call an ambulance, Rebecca!" he shouted. Annie was flopping like a rag doll washed one time too many.

"Miz Patterson!" Pa's voice sounded like the low keys on a piano when he talked and when he bellowed it got deep as a pipe organ that had a bad cold. Miz Patterson was as close as we ever came to a neighborhood nurse. Everybody went to her house when they needed doctoring. There was a path to her door on account of it. She didn't charge anything for her kindness. People gave her what they could; a cup of sugar, a few eggs, maybe a pound cake made with real butter. Bernice Harper gave her a banana crème pie when her son Willie fell over the handle bars of his bike and nearly bit his tongue off. After that, whenever I thought about Miz Patterson, that's what was on my mind. So, my pa's running over to her place, Annie's choking, and I'm thinking about that creamy slice of pie she gave me.

Pa ran back with Annie still hanging upside down. His face looked like a bear had scared him and his eyes agreed. At that tender age, I didn't know there was a word for that look—my father was *terrified*. It certainly got my mind off that pie. Rebecca was on the big black phone with the operator trying to explain where Route 3, Box 949 was.

"Well, it's in Cold Rock, but it's not on a street, ma'am," she said. "It's on a route! Ain't you ever hear of a route? Who hired you anyway?" Rebecca yelled. "Our baby Annie's dying. Get us an ambulance here, you ninny!"

Pa heard it all and realized help was not coming anytime soon. The look on his face got worse. His eyes were crazed as a horse that's been spooked by a snake. It scared me plenty. I dropped to my knees.

"*Pleasegodpleasegodpleasegodpleasegod...*" I chanted sing-song, staring at Annie draped over Pa's arm. She was limp as a stuffed toy that had lost all its filling.

Pa stuck his thumb backwards down Annie's throat. I remember being comforted by the fact it wasn't me. Pa's big thumb stuck backwards down Annie's throat looked like a terrible way to die. But what do you know? That jelly bean popped right up out of her mouth! It spewed out with a bunch of vomit and splattered all over Mama's clean linoleum floor. Annie started coughing real hard and crying. Pa said, "Sssshhhhh, you're okay, baby. S'gonna be alright, now. Daddy's got ya." He hugged her to his chest and patted her softly on the back—like she was a China doll and would break—which I thought was very strange, seeing as he nearly pounded her to death when she was choking. Pa bent his head forward and buried his nose in her blonde curls. His shoulder muscles started dancing with each other.

"Pa's crying," Rebecca whispered.

"Don't cry, Pa!" Clarissa said and ran over and wrapped herself around one of his legs. He reached down with his free hand and rubbed her head, but his shoulders never stopped moving. That started Clarissa wailing, which got me upset, seeing as she was the one I favored. I ran over and hugged her.

Annie struggled to get free from Pa's arms. He eased her down, then wiped his face with the big kerchief he always kept in his back pocket. Clarissa stepped back and looked up at him while Annie toddled about. Pa was taller than a cornstalk with legs as skinny as stilts. He reached down and dried Clarissa's eyes. She was hiccupping and sucking her breath in and out. I rubbed her backside while Pa steadied Annie on her feet.

"No need crying over sorry milk," I said, and "Pretty is when pretty does," and "Do like you said and not like I do." I had the words a bit mixed up and most of their meanings were lost to me, but I liked how they sounded whenever Mama said them, and I was desperate to comfort Clarissa. There was something about the way she cried that day that made me think—if she kept it up—I might stop breathing.

"It's okay, 'Niss," I said. "See?" I pointed to Annie wobbling across the floor. "Her face ain't purple and her eyes ain't lost in her head no more." Clarissa looked up to where I was pointing, and Pa let go of her. I heard the air rush out of his chest. He sat down on our old maroon sofa and pulled a pack of Camels out of his shirt pocket. He tapped the bottom, pulled one loose, and slipped it into his mouth. Mama always said Pa's hands were steady as rain, but when he flicked open his lighter they were bobbing like a fishing line with a bite on one end. It was the Zippo Mama gave him. He spun the wheel with his thumb, and a flame shot high into the air. Pa turned the lighter over, slipped his nail into a tiny groove on the head of a small screw, and twisted. Like magic the flame settled back down. He tilted his chin sideways, leaned forward, aimed the tip of cigarette into the fire, and sucked inward. I watched as the smoke curled into the tail of a cat, zigzagged upward and outward, then disappeared.

"This the *only other* thing should be lighting your fire, hon'," Mama said when he opened the shiny red box it came in one Christmas. They both laughed.

"They have dumb jokes, don't they?" Clarissa said, and I nodded.

"You don't neither one of you know nothing," Rebecca butted in. "You're the dumb ones."

Pa carried that lighter from then on. It had a shiny gold eagle on it that faded over time, but he said he would no more replace it than he would one of us. If he was up and dressed, we knew that lighter was in his back pocket. He had a habit of taking it out and snapping the top open and closed till it drove Mama batty, but we weren't allowed to touch it.

"Could burn the house down with this thing," he told us.

"I'm gonna burn you down, you don't put it away and stop that racket," Mama said. Then something bad happened between them, and Mama took back the lighter. We never saw it again.

That day Annie choked, though, Pa still had it. He lit two Camels up, one right after the other, but he kept his eyes glued to Annie. She waddled over to where that jellybean lay in the middle of all that vomit, snatched it up, and aimed it straight for her mouth. Rebecca grabbed hold of her and slapped it out of her hand. Annie let out a howl like she always did when she didn't get what she wanted.

"Clarissa! You and Adie clean up that mess," Rebecca said. Me and Clarissa were used to her bossing us around since Mama usually left Rebecca in charge and her standard warning was to mind her or else. Most of the time I did like she said, but I wondered why Clarissa did. They were the same age, except Mama said Rebecca came out first and was three minutes older.

"Three minutes—that hardly counts!" I informed Mama and nearly got my head knocked off.

"Clarissa doesn't have to mind you," I told Rebecca during another moment of defiance. "You're not her boss; she's the same age as you."

"Hush, you little brat," Rebecca said, "and you do like you're told 'fore I tell Ma you been sassing me while she's gone. You won't get no supper." Mama was making macaroni and cheese, my favorite, so I immediately grew contrite, behaving like an absolute angel for the rest of the day. Don't ask me why, but Clarissa always behaved, no matter what. Not me. It all depended on what was being offered for dinner. For instance, I hated cabbage. But Rebecca didn't know it. I kept it to myself, and when I wanted to sass her good, I picked those nights so I'd get sent to bed early. It was a good deal for me. I didn't have to do any dishes, I didn't have to eat that darn cabbage that tasted so awful, and I got to lie in bed and read books for hours with no one pestering me.

"You take that sassy mouth of yours to bed, missy," Mama would say. "Won't be no supper for you tonight. I'm making corn beef and cabbage, too." I'd hang my head down and look real sad while I climbed the stairs that led to the bedroom we girls shared. It was next to Annie's—which was really just a little sewing alcove that barely held her crib and a changing table. Mama and Papa had the bedroom downstairs. It faced the train tracks. Mama said the trains lulled her to sleep. But poor Pa, when the whistles blew in the night, he'd jump out of bed thinking it was the alarm clock. Took quite a few of them pesky wake-ups before he stopped getting dressed for work in the middle of the night.

"I got to go in early enough as it is," Pa announced loud enough that the neighbors would hear, if we'd had any. He repaired the machines over at the poultry plant. "I don't need no dress rehearsals at three a.m. What the hell they put them dang tracks next to the house for?"

"Charlie, them tracks was here first!" Mama said. "Now shush and go back to sleep. You forget I'm up same time as you? Who do you think fixes your lunchbox, the fairy lunchbox fixer?" By then we were all awake. Eventually, Pa adjusted to the shrill blast of the whistles as the night trains sailed through Cold Rock.

As for me, I liked lying in bed and hearing the trains rumble past in the dark. On hot nights when the air was too thick to breathe, I'd settle in next to the windowsill, my knees resting on my pillow, my head cradled in my arms. In the fall there was a cool breeze when the cold winds blew down from the mountain. But the nights I remember best were the muggy ones when I couldn't sleep, when the sheets were damp with sweat from Clarissa and Rebecca and me being scrunched too close together in the double bed. Pa had promised to build a bed for me and Clarissa that would fit under the eave, with a trundle bed that would slide out from beneath it. He never got around to it. The sticky bedcovers woke me before the train whistle ever got a chance. I'd kneel at the windowsill while the cicadas held their evening concert. A single magnolia tree rested at the side of the clapboard house. When the wind blew just right, its fragrance drifted into the room, rich and heavy as any treasure, and if I inhaled deeply, its sweet, musky scent made me dizzy. When I felt reckless, I kept breathing it in until my knees grew weak and I'd sink, half delirious, into the pillow parked on the floor. There, I watched the lights from the caboose twinkle past, pretending I was on it, headed to China or Africa or South America to be a missionary, like the women who visited us at Christ the King Holiness Church when they needed more money to carry on their services. Later when I found it took more than trains to get them to where they were going, I dreamt of planes and boats and anything that traveled to distant lands. I was going places; I was going to see the world. My dreams got bigger and brighter with each passing year. Then I met Buck.

But for the time being, seeing as I had the entire world laid out for me up in that little bedroom crouched under the eave of our house, what with my books and the night trains and the future I painted, I planned out most of the times I wasn't going to mind Rebecca and did it on a regular basis. I got out of doing a lot of dishes, and I ended up with much prettier hands than Rebecca. Hers were already beginning to look like Mama's.

Of course, all that misbehaving made me the black sheep of the family. I was always in trouble. I got extra skinny, too, since I missed more suppers than I ate, but I was the best-read one of the bunch. It's a wonder not one of them ever caught on.

"Girls, you stay off that sleep porch till it's time for lights down," Ma would tell Rebecca and Clarissa. "Teach her a thing or two about minding." Clarissa was always quite sorrowful for me—she had such a tender heart. I could have told her Rebecca and Mama were just playing into my hands, but I knew she'd let it slip, so I didn't. Not until we were grown. Then we laughed on it good, even Rebecca. But the day Annie choked was no laughing matter.

We found out later that what Pa did—stuck his thumb down Annie's throat—is the worst thing to do when someone's choking. Well, Pa didn't know that. He did what he thought he had to, and it saved Annie's life. When Mama got home she hugged every one of us and said, "Well, sometimes the worst thing turns out to be the best thing."

Too bad it didn't work out like that the next time Annie needed help. We'd gone up Cold Rock Mountain to fish and swim like we did many Sundays when the weather was nice. What happened changed all of us. But Uncle Burleigh said, "Didn't change ya, it ruined ya," as he sucked on the toothpick permanently housed in the corner of his mouth. "You won't never be the same," he added, "not none of you's."

He kept running his big mouth—as usual—until I wanted to ram that toothpick into the soft spot at the base of his throat and make him take back every word.

I hate to give that old codger credit, but turns out he was right. None of us was the same—not ever.

Acknowledgments

ONCE AGAIN I AM grateful to Ron Pitkin, president of Cumberland House. When I finished this manuscript I sent it to him to see what he thought. He informed me that Cumberland had been purchased by Sourcebooks, but he said that he'd forward it to the editor at Sourcebooks and take a look himself. After reading it, he contacted Sara Kase at Sourcebooks, telling her he enjoyed it immensely and highly recommended it. Sara read it and called it "an authentic coming-of-age tale with a terrific takeaway." I owe both Ron and Sara my deepest gratitude for getting behind this book. Thank you ever so much! Sara is no longer with Sourcebooks and I miss her muchly and wish her all the best in her new endeavor.

The entire Sourcebooks staff worked diligently getting the manuscript ready for publication. My heartfelt thanks to each of you, especially Dominique Raccah, president of Sourcebooks, who warmly welcomed me into the Sourcebooks family and told me she "absolutely loved the title." I want to also thank Heather Moore, my publicist, and Danielle Jackson, who assisted Heather during her maternity leave. In addition, I want to recognize Peter Lynch, Regan Fisher, and Kelly Bale for all their hard work. I couldn't be in better hands.

I've been blessed with a new agent, Rachelle Gardner at Wordserve Literary. Thank you for working so hard on my behalf and for your endless faith in me. I appreciate you each and every day.

I couldn't have finished this manuscript without my husband

Robert, who put up with my tantrums when the writing was not going well. Thanks for your encouragement and for the Chinese takeout on the nights I wrote into the wee hours.

Extra warm wishes to my readers who send emails telling me how much they enjoy my work and to please keep writing. You bring much joy.

Always my best to the man upstairs. Thank you for all the blessings you've showered on me. I'm forever grateful and a firm believer that with you all things are possible.

Reading Group Guide

1. What are some of the emotions Andi experiences upon discovering her father is unfaithful?

2. Andi's brother Alex is killed in a freak hazing incident. Why is she able to forgive his fraternity brothers when she learns there will be no real penalty?

3. With Bridget away at boarding school, Andi is concerned about Madeline intruding on their friendship. Is "three" always a crowd? Have you ever experienced difficulties with three people in a close friendship?

4. Andi discovers that Madeline is shoplifting and could easily get Bridget involved. Why doesn't Andi "blow the whistle" and tell her mother?

5. Andi has trouble relating to her mother because of her drinking. What are some of the ways that her drinking short-changed Andi?

6. There are several themes portrayed throughout the book, such as the way people deal with grief, loss, and betrayal. How does Miles capture or express them? What are some of the scenes that come to mind?

7. Andi gets very involved in the lives of Mavis and Howard at the nursing home during the weeks she reads to them. What parts of her personality allows her to so easily get entangled?

8. Rosa ignores Andi's mothers drinking. Is it to keep her job, or are there other factors involved?

9. Andi seems to have great insight into people and their motives. At one point when she is conflicted whether to tell the truth about the shoplifting she says, "All that's true is sitting on the table like a delicious piece of pie, piping hot from the oven, warm and inviting, waiting for someone to take that first bite and say, yes, this is good, this is what dessert is all about." What do you think she meant by that? Are there other areas of the book where this statement could ring true?

10. Andi is not overly excited when her mother goes to Peachford for alcohol treatment. Why is she so skeptical? Why does she bury herself in her schoolwork thinking getting better grades is the answer to her mother's drinking?

11. Andi had a tumultuous summer. Discuss the different elements she had to deal with, including the death of Henry.

12. Once Andi's mother is home from the hospital, she tells Andi she likes life so much better now that she's sober. Andi gets very emotional and feels her "cup is running over." What are some of the reasons Andi feels this way? What else is going on in her life?

13. Allison Whitley invites Andi to her house for dinner, where Andi gets the idea that Allison would be thrilled to pick out two free

outfits from her and Bridget's boutique. Allison asks, "What for?" and points to her closet. She's perfectly happy with what she has. Andi says she herself has so much, but after watching Allison she is left feeling like she doesn't have much at all. What is she referring to?

14. Andi has a love/hate relationship with her father. How did he contribute to those feelings? Do you feel he did his best to bond with Andi?

15. Bridget is Andi's best friend but grows very close to Madeline while away at school. How did Andi and Bridget's relationship change after that?

16. The counselor Andi goes to visit with at school assures Andi she can always change her mind about her father and what he has done, even though she can't change any of the circumstances themselves. What factors helped Andi change her mind about her father?

17. If Andi's father had not left her mother and married Donna, how do you see the story developing from there? Would Andi have come to the same conclusions about life and her position in it?

18. Beth's sexual preferences change near the end of the novel. Were you surprised? Were their hints in the book that things could go in this direction?

19. Andi was very fond of Rosa and Henry, feeling they were family. How did each of them impact Andi's life?

20. After Andi's brother is killed, her mother struggles with alcoholism, and her   father abandons them for another woman. Do you feel Andi was forced to grow up faster than her friends because of this?

21. What role did Vivian play in Andi's life? At one point she soothes Andi on their cruise when Andi tells her she's told her mother about the affair. She says not to worry, that her mother knew all along and didn't let on because she was afraid Andi's father would choose Donna over her. Vivian says now it's her mother's turn to step up to the bat. She says, "All games eventually need to be played to the end, Andi. Winner take all." What did she mean by that?

22. Before Andi's brother Alex is killed, he gets his girlfriend, Amy, pregnant. What do you think of his best friend marrying her? Do you think they'll be happy?

23. Andi falls head over heels in love with Rodney, who is far too old for her. What do you think convinced her that he felt the same way about her? Have you ever been in love with someone much older than yourself? Was that love reciprocated?

24. When Andi's new little half-brother is born, he makes an enormous impression on her. Do you feel this alone was the reason she reconnected with her father or were there other factors involved?

25. In the end, Andi comes to the conclusion that maybe our own happiness isn't supposed to be our main priority in life. How do you feel about that?

About the Author

JACKIE LEE MILES, A resident of Georgia for over thirty-five years, hails from Wisconsin via South Dakota. She considers herself "a northern girl with a southern heart." Her paternal grandfather was christened Grant Lee by her great-grandmother in honor of the many fallen soldiers on both sides of the Mason-Dixon Line.

Miles resides in Atlanta, Georgia, and Cape Canaveral, Florida, with her husband Robert, and she is a featured speaker at book clubs, schools, and writers' workshops. When not writing or speaking, she tours with the Dixie Darlin's, four nationally published book-writing belles who serve up helpings of down-home humor and warmth. When the Darlin's come to town, they don't just sign books; they give a lively presentation, peppered with advice, animation, and lots of anecdotes. For more information or to schedule an appearance, contact Karin Gillespie at kgillespie@knology.net.

You can write the author at Jackie@jlmiles.com, and you can visit her website at www.jlmiles.com.

Roseflower Creek

"EFFECTIVELY DRAWS THE READER INTO LORI JEAN'S WORLD...
MILES'S STORY PROVES HAUNTING AND EVEN INSPIRATIONAL."
—*Booklist*

JACKIE
LEE MILES

Roseflower Creek

A NOVEL

*"The morning I died it rained. Poured down so hard
it washed the blood off my face."*

It seems everyone in young Lori Jean's life has a secret, but only
one secret will cost her everything. A surprising tribute to our ability
to heal and love in the most difficult circumstances. *Roseflower Creek* will
stay with you long past its final page.

978-1-4022-4001-0 $13.99 U.S./$16.99 CAN/£7.99 UK

Cold Rock River

JACKIE LEE MILES

Cold Rock River

A NOVEL

"...POWERFUL STORY OF FAMILY, LOVE, AND LOSS..."
—*Dorothea Benton Frank*
New York Times bestselling author

Even the best-kept secrets must be revealed...

Seventeen-year-old Adie Jenkins is newly married and newly pregnant, though not necessarily in that order. Unready for fatherhood, her skirt-chasing husband isn't much help.

But in this stunning tale that redefines intimacy, love, and family, Adie discovers hope where she least expects it: from her sweet neighbor Murphy, from the world-wise midwife Willa Mae, and in the worn pages of the diary of a slave girl...

978-1-4022-4004-1 $13.99 U.S./$16.99 CAN/£7.99 UK